LAYTONS GROVE

Books by R.M. Lowery

Laytons Grove
When Kristen Comes Home
What Was Left

—

The Jakob Larsen Mysteries
The Gentle Slope
We Kill Our Own
Time Fades Away

rmlowery.com

LAYTONS GROVE

R.M. LOWERY

WATERVALE PUBLISHING

WATERVALE PUBLISHING

First published in the United States of America

First Edition: March 2026

Cover photo by Amber Kipp
Cover & interior design by Watervale Publishing

ISBN-13: 979-8-9933962-1-7

To my grandfather, Keith Lowery,
who always made Illinois feel like home.

"Sometimes your path is predetermined; sometimes you dig your own grave."

—Unknown

sean

Sean stared out the truck's window at the illuminated night sky, the moon large and low.

Jack pulled to the curb, leaned over to look at the building through the passenger window. "You sure this is it?"

Sean nodded. "This is the place." He picked up the two-way radio and called to Travis. "We all good on your end?"

The radio scratched and squealed. "Yeah. All clear over here."

Sean reached behind the seat, grabbed two Halligan pry bars, handed one to Jack. "You ready?"

Jack shut off the engine, opened the door, and slid out of the truck.

Sean followed, stepping onto the wet street beneath him as the cold November air bit at his face.

The small warehouse on Second Street was out of the way, and out of date. No alarm system, no cameras.

Its sole occupant was a married couple who ran several hot dog carts that catered to contractors outside Menards and other home improvement stores in the area. They paid their employees each Friday. On the first and third Fridays of each month, employees got checks, but on the second and fourth Fridays, they got cash.

Sean learned from an ex-employee that each week, the owners laid envelopes out on a table on Thursday evening so when employees arrived Friday for work, their pay awaited them.

This week was a cash week, and with about sixteen part-time employees working at the company's eight hot dog stands, that meant at least five grand in cash sat on a table waiting to be taken by anyone who found a way inside the warehouse. And since these people had a habit of paying their employees under the table, it was unlikely they'd report the theft because it would draw unwanted attention to them and their finances.

Travis stood guard outside to keep watch for any unexpected visitors as Sean and Jack walked toward the nondescript brick building, sticking to the edge of the parking lot, in the shadows created by the moonlight above them.

Attached to the building's gray metal door—the only way in or out of the place—hung a sign with a clip-art hot dog stenciled in vinyl next to the words ILLINOIS VALLEY VENDING & CONCESSION LLC.

Sean wedged the Halligan bar into the door's seam, just above the lock, then Jack hammered it in with his bar. The door gave way and separated from the frame slightly. Jack stepped in and wedged his Halligan in the newly created gap, and Sean struck the back of the Halligan bar.

The lock released its grip on the frame, and the door swung open.

No alarm sounded. Just as they'd planned.

Sean had been skeptical about the intel on the place that he'd received. Leaving envelopes filled with cash sitting on a table for anyone to take seemed idiotic. But just around the corner from the front door, near an interior office, sat a long table with several white envelopes splayed across the woodgrain top. Five rows of envelopes with the names of each employee written in Sharpie, the rows arranged in alphabetical order: Alyssa, Caleb, Daniel, and so on.

Sean picked up Alyssa's envelope and tore it open to find a handwritten note thanking her for her work, along with a little more than $350 in cash. Caleb's envelope contained about $400. Daniel's had about $300.

Sean collected all the envelopes and slid them into the pocket of his jacket. "All right, let's go."

He turned toward the door, but Jack didn't follow. Instead, he peered through the window of the small office.

Sean paused, waited for him. "C'mon, man. We're done here."

Jack reached for the doorknob, tried to turn it. It didn't budge.

Sean glanced at the exit. Freedom awaited them. "Let's go, man."

"Hold up."

"Why?"

"There's a lock box on the desk in here."

"So?"

"So, there's probably more cash inside it."

"Whatever, man. We got what we came for."

Jack ignored him, wedged his Halligan into the seam of the flimsy office door. The sound of wood cracking echoed across the building.

Sean glanced at the front door again, then returned his gaze to Jack. "Dude, would you let it go? We've gotta dip."

Jack continued jamming the bar into the frame, snapping the casing away from the door lock.

Sean picked up the radio and called to Travis. "How's it look out there?"

The radio crackled. "All good. You about done?"

Sean watched Jack slam the bar into the frame once more. "Yeah, just about." He turned to Jack. "Dude, c'mon. Let's get outta here."

Jack slammed the bar in once more, pulled. More of the frame snapped and the door swung open.

The shrill sound of a siren pierced the silence and echoed off the concrete walls.

Sean hurried toward the exit, shouted over the siren. "Goddamnit. Let's go!"

Jack darted into the office, grabbed the lock box, then joined Sean near the door.

They ran across the parking lot to the awaiting truck. Once safely inside, Jack flashed the headlights to let Travis know they were done. He started the engine and drove away from the building, heading north through downtown Laytons Grove.

Sean watched the town pass by from the window—its vacant stores and deteriorating hundred-year-old buildings slid by in a blur. He glanced in the mirror to see if anyone had followed them. Only Travis' car was in sight, thankfully.

He turned his head toward Jack. "What the fuck, man?"

"What?"

"We were good, but now cops will be all over the place."

He shrugged. "It's cool."

Sean exhaled a sharp breath as he checked the mirror again. It was anything but cool. They'd had a plan, and if Jack hadn't deviated from that plan, no one would know the place had been hit until tomorrow morning. But thanks to Jack, now the cops or the alarm monitoring company were calling the Illinois Valley hot dog magnates to let them know they'd been broken into.

Sean sat silent all the way to Jack's place while Jack cranked up the radio and played drums on the steering wheel.

As soon as Jack parked in the driveway, Sean hopped out, slammed the door behind him.

Travis pulled up to the curb and parked.

Sean stormed into Jack's place. He still lived with his mom, but she worked evenings at a tavern, so the place was theirs most nights. Sean pulled out the envelopes, opened them, emptied the cash onto the kitchen counter. Jack strolled in behind him, plopped down the lock box, pulled out his pocketknife, and started prying it open.

Travis joined them in the kitchen, shifted his gaze between them. "What the hell happened back there? I thought you said there wasn't an alarm."

Sean glared at Jack. "Someone decided to improvise."

The lock box popped open, and Jack pulled out a small stack of cash. "Look at this though. It paid off."

Sean ignored him, turned his attention to counting the cash from the envelopes. Jack, meanwhile, counted the small amount of cash from the lock box.

Travis headed to the refrigerator, opened it. "Who wants a beer?"

Jack nodded his chin toward him. "I'll take one."

Travis grabbed three beers, turned to Sean. "Beer?"

Sean nodded mid count.

Jack slammed the cash from the lock box down on the counter. "Boom! An extra two-forty. Not bad."

Sean's face warmed. An extra $240 that had almost gotten them arrested.

Sean finished counting and stacked the bills on the counter, arranging them by denomination.

Travis set his beer on the counter and leaned in to look at the cash. "How'd we do?"

Sean stepped back, opened his beer. "About fifty-two hundred, by my quick count."

Jack raised his beer in the air. "Shit yeah, brother."

Travis clinked his beer bottle against Jack's. "Plus the two-forty. Nice."

Sean finished a swig. "Yeah. That two-forty will really help. Totally worth almost getting caught red-handed."

Jack scoffed. "If you don't care about it, Travis and I will split your cut."

Sean held out his hand. "Give me my goddamned cut."

Jack grabbed the cash and counted out four Jacksons, then slammed them into Sean's palm. "There ya are, brother."

Sean pocketed the cash, took a swig of beer.

Jack stuck his cut in his pocket. "See, we're good, brother. We got out of there. That's all that matters."

Sean slammed his beer down on the counter. "That's not all that matters. We should never have been in that situation. No one should have known we'd gotten in, but that alarm pretty much guarantees that lots of people know now."

"Relax, bro. We don't even know if they pay for alarm monitoring."

"Exactly. We don't know anything about it. That's why we should have left it alone. This was supposed to be a quick, low-risk job. An easy eighteen hundred bucks each to hold us over until something bigger comes along. These people wouldn't have known for several hours that someone broke in, and they probably wouldn't have called the cops once they did know because what they're doing is illegal, but now, with the alarm, the cops will for sure be involved."

"So what, bro? They still ain't gonna tell 'em about the illegal payroll funds. They'll say someone broke into the office. It's no big deal."

"Except that it is a big deal because now they can claim that all the cash we took was in that lock box, so they can get it covered by insurance. That means police reports will be filed, and it means that cops will be looking into who took it, and on top of all that, the amount stolen adds another felony charge, and that gives the cops more of an incentive to bust whoever took it."

"They'll never figure out it was us, dude."

"We don't know that. Before all this, the owners of that place would have just cut their losses, changed their practices in the future. Now cops are involved, dusting for prints, looking for evidence. Can you say with absolute certainty that we didn't do anything that could lead them to us? They'll probably check security cameras all over the area too. What if we're on one of those cameras? What if they got us coming out, or driving away?"

"So what? We were masked, and all the plates are stolen, bro. They ain't gonna trace them to us."

"Sure, the plates are stolen, but the cars aren't. That was the whole point of this job: it was supposed to be easy. That's all shot to shit now. All we can do now is hope that no one recognizes your truck or Travis' car, or that none of us were caught on a camera without a mask. If you'd just left the office alone, we wouldn't have to worry about any of that shit."

"All right, dude. I get it. I fucked up. But it's done now."

Sean reached into the pile on the counter and counted out his share. "I'm gonna dip. I'll lay low for a few days and see if there's any blowback from this." He shoved the cash into a pocket of his jeans. "I recommend you guys do the same. Keep your cars off the streets for a few days too."

He stormed outside to his car and drove away. It always happened: no matter how much planning he put into a job, Jack always fucked something up. It'd always been that way—ever since their high school days.

Jack was clearly using again too. Sean didn't really care what Jack did in his free time, but now he was fucking with their business. It was probably hypocritical to tell him not to do drugs, especially since they'd gotten through high school by getting high together, but this wasn't high school. Back then, the worst that could happen was a suspension or maybe a few weeks in juvie. These days, mistakes could put them away for years, maybe decades.

Sean shook the thoughts from his head as he pulled into the parking lot of his apartment. Brooke's car sat in the space at the end. He wasn't expecting her, but it wasn't a shock either. She'd been fighting with her roommate a lot lately and had been staying at his place several nights a week. However, right now, he wished she wasn't there because he wasn't really in the mood to be around anyone. It was after midnight, so there was a chance she'd be in bed, but he climbed the staircase and walked through the door to find her sitting on the couch.

She hopped up to greet him, dressed in one of his T-shirts and nothing else. "Hey, babe." She wrapped her arms around his neck and kissed him. "Hope you don't mind that I'm here."

"It's cool."

"Jessica was bugging, so I had to get out of there. Sorry I didn't text first, but I guess I figured you'd be home."

"I was at Jack's." He opened the refrigerator and peered inside. "You hungry?"

She shook her head. “Not really.”

“All right. I’m gonna make a sandwich then.”

“I’ll make you one.” She stepped in front of him, gathered things from the refrigerator.

“Yeah? Okay.” He reached around her to grab a beer.

She set two slices of bread on the counter. “So, hey, your sister stopped by a few hours ago.”

“Oh yeah? What’d she want?”

“To invite us to dinner tomorrow. I guess she’s going to be in town through the weekend.”

“Dinner where? At my parents’ place?”

“Yeah.”

“Is my brother going to be there?”

“She made it sound like he’d be there.”

“Then I’d better pass.”

“Why? I thought you liked Donnie.”

“I love the dude, but my parents are convinced that I’ll corrupt him or some shit. That if he hangs out with me at all he’ll drop out of college and start robbing liquor stores.”

“Your sister made it sound like your parents really want you to be there.”

“Of course she did. Reagan would make it sound like that even if they’d told her not to invite me. She’s always trying to make the family get along.”

Brooke smirked as she shook her head. “You make your family out to be so much worse than they are.”

“You didn’t grow up with them.”

“True.” She shrugged as she spread mustard across a slice of bread. “Still, Reagan seems to keep trying to include you in things. That counts for something, right?”

“She does it because our mom wants us to be one big happy family. But like the rest of my family, Reagan treats me like some kind of special case. Something that's broken and needs to be fixed."

Brooke set the knife down, walked around the counter, wrapped her arms around him, kissed him. "You're not broken, baby. You know that, right?"

Maybe she was right, or maybe she was just broken too. Travis and Jack were definitely broken. It's how they all found each other, so it was possible it was the reason Brooke found him as well. A collection of broken people bound together by the things that kept them from joining the normal parts of society.

reagan

Ma pulled the casserole from the oven and set it on the counter.

"Oh, shoot." She leaned in and inspected it. "It cooked a lot faster than I thought it would. Hope it's not overdone."

Reagan peered over Ma's shoulder to see the dish. It looked great to her, and her dad and brothers would eat just about anything they put on the table, so it didn't really matter. "It's perfectly fine, Ma. Looks amazing to me."

"I don't know. I should have put some foil on top."

"You worry too much." Reagan grabbed a pan from the counter. "Here, I've got the rolls ready to go into the oven."

"Let's leave those until just before dinner. Your dad likes them fresh."

"Oh, right." She chuckled. "I forgot about his neurotic need for oven-fresh rolls."

"He likes what he likes." Ma shrugged. "Anyway, tell me all about your new place. Are you guys about settled in?"

"Not even close. Most of David's stuff is still in storage, and we don't have nearly enough furniture to fill the spaces. But it's a nice place. Newer appliances, wood floors, and it's only a couple blocks to a green line L station."

"I know this will sound very *mom* of me, but it's a safe area, right? I mean, all we see on the news is shooting after shooting in Chicago. It makes me worry."

"It's a safe place, Ma. Oak Park is a good village, and we're in a safe neighborhood. We also have two deadbolts on the door." She chuckled. "You and Dad will have to come see it once we're settled."

"I can't wait, dear." Her expression drooped. "Have you talked to Sean?"

Reagan was surprised it'd taken her this long to bring him up. "I dropped by his place last night, but he wasn't home. His girlfriend was there, so I let her know that they're invited to dinner."

She nodded. "Maybe I'll give him a call later. I'd really like for him to come over while you and Donovan are visiting."

Reagan wasn't sure why Sean avoided the family as much as he did, but she was sure that his constant absence hurt Ma. Sean never had gotten along well with their parents though. When he was a kid, they fought constantly about his performance in school. By the time he was a teen, they fought about him staying out too late or not telling them where he was. And as an adult, well, Sean knew he didn't have to stick around to fight about anything, so he left home at seventeen and had only returned for occasional visits in the five years since.

The old screen door creaked, and her father walked into the house.

He leaned against the door frame of the kitchen. "Hey. I'm home."

It was odd. Normally he'd come in, kiss Ma, have a beer, and talk about his day. His demeanor was different too. Sad, defeated.

Ma went to him and gave him a kiss. "How was work?"

"It was..." He glanced down at his worn, dirty boots.

"It was a long one. I've got some stuff I want to finish up in the garage though. Let me know when dinner is ready, okay?"

Without another word, he walked out the back door and crossed the driveway to the detached garage.

His distant, sad mood was eerily familiar to Reagan. He'd acted the same way when he got laid off from the Johnson-Power Glassworks plant nearly a decade ago—a place he'd worked since he was eighteen. In the months that followed the plant's closure, he struggled to find steady work, taking lots of odd jobs for low pay. But then he found his current job at Midland Ceramics, a factory that made bricks for homebuilding and landscaping. Although, even after working there for years now, he still wasn't making what he'd made at Johnson-Power. He also had to drive to Streator, about thirty miles southeast of Laytons Grove, and the commute took longer, cost more in gas, and put more miles on his already old truck. He'd never loved the job, but there weren't a lot of other options because most of the factories across the Illinois Valley had closed years ago, making Midland Ceramics an endangered species. If Midland were to shut down, Reagan wasn't sure what her dad would do.

Reagan leaned against the counter to face her mother. "Think everything's okay?"

"I'm sure it is, dear. He's been working pretty hard lately. Lots of overtime. He's probably just worn out."

It was obvious Ma didn't believe her own words.

"You sure that's all it is?"

"I am, dear." Ma grabbed a dish full of potatoes and peeled back the foil covering it. "I think these are going to need more milk than we have. They seem dry. Unfortunately, I used the last of the milk a little bit ago."

It was Ma's way of asking Reagan to go get more milk. It was also an obvious ploy to get rid of her because the potatoes looked fine.

Reagan decided to give in. "I'll go to Morelli's and get some more milk, Ma."

"Are you sure you don't mind? You're supposed to be on vacation."

"It's not really a vacation, Ma. It's just a weekend."

"If you're sure." Ma walked toward the living room. "Let me get my purse."

Reagan followed her into the living room. "Ma?"

"Yes?"

"Are you sure everything is okay with Dad?"

Their voices awoke Baxter, the family's cat. Ma patted his head as he stood and stretched on the back of the sofa where he'd been sleeping. "I'm sure, dear. You don't need to worry about anything." She looked out the front window. "Oh, shoot. Your father blocked you in the driveway. Let me get my keys. You can take my car."

"That's okay. I think I'll walk."

"Are you sure? It's pretty cold out there."

"I'm sure. It's been a while since I've wandered around town."

"Okay, but in that case, just get a half gallon. It'll be easier to carry."

The town hadn't changed much since her last visit. It rarely changed. For most of her life that lack of change bothered her, and she'd spent most of her life trying to get out of Laytons Grove. But now—walking its charming streets, admiring the plentiful trees and well-kept lawns of the old homes—she couldn't remember why she'd wanted to leave.

It wasn't an exciting place to grow up, and that was a given since no small town was ever particularly exciting. While many small towns were located close to larger towns with more things to do, only farmland surrounded Laytons Grove—acres and acres of corn and soybeans planted in straight rows. The standing town joke went: on a clear day, you may even see a cow or two.

Time had weathered the once vibrant town too. Downtown Laytons Grove was nothing like it had been a decade or two ago. For years, many of the town's family-owned businesses had been struggling, and the aftershocks of the pandemic only made things worse. Any direction Reagan looked, she saw crumbling sidewalks, deteriorating buildings, shuttered stores, and even boarded-up homes.

As Reagan turned onto Main Street, Morelli's Convenience Store came into view. Morelli's was one of the few family-owned businesses that still thrived—a welcomed sight. Reagan had spent much of her childhood riding her bike to Morelli's to buy candy, and many times over the years, her mother had sent her there to get basics like bread, eggs, and of course, milk.

A chime rang as she opened the big glass door and within seconds of stepping inside, Tony Morelli greeted her.

"Reagan! It's so good to see you."

"You too, Mr. Morelli."

Tony had owned the store since Reagan was a baby. His father ran it before that, but in all of Reagan's memories, Tony was the only one proprietor. But Tony was in his late sixties now and was supposedly considering retiring, but that decision rested on which one of his two kids would take over the business. Tony's only son, Michael, was far more interested in running the store, so everyone in town figured he was the most obvious candidate. However, his oldest child, Mary, helped out at the store a lot and seemed to enjoy it, but she was also a detective with the Laytons Grove Police Department—a job she seemed to love—so it seemed unlikely that she'd give it up to run a gas station.

Reagan knew Mary well. They'd worked on a few community projects together over the years, but she didn't know Michael well, aside from interactions with him while shopping in the store.

She grabbed a half gallon of milk from the cooler and brought it to the counter where Tony had *The Daily Telegraph* spread across the other side of the counter.

He peered up at her over the rims of his reading glasses. "What brings you back to town?"

"Just visiting my family. I had a couple vacation days to use, so I came down for a long weekend."

"Well, welcome home."

"Thank you. It's good to be here."

"How are you liking life in the big city?"

"I like it a lot. There's always something going on, and there are lots of great restaurants. I also have a great job that I really enjoy."

"That's fantastic to hear. I have to confess though, I always thought you'd move back after graduation." He smiled. "Guess I'm a little disappointed that you didn't."

"You and both of my parents."

He chuckled quietly. "I can imagine. How are your parents? I don't believe they've been in lately."

"They're good. Ma and I are making dinner for the entire family tonight. That's why I'm here for more milk."

It was always a bit of an adjustment returning to Laytons Grove. In Oak Park, even though she frequented the same market on Madison Street, no one there knew much about her. The employees were always friendly, but no one ever asked about her parents, or her brothers, or asked how she was doing—probably because they didn't know her family and hadn't known her since she was a child. A couple people there knew her by name, but they didn't know her well enough to know she'd been named after her aunt and uncle, not the fortieth president of the United States, as most people assumed. In contrast, Laytons Grove was the antithesis of life in Chicagoland: everyone knew her and her family, and they knew every detail of her life whether she wanted them to or not.

Tony clicked some buttons on the register as Reagan stared at the candy bin lining the front of the checkout area. As a kid, she and her friends often rode their bikes to Morelli's after doing chores so they could spend their newly earned cash on something from the bins.

Tony clicked a couple more buttons and the register beeped. "Just the milk today?"

"That should do it."

"You sure you don't need a Push Pop for old time's sake?"

A smile slid across Reagan's face. "I haven't thought about those in years."

"I remember when you were a little girl. You'd always buy a Push Pop. Truth be told, I kept stocking them because you liked 'em so much."

"Really? Well, we did buy a ton of them, and those silly jewel-shaped candy rings too."

"Ring Pops." He chuckled. "Yup, we still sell those as well. Can I get ya one?"

"No, that's okay. Just the milk, I guess."

"If you're sure." He pushed some more buttons and gave her the total.

She handed over the cash that Ma had given her, and Tony gathered her change from the drawer.

He dropped it into her hand with a smile. "Just a second, Reagan." He walked around the counter and disappeared into the candy aisle. He returned moments later with a Ring Pop in his hand. "Tell ya what: this is on me. It's for being such a good customer all these years."

"Oh, you don't have to do that."

"It's already done." He smiled as he placed a red Ring Pop in her hand. "Consider it a homecoming gift from Morelli's."

"Well, thank you. That's very sweet of you."

"Don't mention it. And please, tell your parents I said hello."

Once in the parking lot, Reagan slid the Ring Pop onto her finger. It fit tighter than it did a few years ago, but it brought back a lot of good memories of bike rides home, struggling to steer as she sucked on the Ring Pop. The trickiest part was turning the corner at Peoria Avenue and Monroe Street because the Thompson's house on the corner was surrounded by a chain link fence, and if you weren't paying attention, the fence would seemingly reach out and grab the end of your handlebars.

That route was the fastest way home from Morelli's, but tonight, Reagan decided to take the long way home, which would allow her to see more of the town. It would also give her parents ample time to discuss whatever it was that was bothering her father.

When the evening news ended, Reagan went upstairs to her old room and browsed the bookshelves. She'd vacated the space years ago when she first moved to Chicago for college, but with space in her dorm room extremely limited, she was forced to leave most of her library behind. Over the years, she'd moved into bigger spaces but still hadn't migrated her older books to Chicago. Now that she and David had a more permanent space to call home, it was probably time to pack up her old books.

She pulled *If I Stay* from a shelf, a book she'd loved as a teen. Reagan curled up in the window seat—a spot where she'd spent many hours of her childhood sitting and reading—and opened the book. Within minutes, she became engrossed again, diving into Mia's love of Beethoven and her hopes of getting into Juilliard, but the muffled sounds of her parents' conversation downstairs proved too distracting. Their murmurings resonated in the floorboards beneath her as their voices raised and lowered. It sounded serious, whatever they were discussing.

Reagan crept to the doorway, careful to avoid the squeakiest parts of the old wooden floor. She sat down at the top of the staircase, like she'd done so many times as a child when her parents thought she was in her room doing homework.

Ma spoke softly. "What about your position?"

"It's safe. I talked to Ron today. He told me they'd trimmed all of the fat they need to. Things will be just fine. I don't want you worrying about it."

He seemed worried about it himself though.

Ma's voice softened even more. "I just..." She exhaled a long sigh. "I can't imagine what we'd do, Frank. If you lost your—"

"I said you don't need to worry about that. Ron assured me that the four guys they cut loose today was it. It's gonna save the company a lot of money, and that's good for the long run."

"I hope so. I really do." She sighed again. "I just don't know what we'd do. Things are tight as it is. What if we lose the house?"

Reagan's stomach tightened. The small Victorian on Monroe Street wasn't much—nothing like the perfectly restored Victorians you saw on HGTV shows—but it was *their* house. The McKenna home. The only home she'd ever known. The one place she could always return to no matter where life took her. Even with the squeaky wood floors, the little window in the dining room that never fully closed all the way, or the weird smell that wafted up from the unfinished basement, it was still the one place she felt completely safe.

sean

The banging sound woke him. It seemed to be coming from the front door. Whoever it was, they obviously didn't plan to leave without talking to him.

Struggling to pull a shirt over his head, Sean stumbled toward the door. "Who is it?"

"The police. Open up!" It was Jack's voice. He didn't even try to disguise it.

"What the fuck do you want?"

"To come inside, dipshit."

Sean opened the door and stepped aside, giving Jack room to walk into his apartment.

Jack slapped him on the chest. "Thanks, brother."

Sean squinted at the sunlight streaming into his home. "What time is it?"

"Noon. That too early for you?" Jack laughed at his dad joke and plopped down on the couch. "I texted, but you never responded."

Sean closed the door, darkening the room. "That give you any clue that I wasn't looking to entertain guests?"

"Oh, shit." He careened his neck toward the bedroom. "Is Brooke here? You guys doing some nasty shit I don't wanna know about?"

"She's at work, asshole."

"Good. I don't want to think about you two in bed." He plopped his feet on the coffee table. "What the hell is a girl that hot doing with a fuck-knuckle like you anyway?"

"Fuck-knuckle?"

"You heard me."

Sean headed toward the fridge. "You want something to drink? Pop or something."

"You outta beer?"

"No. Is that what you want?"

"Shit yeah, bro."

He grabbed a bottle for Jack and some apple juice for himself, then sat down on a stool by the kitchen counter. "I assume you didn't drop by just to drink my beer?"

"You assume correctly. I got a job I want to run by ya."

"I'm listening."

"Watches."

"What about them?"

Jack opened the beer, swallowed a swig. "I got a line on a shipment. High-end shit. I'm talkin' Movado, Tag, Omega. Serious drip, man. These things are worth at least several hundred each, but most will fetch several thousand each."

"Sure, in a retail store."

Sean had never liked taking merchandise. Technology was making it easier and easier for manufacturers and cops to track products, plus, to sell the goods, they needed a fence. That meant involving another person—a person with less loyalty to them, which made it more likely they'd roll on them if the cops came knocking. And even if the cops were never involved, including an outsider always came at the risk of the fence screwing them over in order to keep a bigger cut.

Sean shook his head. "Things like watches are too tricky to unload."

Jack finished a swig. "They're a little tricky, but we stand to make plenty off them, even if we unload them on the cheap."

"Yeah? Who we gonna sell that shit to?"

"I got that part covered, bro. I know this dude up in Joliet. He'll buy 'em at forty percent of retail."

"Forty percent? Seriously? Seems like a lot of risk on our end for forty cents on the dollar."

"Dude, it'll be huge though. Big payday for a little bit of work. I got a hold of some shipping manifests from a guy that works over at Snyder Trucking. Every fucking week Snyder transports these kinds of watches. They travel down I-80 on their way from a dealer out west to stores in Chicago. Like more than a hundred at a time. Like I said, shit is high end. Selling them at forty percent of retail will make us seventy, eighty grand, easy. Maybe more."

"Okay, so what's the job? We gonna get some black Honda Civics and hijack a semi, full-on Fast and Furious style?"

Jack laughed. "No, dude. Nothin' like that. These trucks come through the Illinois Valley all the time on their way to Chicago, and they stop off at the Wentworth Shipping warehouse over in LaSalle."

"So? We what, have a little picnic in the parking lot and wait for them to fall off the truck?"

"No, man. We take 'em off the truck. See, the trucks, they stop there, and it's a long stop. Lots of other shit gets unloaded there, and it's just a couple guys that do all the work, so I figure we create a distraction—a fire or small explosion—something that gets their attention and pulls them away from their work. Then we roll up, hop in the open trailer, grab the boxes that contain the watches, and we're out of there."

"An explosion? That's a good way to make sure the entire area is swarming with cops, maybe even federal agents."

"I don't know, bro. It was just an example. It don't have to be anything that major. Maybe we just set a dumpster on fire. Maybe drop an aerosol can in there so it pops when the fire heats up. Just something that gets their attention, and then, while they're putting the fire out, we grab the watches and go."

Sean thought it over for a moment. While not a terrible idea, Jack surely hadn't thought it all the way through. "They got cameras at this warehouse?"

"A couple that I've scoped out, both are near the entrance. I figure we wear masks, use stolen plates, or maybe even a stolen truck. We'll be long gone by the time anyone checks the video, and once they do, it's just a couple of masked guys in a stolen truck."

"What's the entrance and exit situation? Guard shack? Gated property?"

"No guard shack or nothin' like that, but yeah, the place is fenced in. Gate's open all day though."

"That gate, it's the only way in and out?"

"Yeah."

"So, if something blocks our exit, we're stuck there?"

"In theory, yeah, but the odds of that happening are low."

"Okay, but you're talking about stealing a truck, and setting some type of fire. All of that brings more attention, and more potential charges if shit goes south."

"Shit won't go south, bro. We'll just borrow a truck, you know?"

"*Borrow* one?"

Jack chucked. "Yeah, man. The morning of the heist, we just hit up the parking lot of a tavern and find a car or a truck with the keys left in it. You know, from someone that had a few too many the night before and walked home or whatever. We borrow the car for a couple hours, then drop it off back at the tavern. By the time the drunk fucker gets a ride to pick it up, we'll be done. Bitch won't even have a clue we used it."

"Assuming that all of it went that smoothly, there's still the matter of starting a fire. That'll draw some attention. Fire trucks, onlookers, maybe even reporters from the local paper. And even a small fire is likely to draw cops to the area."

"It doesn't have to be a fire, bro. That was just one idea. Maybe we just have Travis call the warehouse and act like a pissed off customer. Draw shit out, get the other guy on the phone too. Or anything else. We just need something that pulls the workers away from the truck for a minute or two while we go in and grab the watches."

Sean thought about it in silence. Jack's plan still had plenty of holes in it, but with some work, they could be filled. The thing he couldn't get over was the fact they'd be stealing watches—merchandise with serial numbers. Stealing cash was much safer and nearly impossible to trace. If they got pulled over with a lot of cash on them, it would raise suspicions, but cops would have a hard time proving it was stolen. Several boxes filled with expensive watches was a different story. If they were caught with those, they'd be headed for prison for sure. If Jack estimated a hundred grand worth at a sixty percent discount, that meant they'd be in possession of more than $200,000 in stolen merchandise, an amount that constituted the second highest felony in the state with a multi-year prison sentence attached. And even if they managed to avoid being caught with the watches, the biggest problem was that they'd have to trust an outsider to fence them, greatly increasing the risk while depleting the potential reward.

Jack tossed back the final drops of his beer. "So? What d'ya think? I figure one of us creates the distraction, one of us drives the truck, and one of us grabs the watches. The whole thing could be done in under two minutes. Ninety grand in about two minutes, bro."

The dollar amount, if accurate, was enticing, but the risk that came with it was glaringly hefty.

Sean took a deep breath before responding. Jack tended to get pissed off whenever he turned down his ideas. "Look, I get there's a decent payout here, but with that high dollar value comes the potential for massive felony charges. We're talking at least four years in prison, with the potential for a decade or more."

Jack lifted his hands slowly, palms in the air. "Nothing ventured, nothing gained, right?"

"Sure, but if *one thing* goes wrong, we're all going to prison. It's not worth it to me, man. We'll find something else soon. Something with less risk."

Jack stood, glared. "Like what? Some other little bullshit score worth five grand, split three ways? We're looking at nearly a hundred fucking grand here, bro. Thirty grand each for a few minutes of our time."

"Sure, thirty grand apiece would be great, but doing fifteen years in prison would kind of suck, if you ask me."

"So, that's it? We're not doing it just because you're afraid of what *could* happen?"

"It's not about fear, man. It's about weighing risk versus reward. It's about being safe, and smart. Planning things well. Then planning some more. A hundred grand would be amazing, but it also comes with more risk, and more people looking for those who did the job. Even if we got away with the watches, the investigation into who did it will be way more intense than anything we've ever been a part of. We're talking about intercepting a trucking company's shipment, which could bring heat from local police, state police investigators, possibly even the feds. We don't need that kind of attention. There are much safer jobs out there, and we'll find one soon."

Jack headed to the door. "Sorry I bothered you with my stupid plan to make us rich by earning twenty times what we usually get."

"It's not stupid, dude. I'm just saying we need to be more careful. To attract less attention."

Jack stormed toward the front door. "Whatever."

He slammed the door behind him.

Sean plopped onto the sofa. There was no point in going after him or trying to make him see the realities of what could happen if things went wrong. When Jack got an idea in his head, he stuck with it, blinded by the possibilities, and in this case, the possibility of having a hundred grand in his hands was particularly blinding and kept him from seeing the enormous risk staring back.

As nice as it would be to pull a job worth a hundred grand, they also didn't need that much. By taking smaller scores, by focusing on cash—a couple grand here, five grand there—they'd avoided the spotlight. While some of their jobs landed in the pages of *The Daily Telegraph*, plenty of others got no coverage at all. Presumedly, the same was true for the local police department. Some of the larger jobs probably got the attention of detectives, but plenty of others had nothing more than a police report filed. Jack viewed it as them thinking too small, but the dullness of it all is exactly what had kept them safe all these years. In fact, the most they'd ever grabbed during a single job was twelve grand. By taking in small amounts of cash here and there, they were all able to pay their bills and make some splurges on things like TVs and video game consoles. Sticking to smaller scores had allowed them to operate undetected all this time, and because they'd focused on smaller jobs, the cops hadn't devoted many resources to looking for them. It also kept them from gaining the attention of larger law enforcement agencies.

Those were details Jack couldn't seem to understand. He'd never cared much about details and had always rushed into things without a plan in place—without fleshing out what could go wrong and then coming up with contingencies. He thrived on risk, and it rarely paid off.

On one of their first jobs, back in high school, they'd planned to break into the gymnasium after a big basketball game. Their Lincoln High Warriors played the Serena Huskers that night. Serena was Lincoln's top rival, so most of the town had crowded into the Lincoln High gym to watch the game. Each one of those spectators had paid five bucks to get in, and by the end of the night, all that cash was sitting in an envelope in the coach's office.

Jack had come up with a plan to sneak back into the gym after the game and steal the cash, and so, Sean attended the game with his family—cheering along with Reagan and Donnie—playing the role of one more spirited Warriors' supporter who'd paid to watch the team play. After the game, he went home and carried on with a typical evening routine, at least until around midnight when he climbed out his bedroom window, down a nearby elm tree. He walked up the street where he found Jack behind the wheel of a green Volvo he'd borrowed from his mom while she slept. Travis was already in the passenger seat when Sean climbed in, and Jack drove them back to the school where they parked along the curb, just across the street from the gym. The janitor was still inside, cleaning up after the game. After just a few minutes, Jack started bitching about how long it was taking, kept wanting to charge inside.

"Fuck, man," Jack said as he leaned over Sean to get a better look at the gym. "Let's just do this. He may not even be there. He coulda gotten a ride with someone else and just left his car here."

Sean assured him he hadn't gone anywhere, urged him to wait.

Jack plugged his iPod into the car's stereo and cranked up some Black Flag. The longer they waited though, the more impatient Jack became. Sean and Travis distracted him with conversations about how much homework their English teacher had assigned, and the topic soon shifted to whether Ms. Gustafson was hot or not. Jack thought she was "kinda fat," Travis called her "curvy," even though he didn't go to Lincoln High and was homeschoolcd by his parents.

Jack turned quickly to Travis and said, "Do you even know who we're talking about?"

Travis nodded. "Short brown hair, big tits."

Jack shrugged and said, "Yeah, that's her. How do you know her?"

"She was at the game tonight. At the ticket table."

"Oh. Yeah."

The pointless conversation carried on too long, but at least it kept Jack from doing something stupid or impulsive. Before they'd settled on a decision regarding the attractiveness of Ms. Gustafson, the janitor stepped out the front door carrying a huge bag of trash. He tossed the bag in a dumpster, got in his car, and drove away.

Jack hopped out, headed for the building. Sean and Travis followed.

Their entire plan centered on the fact that the old doors on the side of the building didn't latch well. It was widely known across campus that if you yanked on them hard enough, they opened without needing a key.

Jack walked up to the brown metal door and gave it a solid tug. It popped right open.

The gym's lights were off, but one light left on in the office provided enough guidance to allow them to walk across the gym floor without turning on any of the fluorescent lights overhead. They headed straight for the thick wood door to the office, and Sean reached out and turned the handle.

It didn't turn.

Upon inspection, he noticed a small key slot in the center of the door handle. "Shit. It's locked."

As if Sean were making up the problem, Jack stepped in front of him, attempted to open the door. It didn't budge for him either.

Sean balled up a fist and hammered the door. "Shit. Now what?"

Jack stepped forward and said, "We'll pry it open."

"With what?"

"Uh, well, we could..." Jack looked around the gym but found nothing of use. "Shit!"

While Jack and Travis scoured the gym looking for anything they could use to pry open the door, Sean examined the area around the office, hoping they could gain entry somewhere else, maybe even from above. But the side walls were concrete and ran straight up to the upper mezzanine where the weight room was. The entire office was solid, with no way in except the door, or by breaking the glass windows that looked out across the gym.

"Fuck it!" Jack shouted as he stormed toward the door. "I'll kick it in."

Before Sean could object, Jack took a big step and thrust his foot into the door.

It didn't move at all.

Jack gave it another try, but again the door didn't budge.

Travis chuckled and said, "Dumb-ass. The door frame is made of steel."

Jack stormed away, headed toward the east doors, then disappeared outside.

Travis turned to Sean and said, "Where the hell is he going?"

Sean shrugged. By then he barely cared where Jack was. The whole thing was so fucking stupid. Of course the office door was locked. Why wouldn't it be? Who would leave a bag full of cash unattended in an unlocked office? If any of them had put even a little thought into the plan, they'd have realized the door would be locked and they could have made a plan for how to get into the office.

The gym doors swung open again and Jack stormed back inside carrying a large rock.

Before Sean could say anything, Jack cocked his arm back—extending it and the rock well behind his head—then heaved it at the glass.

It connected with a loud thud.

It made an even louder thud as it hit the wood floor below.

The window didn't shatter. It barely wobbled. The rock made a noticeable dent in the floor though.

Jack picked the rock up—again hoisting in above his shoulders—then chucked it at the window.

It bounced off the window and crashed to the floor.

Travis stepped between Jack and the rock, waved his arms, and said, "Dude, stop it. This window is designed to take lots of abuse. All you're doing is making a bunch of noise."

Sean headed toward the main doors. "Let's get out of here."

"We can't leave," Jack said as he paced back and forth in front of the window. "We can't leave with nothing."

Sean didn't care. He'd had enough. "Whatever. I'm out of here, man."

"Me too," Travis said as he picked up the rock. "We've made too much noise. Someone might have called the cops."

As they stepped outside, Travis tossed the rock to the side of the building.

Jack had the car keys though. If he didn't come outside soon, Sean was prepared to walk home.

Jack emerged soon though, carrying something in his right hand.

Sean squinted to make sure it was what he thought it was: a volleyball. "What the fuck are you going to do with that?"

"Shit, dude. I dunno." Jack tossed the ball in the back of the Volvo and climbed into the driver's seat. "Let's get the fuck out of here."

With no plan, they'd risked going to juvie for the rare opportunity to steal a partially deflated volleyball from a public high school. Jack never did seem to understand how stupid that was, but that night was permanently burned into Sean's memory. A constant reminder of why he couldn't fully trust Jack.

mary

Snow fell overnight, the first measurable snowfall of the season. It hadn't accumulated on the roadways much, but it'd made them slick and dangerous for anyone without good tires. It didn't seem to stop the regular customers from coming to Morelli's Convenience that morning though. Mary had only stopped in to check on Papa, but given the increased foot traffic in the store, she ended up putting on an apron and pitching in, especially after learning that he was working alone.

Helping customers *and* keeping the floor mopped was a little too much for him to keep up with these days, and many of the morning regulars were elderly as well—most venturing into the store to get their morning coffee or grab a newspaper. She didn't want one of them slipping and falling, so she kept a vigilant eye on the floors, and in between mopping, she restocked the grocery aisle.

Papa handed some change to Mrs. Ovanic and wished her a good day. "Come see us again soon."

"I'll be in tomorrow, you know I will." She smiled, then turned toward the grocery aisle. "Nice to see you again, Mary."

"You as well. Have a good day."

Papa closed the register drawer and turned to Mary. "How's our inventory looking?"

"We're out of every soup except cream of broccoli. We haven't sold one can of that." She chuckled. "I almost feel bad for broccoli."

Papa smiled. "How about coffee supplies? I know we were low on filters."

"I cleaned out the storeroom last night and found a few. We'll be okay for a while. We are low on the little creamers though. I think the Kurtz's kids were in and took a bunch again."

"What on Earth would they want with coffee creamer?"

"They drink them for some reason."

"Really?"

She nodded. "About a month ago, I caught them out back, peeling them open and drinking them straight. At least a dozen of the little cups. They were just going to leave the trash all over the place too."

He shook his head in a *kids-these-days* kind of way.

Mary went to the front to check how many boxes of bags they had beneath the counter. The door chimed. She looked up to see her brother standing just inside the double glass doors, scowling at the display of Illinois-themed merchandise she'd placed there just before close last night.

He leaned in for a closer look. "What is this?"

"What's what?" She wasn't being sarcastic. She thought Michael was referring to a specific item on the display and she wanted to know which one.

"This tourist-trap nonsense." He pulled a keychain from a hook and waved it around. "No one coming in here is looking to buy a keychain in the shape of Illinois."

"I'm trying to get rid of them. I found a whole box in back."

He snorted as he grabbed something from another hook. "And this top hat Land of Lincoln magnet?"

"Same story. Found an entire box in back. I put both of those on sale. I'm just trying to sell through them and get 'em out of our inventory. If no one knows we have them, we can't sell them, so I put them right up front."

He scoffed. "It's freezing outside. We need to move hats and gloves up here. Ice scrapers too."

She pointed to the wicker bin on the checkout counter. "You mean those hats and gloves? That's all we have left: three beanies and a couple pairs of gloves. We sold out of ice scrapers two days ago. A shipment comes tomorrow though. It's supposed to have hats, scarves, gloves, ice scrapers, ice melt, and windshield washer fluid. Anything else I can answer for you?"

He shoved the magnet back onto the display, then stormed toward the office in the back.

She turned to Papa, hoping he'd offer some kind of support, maybe a few words of encouragement on how to deal with her impossible know-it-all brother. Instead, he turned his palms up in the air and offered a small shrug.

Papa never said anything bad about Michael and blindly supported his hopes of taking over the store once Papa retired. Problem was, Michael rarely spent any time at the store. Conversely, Mary was there fifteen or more hours a week, on top of her job with the police department. Michael had a business degree though, so apparently, that meant he knew everything there was to know about running a convenience store, even if he acted like working in one was far beneath him.

Her phone buzzed with a text from her boss. Papa was busy ringing someone up, so she whispered to him. "I'll be back a little later to check in, Papa."

He gave her a nod and she rushed out the door and to her SUV where she dialed Flanigan's number.

"Hey, Morelli. I need you over here at 1680 Sixth Street. We've got a real fucked up situation on our hands."

She started her SUV and headed to the scene on the city's southwest side as Flanigan explained the situation. Uniformed officers had responded to a call at the home after neighbors called dispatch to report that two small children had been alone and unattended in the front yard for nearly an hour. Officers arrived to find a two-year-old boy and a four-year-old girl alone in the yard. The boy was shirtless, wearing only a badly soiled diaper. The girl was clothed, but not warmly enough for the wet and cold fall weather. The children's mother answered the door when the officers knocked, but the woman was heavily intoxicated, possibly under the influence of narcotics.

Responding officers stated the house smelled like rotting eggs and they detained the two adults inside the filthy house. In the kitchen, officers found jars, tanks, and a pile of empty blister packs that once contained cold medicines—all signs of a meth lab. It was a familiar sight, especially lately. LGPD had busted three makeshift labs this month alone, and it seemed this was going to end up being the fourth.

Mary pulled up to the curb outside the small ranch house where Flanigan waited for her on the lawn, and specialty crews in protective gear were already clearing items from the house.

She stood beside Flanigan and studied the unfolding scene. "This a confirmed lab?"

Flanigan nodded. "And worse than that, it looks like we interrupted the making of breakfast for their children. These folks were cooking eggs and toast inches from where a batch of meth had just been cooked."

"My god."

Parents were supposed to protect their children. It was further unfathomable that someone would endanger any child—especially their own—just to make a few bucks, or even to support an addiction. Mary had two girls. Ashley, sixteen, and Emma, fifteen. She'd given birth to Ashley just as she finished high school and struggled to raise both girls on her own after their father left. It wasn't always easy, but she would do anything for them and would never place them in harm's way. It was a philosophy not shared equally by all parents, it seemed.

Flanigan pointed toward a window at the front of the house. "In the bathroom there, just off the family room, we located a separate lab, apparently used to make a different kind of meth. More jars and two propane cylinders, and in the closet of a bedroom shared by both kids, we found two large tanks. One of 'em contained anhydrous ammonia."

It wasn't uncommon for them to find anhydrous ammonia inside labs during busts. The chemical compound was routinely used as a fertilizer on many farms in the area, but it was also often stolen from those farms because it could also be used to manufacture meth. The chemical was dangerous, so dangerous that it could cause severe burns to any human skin it made contact with, and the vapors alone could cause severe destruction to lung and eye tissue. Even so, these parents were storing it in the same room where their children slept, apparently without concern for their health.

Mary's stomach turned at the thought of what irreversible damage the kids had endured already. "Are the kids okay?"

"Hard to say. They've been taken in for an evaluation. Of course, you never know what long-term issues they'll have from exposure to all this shit."

She released a deep sigh. "Where are the Parents of the Year right now?"

"One's in Officer Mulner's vehicle. The other's with Figenbaum. I want you to follow them in. Interview them, see what they'll tell us."

Mary followed the squad cars to LGPD headquarters. Even after multiple lab busts like this one, it still upset her. Laytons Grove had been home to her family for generations, and she'd lived in the town all thirty-four years of her life. She'd always figured it was the perfect place to raise Ashley and Emma, but lately, she'd been wondering if she'd been wrong about that. Things were changing. Drugs were taking over, which made it an increasingly dangerous place to raise teenagers, and more dangerous to be a cop.

About a month ago, a LaSalle County Sheriff's deputy was shot during a traffic stop, just a mile outside of town. The deputy had pulled the car over along Highway 21, and as the deputy approached the vehicle, the driver fired a single round that struck the deputy in the shoulder, just beyond the coverage of his bullet-proof vest. Following a chase involving sheriff's deputies and the Laytons Grove PD, a deputy performed a PIT maneuver and brought the suspect's car to rest. They arrested the driver and a passenger, and a search of the vehicle turned up two handguns, a sawed-off shotgun, and just over seven pounds of meth. Drugs and guns destined for the streets of Laytons Grove.

The idea that her girls could be exposed to something as devastating as meth was terrifying, but the fear of the violence that came with it was more concerning. That fear was the reason she'd become a cop—a job that gave her the opportunity to serve the community she loved and to make life a little safer for her family. Lately though, she worried it could be a losing battle.

reagan

Reagan sat down at her desk and stared toward the small window that looked into an alleyway. As uninspiring as the view was, she'd always enjoyed it because it reminded her that she was in Chicago, the place she'd wanted to live since she was a little girl. Even though she was trapped inside an office all day, that alley view reminded her that she lived in a city that was vastly bigger than the small town she'd grown up in—reminded her that once she was off work, she'd have dozens of restaurants to dine at, shops to visit, events to attend. And she could do all those things until late into the evening, unlike Laytons Grove where most things closed by eight o'clock.

The view from that window—and the possibilities it represented—always made it easy to return to work.

Except for today, for some reason. It was odd. Usually when she spent a few days in Laytons Grove, she couldn't get back to Chicago fast enough, and when it came time to return to Laytons Grove for a visit, she dreaded it. Today, she felt the opposite. She didn't want to be in Chicago. She wanted to be home with her family.

One obvious reason was that she felt concern for them. Despite her father's words, she wasn't sure that his job was secure or that her parents wouldn't face losing the house again. She'd seen the same signs before, years ago, when she was still in high school.

When Johnson-Power Glassworks laid him off, the family had to cut back on everything, and before long, her parents had fallen behind on several mortgage payments. For weeks she listened to them from the top of the stairs as they discussed potentially selling the house, and on occasion, they even discussed letting it fall into foreclosure and making the bank evict them.

Thankfully, Ma's sister and brother-in-law stepped in with a loan that covered the mortgage until her dad found work at Midland Ceramics. They'd come close to disaster, and Reagan thought all of that was in the past, until this weekend. Now she felt she should be with them, even if there wasn't much she could do.

The struggles she watched her parents navigate throughout the years led to her taking her current job at Lifeswork. Her role with the nonprofit wasn't an important one, just a basic entry level position that came with the title of "office assistant," although everyone knew she was little more than a glorified receptionist. Her main job was to welcome the people who came in, give them paperwork to complete, and ask them to sit and wait in the drab lobby until someone called their name. It wasn't thrilling work, but Lifeswork helped out-of-work people get back on their feet, and it felt good to play a small part in their successes.

While some of those who came through the doors of Lifeswork had struggles with drugs or alcohol, the vast majority had simply fallen on hard times. They'd missed a paycheck or two, or had to empty their bank accounts and max out their credit cards to cover an unexpected medical expense.

One thing she'd learned by watching her father struggle was that society wasn't always fair to those who had lost their jobs, even when it was due to no fault of their own. While there was little she could do about that on a large scale, her job at Lifeswork provided her the chance to change how a small number of people were treated. That began when she first greeted the people coming into the office. Most of her coworkers did that and nothing more. They also tended to talk *at* each person who came into the office, rather than talking *to* them: "Have a seat over there" or "We'll call you when we're ready for you," all without looking up from their computer monitors. It was so routine, so cold, so scripted. They never even addressed anyone by name, and it seemed unlikely that they would even be able to recall what color shirt someone was wearing, let alone be able to describe their physical features with any sort of detail.

Reagan recognized the look on the faces of the people in there though—most wore the same look her dad wore on his face after being laid off from Johnson-Power. The look of being tired, discouraged, and humiliated by the process of having to look for a job after putting in several years of hard work with their previous employer.

After just a few weeks working at Lifeswork, she fully understood, for the first time, what her father must have felt. He'd probably been treated just like the people that came into Lifeswork: like nothing more than a number in a line.

The hardships her family endured, and those of everyone who walked into the Lifeswork office, could usually be traced to one thing: corporate greed. Johnson-Power laid her father off because the employees had wanted to be treated better, wanted safer work conditions, and wanted more money for the hard work they did. In fact, they'd been trying to form a union to help get all those things, and they'd come close to succeeding, but when the company saw that unionization was about to become a reality, the owners shut down the plant, deciding it was cheaper to move operations to another facility rather than pay experienced workers a little bit more money each month.

Her trip into the Morelli's convenience store over the weekend had brought back a flood of memories too, memories of fighting corporate greed alongside Mary Morelli. Several years ago, Mary headed a group of citizens in an effort to stop a major big box retailer from opening a massive store in town. All across the region, the company had been forcing small shops out of business by undercutting them on price. The company also forced manufacturing plants to move operations out of the entire Midwest to overseas locations so they could produce goods at the low cost the retailer demanded. As the daughter of a small business owner in Laytons Grove, Mary set out to stop the massive retailer from opening a store in town by joining with other small business owners to launch the Coalition for a Better Laytons Grove. Reagan joined the Coalition a few months after it formed, protesting throughout town, gathering signatures on petitions, and delivering flyers door-to-door across town to spread the word about how other small towns had been devastated by the company's unfair business practices.

Their efforts paid off when the city council voted against the company's zoning requests, effectively preventing the store from opening in Laytons Grove. It was a big win for Reagan and her fellow protesters. It felt good to take a stand against something that threatened to harm the community, an experience that taught her that she could make a difference.

Speaking up was something she still believed in, and so she had gotten permission to leave work early today to attend a protest that she and David had organized in front of the downtown Chicago headquarters of a cosmetic company that routinely tested its products on animals. It was David who first opened her eyes to the atrocities of animal testing, back when they were attending the University of Chicago together. She was already a vegetarian when they met—shunning the industry that exploited animals for profit when she was just thirteen. David was a vegetarian too, and he pointed out things she'd never considered. Things like the use of animals in the testing of everyday products, such as the makeup she wore.

At the time, she felt totally ashamed for never considering how many companies tested their products on animals. For a time, she thought about giving up makeup altogether, but without much effort at all, she found several companies that produced the products she needed in more ethical ways. That discovery sparked something inside her.

Despite finding dozens of companies that managed to produce ethically made products—proving to the industry that it could be done—hundreds of others continued to needlessly torture animals. It angered her, but instead of being mad all the time, she set her sights on doing something about it. Something that could bring awareness to the situation and maybe even make companies stop testing on animals altogether.

The problem, as she saw it, was that not enough people knew that companies still tested on animals, and not enough knew there were so many other options. That's why she and David decided to organize today's protest against Armmon Industries.

Turnout would be key, so she and David made dozens of phone calls and plastered their alma mater's campus with flyers, seeking people to join them. A couple dozen had already said they'd be there, but she hoped a lot more than that would show up.

Reagan got off the train at the State-Clark Station and walked to the Armmon Industries building a few blocks southeast, on Randolph Street. The weather wasn't bad for a fall afternoon in Chicago—cool but with some sunshine peeking through the clouds—and about twenty people had gathered in front of the building, most of them carrying signs and chanting slogans.

David spotted her crossing the street and hurried toward her. "Hey, hon." He greeted her with a kiss. "Good turnout so far, don't you think?"

Reagan looked at the small crowd and nodded. It was a decent gathering, though admittedly smaller than she'd anticipated.

Some people they'd gone to school with had made several protest signs the night before, which were now propped against the building for anyone who wanted one, so Reagan grabbed one that read: DON'T CHOOSE TO ABUSE. Hoisting it in the air, she joined a group in front of the building's entrance and marched back and forth as they chanted a series of slogans in unison. Four other people stood on the sidewalk and passed out flyers to people walking by. One side of the flyers explained the horrors of animal testing while the other side listed companies that offered products made without testing on animals.

As she marched and chanted, the crowd swelled, doubling in size within a few minutes, and nearly doubling again when a bus carrying more protesters arrived at a nearby stop.

Most of the new arrivals appeared to be college students, and judging from the clothing they wore, many hailed from the University of Chicago, but plenty Chicago-area schools were represented as well. It didn't take long for the cache of signs to deplete, and so Reagan ceded her sign to a woman in a Northwestern sweatshirt and then joined David and his friends, who were busy making more signs to meet the increased demand.

She sat on the curb beside him and picked up a Sharpie. "Seems like we're getting a huge response."

He nodded as he wrote on a piece of tagboard. "A friend of mine at DePaul got some social media influencer to repost some stuff about it. I honestly didn't expect anything to come of it, but I guess I was wrong."

"Think we have enough materials for all the signs we'll need?"

"I'm not too worried about it. Not everyone needs one, and I think this massive turnout makes more of a statement than anything we can write on a sign."

Reagan gazed toward Dearborn Street to see another large group of nearly two dozen people walking toward them. Another large group soon joined from the elevated tracks to the north. At the same time though, foot traffic on the sidewalks had decreased, leaving fewer people to take flyers and those who did walk by refused to take a flyer and most wore expressions of annoyance on their faces. Still, the mission was intact. People for sure knew about the protest. Even if most of those passing by thought the demonstrators were a nuisance or a bunch of idealistic dreamers, they were bringing attention to their cause, and even if one or two people considered alternatives to products tested on animals, it was all worth it.

She turned to David. "How many followers does this influencer have?"

"Not sure. A million or more, from what I'm told."

"Wow! It seems to have helped." She pointed toward Wabash where another dozen or so people had just gotten off a train. "There has to be nearly a hundred and fifty people here already." She contemplated the gathering for a moment. "I wonder if we were supposed to get a permit or something for this many people?"

"A little late for that now." He laughed. "Besides, it's a free country. People are allowed to protest things that piss them off, with or without governmental approval."

He had a good point. It wasn't like they'd organized a street fair or something. All they'd done is asked likeminded people to come out and let Armmon Industries know they weren't happy with their business practices. They also hadn't put their names or phone numbers on any of the flyers, so it was unlikely they'd get in trouble for organizing the demonstration.

Just as she began to feel good about things, David yelled toward a group gathered near the building's covered entrance. "Guys! Get away from the doors!"

Reagan stood, turned toward Armmon's building where a group of about fifteen people sat on the ground, blocking the doors, preventing anyone from entering or exiting.

David walked closer, pleaded loudly. "Guys, this isn't what we're here for. It's not going to help our cause."

They ignored him.

Reagan sidled beside him. "Hey, everybody. Let's just stick to the sidewalks, okay?"

No one budged.

Again David pleaded. "This isn't fair, guys." He leaned in to speak directly to one of the men sitting in front of the door. "C'mon, man. This building is shared by companies other than Armmon. It's not right to disrupt their business."

The man flipped off David. "Shut up, loser."

David let the insult go and again addressed the entire group. "Guys, this isn't our strategy. We want to raise awareness, not create a fire hazard."

Someone else from the group shouted at him. "Piss off, douchebag."

Reagan gazed into the building where several people pushed against the doors, trying to exit. Some banged on the glass. Others shouted at the protesters. They didn't move. Instead, many of them flipped off the people on the other side of the glass.

David walked over to Reagan. "I don't know what to do." He released a deep sigh. "This wasn't the plan. We want people to be aware of what Armmon does to animals, not see us as a bunch of idiots who antagonized everyone."

"Do you know those guys?"

He shook his head. "No. I've never seen any of them before." He sighed again. "This is turning into a total disaster. I don't know what to do."

His gaze shifted to something over her shoulder.

She turned around to see four police officers approaching the building.

The officers marched past them and up to the protesters in front of the door. It was difficult to hear what the officers said, but they seemed to demand that they move out of the way.

No one budged.

More cops joined, demanding that the protesters move, but instead, those gathered in the doorway shouted insults at the cops, calling them pigs and telling them to fuck off as they interlocked arms, forming a chain.

A man in front of the building chanted: “A-C-A-B! Defund the police!”

Many seated by the doors echoed back in unison: “A-C-A-B! Defund the police!”

The man chanted: “A-C-A-B! Fuck the police!”

The crowd echoed him.

As more cops entered the area, more people joined the group in front of the doors.

A woman raised a megaphone and shouted: “Cops and the Klan go hand in hand!”

The others echoed it back in unison.

The group seemed organized. Seemed like they’d planned to confront the police today. Seemed like they’d done this several times before.

In an up-down, up-down cadence, the woman with the megaphone shouted: “Blue lives murder!”

Those linking arms in the doorway echoed her words, their chant ricocheting off the bricks of the semi-enclosed entrance. “Blue lives murder!”

Several more cops arrived from the east end of the street, some carrying shields and wearing helmets. Through a PA system mounted to one of the squad cars, and an officer ordered the protesters to disperse.

No one moved.

An officer stepped toward the seated group, but when

he got close, one of the protesters from the sidewalk stepped in front of him and blocked his path.

They exchanged some words—Reagan couldn't hear what—and then the protester shoved the cop.

The cops with the shields charged the building. Water bottles, rocks, and other debris flew toward Reagan and David from the direction of the protesters in the doorway.

More uniformed cops arrived and grabbed the peaceful protesters from the sidewalk, threw them to the ground, and handcuffed them.

David grabbed her wrist and tugged, pulling her away from the sidewalk and into the street. He dragged her west on Randolph, pulling so hard she struggled to keep her feet stable beneath her.

A couple blocks away, they stopped briefly. She struggled to catch her breath, but before she could, he yanked her arm again directed her south for a couple more blocks before he pulled her toward some stairs to an L station.

A train pulled in as they reached the platform, and as a cluster of people exited the car, he pulled her inside.

Out of breath, she took a seat near the doorway.

He sat down beside her. "I'm so fucking sorry."

"For what?"

"The whole thing. All of this is my fault. I put us in danger, and I'm sorry. I have to be more responsible than that."

"You didn't put anyone in danger. You didn't cause any of that."

"I don't know what happened. I don't know why those guys acted like that. It all happened so fast."

"That wasn't your fault. It's okay."

And it was okay. Things could have been worse. They

could have been the ones thrown to the ground and handcuffed. She could have made a call to Ma from jail to say she needed bail. They could have been injured. But they weren't. They were fine. They were headed home tonight, a luxury that others didn't have right now.

sean

The sound of gravel crunching beneath tires pulled Sean's attention away from the movie on his TV and centered it on the parking lot outside his apartment. He glanced out the window to see Jack's truck pulling in, with Travis seated in the passenger seat.

Jack had been vague when he texted and said he wanted to discuss something, but Sean knew what he wanted, knew that he'd surely pitched his watch-heist plan to Travis and that Travis must have been on board with it. In just a few moments, they'd both be standing in his living room trying to convince him to join them.

Jack's plan wasn't terrible, but he'd known Jack long enough to recognize that he had trouble finding weak points in his ideas once they came to him, and instead of looking for solutions to potential problems, Jack tended to blindly and stubbornly stick to his original plan. The only way to change his mind was to offer a better idea, which Sean had, but now he needed to convince Jack that the new plan was the better, safer option for all of them.

He opened the door before they knocked, and Jack headed straight for the fridge to grab beers.

Jack popped the top off the bottle, flopped onto the sofa, kicked his feet up on the coffee table. "Brooke here?"

Sean shook his head. “Naw. She’s at her place.” He sat down across from Jack in an armchair that he’d inherited from his uncle. “So, what’s up?”

Jack finished a swig. “I know you don’t like it, but that thing with the watches... I’ve told Travis all about it, and he wants to do it.”

“Is that so?”

Travis grabbed a beer and sat down beside Jack, nodded. “I mean, that’s one helluva payday, right?”

Sean inhaled deeply, steadied the boiling anger inside. “It would be a massive payout, sure. I can’t deny that, but there’s also a lot that could go wrong. With one way in and out of the yard, we could get stuck there if we don’t have a contingency plan, and even if everything goes perfectly, selling merchandise is a slow and expensive process. It could be months before we collect our pay, and the fence is going to take a massive cut.”

Travis nodded in agreement. “Yeah, I’ll admit, I’m a little concerned that we’d never be able to collect on all of it. Still though, even if we’re only able to sell half of the watches, we’d make a killing, even after the fence’s cut.”

Sean traced the rim of the beer bottle with his thumb. “What if we set the whole thing on the back burner for now and focus on something that has a more immediate payday?”

Jack removed his feet from the coffee table, sat up straight. “Why are you so against making a hundred grand?”

“I’m not, believe me.” He lit a cigarette. “But a hundred grand is a best-case scenario with that job, assuming we’re able to secure a good buyer and move every one of those watches, and that we don’t get arrested in the process. But look, you said it yourself, those watches are shipped through town all the time, so it's always an option down the road. What would you say if I said that I had a way to make eight to ten grand right now, all cash, with no fence needed, and with no merchandise to offload?"

Jack's posture relaxed. "All right, I'm listening. What's the job?"

"There's this guy I've been watching. He sells sports memorabilia—baseball cards, autographed jerseys and photos, shit like that."

Jack snort-laughed. "You want us to steal a Mickey Mantle rookie card or some shit? And that's better than nabbing high-end watches?"

"I'm not talking about hitting the guy's merchandise. I'm talking about going after the cash he has on hand."

Travis finished a swig of beer, leaned back on the sofa. "How much cash could someone like that possibly have?"

"Plenty." Sean exhaled a cloud of smoke. "This dude sells lots of memorabilia, and all of it is pricey shit. Now, he sells some of it online, but where he really makes his money is at special events. In-person gatherings of sports nerds."

Jack scoffed. "I'm sure most of that is credit card and Venmo sales though."

Sean shook his head. "Not all of it. The majority of it is still cash. He takes cards and payment apps, but he also passes the processing fees onto his customers, which pushes most of them toward paying in cash. The guy rakes in thousands in cash sales at each show he attends, and he's signed up to be a vendor at a big show at the mall over in Peru in a couple weeks. That show is geared toward holiday shoppers—people looking to buy early Christmas gifts—so it should be extra lucrative for the guy."

Travis finished another swig. "How much can the guy really make from shit like baseball cards though?"

"He specializes in rare items—baseball cards worth two, three grand each, signed jerseys worth five grand or more."

Jack chuckled. "So, we what? *Hope* that he happens to sell some expensive cards at this show? Why hope when we can just grab watches that we know are worth a fuck-ton?"

Sean finished his cigarette and stubbed it out. "I've been researching this guy's company. During a weekend show, he rakes in eight to ten grand, on average. We're not *hoping* for anything. I know how much he's making, and if he has even an average weekend, he'll make a ton, which means we'll make plenty for our efforts."

Travis set his beer on the coffee table, leaned closer. "Okay, so the dude earns a ton. How do we get to all that cash?"

"The guy runs the business from a small commercial space up in Mendota. An old building that he rents cheaply. I trailed him after a show last Saturday and watched as he took everything back to that building. Dude never went to the bank, which means he keeps the cash in there too."

Jack finished his beer and slammed the bottle on the table. "That seems like a big assumption."

"Perhaps, and I will absolutely do more recon before we move on this, but last week, I waited for him to leave and then slid a borescope camera under the garage door to see what's inside. He's got a two-door safe in there. Nothing fancy at all. I looked up the manufacture, and it's something you can get at big box stores for under two-hundred bucks. Seems flimsy as hell, so it's not going to take much to pry it open."

Travis set his beer down. "He got cameras? Or an alarm system?"

Sean lit another cigarette. "One basic Wi-Fi camera, mounted over the front door. I was able to see the alarm keypad with my borescope. Again, nothing fancy. Cheap wireless alarm with door sensors and one motion detector. It'll be no problem jamming the wireless sensors, probably with the same jammer we used on that property management office we hit last year."

Jack stood and went to the fridge for another beer. "So... what's your plan?"

"It's pretty straightforward, really." Sean exhaled a long drag of the cigarette. "We eliminate the Wi-Fi camera by cutting the internet to the building. The main connection comes from a utility pole to the roof. Cutting the internet also prevents the alarm from sending alerts to the guy's phone. Plus, whoever's on the roof can stay there as a lookout."

Jack plopped down on the sofa. "Then we jam the alarm?"

"Yep. I'll check the specs of his specific alarm, but that little remote transmitter we already have should create enough interference to prevent the door sensors and motion detectors from communicating with the base station."

"Allowing us to walk right in, undetected." Jack smiled at the idea. "What's your plan for the safe?"

"Simple, really. Push it over, take a couple pry bars to it, and force it open. As a backup plan, we can wheel it out on a dolly and load it into a truck, but I don't think it'll come to that. It looks cheap as hell."

Travis got up for a second beer. "What's our personnel situation? One lookout on the roof, and two of us inside?"

Sean nodded. "That's my plan, yeah. The whole thing shouldn't take more than five minutes, probably a lot less."

Travis sat down. "Ten grand? You really think we'll get that much?"

Sean nodded. “Maybe more. It’ll be more than worth our minimal efforts.”

Travis looked at Jack. “Sounds good to me.” He turned toward Sean. “I’m in.”

Jack sighed. “Yeah, me too.”

Sean stubbed out his cigarette. “Good. I’ll do a little more research. Nail down the specifics, but we’ll be set to go well before the show at the mall.”

Jack stood, clasped Sean’s hand, pulled him in for a man-hug. “Shit yeah, bro. I love this idea.” He turned toward the door. “Sorry, man, but I gotta dip.”

Sean laughed. “Why? Is your mommy expecting you?”

“Actually, I’ve gotta go bang *your* mommy.”

Travis laughed, slapped Jack on the back. “Whatever. Little bitch is meeting his dealer.”

Jack shrugged, turning his palms upward. “Bro? What the fuck? I don’t go around broadcasting your business to everyone.”

Travis laughed and stepped out the door. “You’re my ride, so I guess I’m leaving too.”

Sean joined them in the doorway. “All right, cool. I’ll get to work on some more recon, get the alarm specs and all that. I’ll let you know what I find.”

Travis stepped out the door. “Cool, dude.”

Jack followed him, turned to Sean. “You sure you don’t want to also do the watch job, bro?”

“I just don’t think it’s worth the risk. Like I said, maybe one of these days. Sorry.” Sean shook his head. “You good with this job instead?”

Jack stared at the ground in silence for a moment, then nodded. “I’m in, for sure.”

Sean watched from the top of the stairs as they drove away and then returned to his chair. Jack was obviously upset about the rejection of his plan, but in the long run, Sean was protecting him. He owed Jack that for all he'd done over the years. From Sean's earliest days of public school, where he was sent when his parents could no longer afford the church's private school, Jack had been there for him.

At first, Sean was happy to switch to Lincoln High from the stuffiness of St. Thomas, with its uniforms, strict rules, and heavy religious leanings, but it was more of an adjustment than he'd expected. It felt like he'd moved to a new city. Everyone at Lincoln High already knew each other since elementary school and had formed cliques long before high school began. As the new kid, no one spoke to him, and the teachers treated him like shit too, like they thought he should know everything they were teaching because he'd been attending a more advanced private school.

Everyone soon learned something Sean had known for years: school wasn't really his thing. Donnie did well in school, and Reagan had always gotten insanely good grades with ease, but Sean certainly didn't follow in his big sister's footsteps. To make an already terrible situation even worse, within the first few days of school, a kid named Tommy Nelson started fucking with Sean every chance he got, harassing him, jumping him in the gym's locker room.

One particularly bad day, Tommy and his friends cornered Sean in the locker room just after he'd changed into his gym clothes. Tommy approached on his right as Cory Williams and Brad Ovanic blocked his escape on the left. When Sean turned around, Tommy shoved him against the lockers, and when he bounced off, Cory shoved him into the stone wall. When Sean protested, Tommy punched him in the stomach. The impact forced the wind out of Sean's lungs and, too out of breath to fight back, Sean attempted to leave, but when he tried to squeeze by Brad, he punched him in the jaw. It was a hard, shocking blow that Sean hadn't even seen him wind up for.

Everything went white for a moment, then his face throbbed.

As he struggled to focus, Tommy shoved him into the wall and again punched him in the stomach, and said, "What's the matter, pussy? You gonna cry?"

Before Sean caught his breath, Tommy punched him in the face. It wasn't as hard as Brad's punch, but it still hurt.

Brad laughed.

Cory laughed.

Tommy shoved Sean again. "Fucking pussy."

Sean tried sliding by the wall again, and again tried to squeeze past the lockers, but Tommy shoved him into the wall yet again, and then all three stepped in closer to close off any possible escape route.

Trapped, Sean struggled to get air to his lungs, then Cory punched him in the face.

"Knock it off!" Sean didn't recognize the voice, but it caused the group to back off and gave him room to get out of the corner, a chance to refocus from the blurred vision.

When his vision cleared, he saw Coach Ferraro.

Coach stepped closer and shouted, "Get out there and start warming up or I'll have all four of you running laps."

Tommy and his friends hurried toward the door.

Sean stood there, struggled to regain his breath.

Coach told him to go get warmed up and threatened him again with laps.

That was it. He didn't say anything about the attack he'd obviously witnessed, didn't even ask if Sean was all right.

At lunch period that day, wanting to avoid another run-in with Tommy, Sean skipped going to his locker and headed straight to the cafeteria, then out the doors to the lawn where he could be alone. He sat down on the steps, peered into the bagged lunch that Ma had packed him.

Someone interrupted. A rangy, long-haired kid with a skateboard under his arm. "Mind if I sit here?"

"Uh, sure."

"I can't deal with the fucking losers inside that place." He sat down, jerked his head back to flip his stringy hair out of his face. "Jesus fucking Christ. Yesterday, I sat in there and some dipshit sat down next to me and started asking me about music. Stupid shithead asked if I liked Drake. I thought he was kidding at first, but he wasn't. Do people at this school really listen to shit like that?"

Sean chuckled nervously and said, "Yeah. They do."

"Fuckin' farm boys. These dipshits probably think that shit is hardcore gangsta rap."

"I fucking hate this school."

"I'm Jack, by the way."

Sean introduced himself and Jack pulled out a pack of cigarettes and lit one. He tilted the pack toward Sean and said, "You smoke?"

"Uh..."

"It's cool if ya don't." He tucked the pack back into his pocket.

Already afraid he seemed like a loser, Sean searched for something to say, settled on saying, "You new here?"

Jack took a drag from the cigarette and nodded as a cloud of smoke encircled him. "Yeah. I just moved here."

"Cool. Where from?"

"Saint Louis. My mom finally dumped my loser dad, so we moved up here to get away."

Jack finished his cigarette, hopped on his skateboard, did a few tricks—a couple kick flips, some grinds on the stairs. After landing a couple more kick flips, Jack stopped in front of Sean and said, "You skate?"

Again he felt like a loser, but he had to say that he'd never even been on a skateboard before.

Jack offered to teach him and said he had a friend he should meet. "I got an extra board at home. I'll bring it tomorrow. Show you some cool shit."

"That'd be awesome."

"We'll go downtown. There are a lot of good spots to skate down there. I'll have my boy Travis meet us. You'll like him. That dude is fuckin' sick on a board, bro. He can probably teach you better than I can."

Sean agreed, thinking it all sounded awesome.

Jack stared at him, then said, "Can I ask you something kinda personal?"

"Uh, I guess."

"What the fuck happened to your face?"

He reached up to touch it, found it tender to the touch. "Some prick hit me earlier."

"Your dad?"

"No. Someone I don't even know, really."

"You hit him back?"

"Coach Ferraro came in before I could."

Jack nodded, then changed the subject.

A few days later, Sean and Jack were walking through the halls of Lincoln High when the force of someone's shoulder thrust into Sean's back. The jolt knocked him into a couple of students who were standing near him.

Tommy.

"You've gotta watch where you're going, bitch," Tommy said with a laugh.

His words were met with the approving laughter of his friends.

Sean turned to Tommy, faced him, and said, "Fuck off."

Tommy seemed surprised but stepped closer. "You wanna go, bitch?"

Jack shoved Tommy, stepped between them, and said, "You got a problem, motherfucker?"

"Not with you." Tommy pointed at Sean, "Just that little bitch."

"Yeah? Well, that's my boy there, so if you've got a problem with him, you've got a problem with me."

"Man, fuck you."

Jack stepped even closer, his face inches from Tommy's face, then said, "Look, bitch. I ain't some small-town pussy like you're used to fucking with. Where I come from, little cunts like you get shanked in the hallways, so if I was you, I'd choose my next words really fucking carefully."

Jack's voice and demeanor were frightening, even to Sean. His head hung low, his gaze straight at Tommy's eyes. No sign of fear or even of slight discomfort on Jack's part. Sean had never seen anyone act quite that intense before, and Jack's words seemed sincere, like he'd made good on similar threats in the past.

Tommy must have sensed it too because he backed down immediately.

"It's cool, man." Tommy took a step back. "We ain't got a problem here. I just thought he was disrespectin' me."

Jack stepped closer, closing the distance Tommy had created. "Yeah? You fuck with him again and they'll be pulling your fat corpse out of a dumpster somewhere. Got it, motherfucker?"

"We're good, homie," he said as he again stepped backward.

About a month later, Sean was skating with Jack and Travis downtown when they spotted Tommy walking into Morelli's. Within seconds, they'd hatched a plan, so Sean and Jack went around the back of the Morelli's building, pulled their shirts over their mouths and noses to cover their faces, and waited in the loading dock area. Travis, who Tommy had never met, went around to the front of the store and waited for Tommy to exit.

As soon as Tommy stepped outside, Travis grabbed the bag from his hand and ran toward the back.

Tommy followed, and once he came around the corner, Sean and Jack jumped him, tackled him to the ground, beat the shit out of him with a flurry of punches and kicks.

Afterward, they rode over to Hossack Park, dumped the contents of the Morelli's bag onto a picnic table, and evenly split the proceeds of their first score together: six candy bars.

From there, they stole answers to an upcoming test, stole all the cash from a school dance, then cash from a school concession cart. By now, it was impossible to remember every job they'd pulled together, or how much they'd earned over the years.

At the start, they did it out of boredom, and partly for the thrill. As the jobs got bigger, it became clear they could earn a good living while having fun. For Sean, it meant that, instead of putting in decades working in a hot, loud factory like his father—only to be rewarded by being laid off—he could spend his days any way he wanted, earn more money than people working forty or more hours a week, and still have fun doing it. Problem was, he wasn't sure he was still having fun.

mary

Mary's stomach twisted as she read the autopsy report. Both men were in their twenties, both from nearby Spring Valley. The coroner determined the men died in a fire. Their bodies were found by a farmer, dumped in a ditch off Highway 71. With no signs of a fire anywhere nearby the bodies, it meant they'd been burned somewhere else before someone transported their charred bodies to Laytons Grove. No attempt was made to bury the bodies or even cover them, and they were placed alongside a busy road, which meant that whoever had murdered the two men wanted the bodies to be found, perhaps to send some kind of message to others.

Family members said the two cousins had been "involved" with some people from Chicago, people they described as "sketchy." They also believed they might have been selling methamphetamine for those sketchy people.

Both victims had criminal records. Small drug possession charges, but nothing major. One of them had a misdemeanor battery conviction as well, but nothing about the mens' records indicated either one would be involved in the kind of drug trafficking operation that would end with them being burned alive and dumped in a ditch.

The case, just a few weeks old, had stalled though. The families claimed they didn't know who the sketchy guys from Chicago were, and after being cooperative initially, in recent days, they'd stopped answering Mary's calls. That left her with no leads on who might have wanted to kill the men, and attempts to link them to recent meth lab busts in town had been unsuccessful as well.

She tucked the folder in the drawer of her desk. It was getting late, so she gathered her things and headed to her SUV. She'd promised Papa she'd check in with him at the store, and she didn't want to make him wait for her all night. Michael was supposed to relieve Papa at six and then work a closing shift, but Mary didn't feel confident that Michael would remember, or that he'd be on time, or that he wouldn't get distracted by something more important to him. He constantly claimed he was ready to run things on his own, but so far, his actions told a different story.

Mary pulled into the store's parking lot and parked near the road, leaving the closer spaces for customers. To her immense surprise, she spotted Michael's Audi parked on the side of the building. It was a miracle. He'd apparently deigned to show up to the store and work like a regular employee.

Inside, Papa stood behind the counter and Michael stood on the other side of the counter, in front of him. They both stopped talking as the chime announced her presence. She'd apparently interrupted a very serious conversation.

She looked at Papa, then at Michael. "Am I intruding?"

Michael shook his head, then walked away from the counter, clearly upset about something.

She turned to Papa. "What's going on?"

"Oh, Michael was just running an idea by me."

"Oh, yeah? What kind of idea?"

Michael returned to the counter. "Nothing. Just forget it." He paced the floor briefly, then wandered toward the back of the store.

"Forget what? What did I miss?"

Papa leaned on the counter. "Michael thinks we should open a second location."

"A second Morelli's?"

Papa nodded. "Wants to do it out by Utica."

"Utica? Why?"

Michael rejoined them. "I said to just forget it."

"No." She shook her head. "Clearly you gave Papa some kind of sales pitch for your idea. I think I deserve to hear it too."

"Let's just move on."

"No, I want to hear about this second location."

He sighed sharply. "Okay, basically, I've scouted a great plot of land with a small building for sale."

"In Utica?"

"Yeah. It's just minutes from Starved Rock State Park. Everyone heading out to fish or hike is going to need gas and snacks at some point, either on their way in or on their way home. It's possible that the revenue from the new store could surpass this one within five years, quite possibly sooner."

"Seems like you've put a lot of work into this."

"Don't do that shit."

"What shit?"

"The shit where you talk to me like I'm one of your kids. Like you're shooting down their idea to get a puppy or something."

"That's not what I'm doing, Mikie." She took a deep breath to sooth her anger. "I just don't see why we would need a second location."

Papa scoffed. "It's more than that. Michael has a whole franchising plan in place too. He wants to expand all over the Midwest."

Mary turned toward her brother. "Franchising?"

"I said forget it." Again he wandered toward the back of the store.

All of this was odd news. Sure, ever since entering business school Michael had wanted to become the next Mark Cuban or Jack Dorsey or whoever, but she didn't know he'd planned to join the one percent by expanding Morelli's Convenience. The whole thing seemed absurd. Morelli's was, and always had been, a small store in a small town, and no one in the family had any plans for it beyond that because it'd supported the family for generations.

Her father had run it her entire life, and before that, her grandfather Carlo was behind the counter. Carlo purchased the place decades ago, when it was called the Fox River General Store. He renamed it Morelli's General Store, and for years, the little spot on the corner of the two busiest streets in Laytons Grove—Main Street and Peoria Avenue—was the only place in town to buy basic goods.

Grandpa Carlo's main hope was that the store would remain in the hands of his family and allow future generations to provide for their families just like he'd been able to do. That plan was going well. Really well. Papa had always provided for them, and he'd put Michael in the position to take over and do the same for his family, if he ever settled down long enough to start one. What he'd proposed threatened all of that though.

Mary turned toward her father. "Is franchising the store something you're okay with doing?"

Before he could respond, Michale stored back to the counter. "I said drop it. Obviously everyone thinks it's a dumb idea."

She softened her tone and turned to face her brother. "No, I think we should discuss this, but help me understand where this is coming from. I mean, what gave you the idea to expand? That's nothing we've ever talked about, and I can't imagine it's something Grandpa Carlo would want to see."

"You don't know that. Why wouldn't he want to see us expand? He expanded on his idea. Papa expanded on what he inherited. Why can't we do the same?"

He'd made a surprisingly decent point. It was Papa who'd transformed the small grocery store into a gas station and convenience store, but he'd done it in response to threats to losing the business, not for the sake of more profit. His expansion came not long after he took over the business—months after a large grocery store opened just a few blocks west, taking a lot of business away from the family store. He also noticed a shortage of gas stations in the area, so he took out a loan and expanded into what Morelli's is today. Michael's idea seemed based in greed, not need.

Again she took a deep breath. "It's not a bad idea, Mikie, but it sounds incredibly expensive. There'd be licenses and zoning hurdles, plus installing tanks and pumps. There's also the renovations to the existing building in Utica, and I'm guessing it's not a new building, right? Renovating older properties can get expensive. We'd probably have to do asbestos or lead abatement, and aside from getting the building ready, we'd have to increase our orders from vendors in order to stock the shelves. By the time it opens, we'll have spent an insane amount of money."

"I know that, and I'm willing to pay for all of it on my own. I'm not asking to leverage the business or anything like that."

Her muscles tightened. "I don't want to pry into your life or whatever, but how can you afford to pay for all that?"

"If I sell some of my shares in Courante Systems."

She'd walked right into that one. A few years ago, Michael invested a few thousand dollars into a company that was developing an app to help people find new bands to listen to. He loved bragging about his involvement in the company, loved flaunting the fact he owned those shares, but she doubted they were worth as much as Michael said. She certainly doubted that they were worth enough to expand Morelli's to the extent he was proposing.

Again she sighed. "You believe in a second location that much? Enough to sell off your best investment."

"I do." He turned toward Papa. "But *he* thinks I'll destroy the family business."

Papa slapped the counter with his palm. "That is not what I said, Michael. Don't put words in my mouth. My concern is that you won't be able to effectively run two locations, and that stretching yourself too thin could lead to both of them falling apart."

"You're only focusing on the negatives. The other side of that argument is that I'll end up with twice the revenue we have now. Twice the name exposure. And with that name exposure comes the possibility to franchise. To have people pay *us* to put the Morelli's name on stores they open. The licensing fees alone could support every member of this family for generations to come. It's possible that Mary's kids, or at least her grandkids, would never even have to work in a Morelli's store."

Papa sighed again. "Or the whole thing could go bust and we're left with nothing."

Mary interjected. "Mikie, I get that you're comfortable taking risks, but this store has supported this family for generations, and we've all enjoyed working here. I think what Papa is saying is that, to him, it's not worth risking the whole thing."

Michael grunted. "This isn't about taking on extra risk. It's about *reducing* risk. As it is, this store comes with plenty of risk. Nothing's guaranteed here. Any number of things could happen, and we could be out of business tomorrow. With each new location we open, we reduce the risk that something catastrophic could put us out of business."

"Michael..." Papa released a deep breath before speaking again. "We have everything we need with this location. It has provided for us for years—for decades—and if we're careful, it will continue to do so for many more."

"I know that, Papa, but imagine if there was a Morelli's Convenience Store in every town across the Illinois Valley, or in every sizable town in the state, for that matter. What if, someday, there were Morelli's stores in *every* state in the country?"

Mary scoffed. "But why do we need that, Mikie?"

"Why the hell not? I'm just trying to look ahead, you know? But if you're hellbent on preventing this place from getting better, or from the family prospering, then I don't know what to do."

He turned and stormed toward the front doors. She called after him, but he ignored her, flung open the doors, and stormed outside.

She followed him to the parking lot. "So, I guess I'm closing the store by myself tonight?"

He stopped at his car. "Why not? You love the place as it is so goddamned much. If I work tonight, I'll probably just try to improve it and ruin it."

He climbed inside his car and started it. The tires squealed as he took off down Main Street.

His need to expand Morelli's was something she couldn't understand. Papa was going to retire someday soon, and someone had to take over, someone responsible. She'd never considered leaving the force, but thinking about what could happen to the family business with Michael in charge upset her more than the prospect of leaving a job she loved.

reagan

Ma pulled the cookies out of the oven and set the pan on the counter. "Those look done enough, don't they?"

Reagan nodded in agreement. "They look perfect, and I'll bet that Dad will never know they're vegan."

"I think he might be okay with the idea of vegan cookies." Ma chuckled. "Now, that recipe you have for vegan hamburgers, well, that would be tougher to get by him."

"I bet he'd like them just fine, but I get what you're saying. One small step at a time, right?"

"Something like that." Ma smiled. "I'm so glad you were able to come down and visit again."

"Me too. I miss you guys."

She'd chosen the phrase because she didn't want to say that she was worried about them, but the words were true, nonetheless. She did miss her family, and Laytons Grove, an unfamiliar feeling she was still adjusting to. For most of her life, she'd wanted nothing more than to leave—to move basically anywhere else. She'd hated that everyone in town knew nearly everything about her. She hated that when she broke up with her first boyfriend, everyone at school knew about it instantly, and that when he'd lied and said they'd had sex when they hadn't, everyone took his word for it. She hated that there wasn't a mall, or a large movie theater. Everything about the town seemed discordant with the life she wanted, and so all she'd ever wanted was to move away.

When she began applying to colleges, she focused on places like Michigan, Wisconsin, and Minnesota because they seemed far away from Laytons Grove, yet close enough that Ma would find a way to be okay with it. Then she got into the University of Chicago and even landed scholarships to pay for it. Even though she'd often dreamed of someday living in Chicago, part of her felt she was settling because Chicago wasn't quite far enough away. But after four years of school in Chicago, and after she and David settled in the area with jobs and a nice apartment, it felt a million miles away from Laytons Grove. At the time, that helped, but now, oddly, living in Chicago seemed like a bad thing.

Ma scooped the cookies off the sheet and onto a cooling rack. "I'm excited to try these."

"I think you'll like them." Reagan leaned against the counter. "David loves them, and in all seriousness, no one would ever know they're vegan."

"We'll see. I won't say anything to your father or Donovan so we can get an honest review."

"Donnie's coming?"

"Oh! Did I not tell you? I talked to him this morning and he's agreed to come up for dinner tomorrow night. He can't stay long because he needs to get back to Champaign for classes, but we get him for dinner."

"That's awesome!"

Ma's face turned serious. "I don't suppose I could talk you into working on Sean, could I? It would be really nice for the whole family to have a meal together."

Reagan couldn't turn down the plea, and Ma knew it. She could be very cunning when she needed to be. "I'll see what I can do. Maybe I'll swing by his place a little later, see if I can catch him at home instead of calling or texting."

He'd have a harder time turning her down in person. Reagan could be cunning too.

Sean's apartment was about ten blocks east of their parents' house, on the edge of downtown. It was a small one-bedroom place located on the corner of Elgin Avenue and Adams Street, inside an old house that'd been divided into multiple units, and his second-floor unit offered an uninspired view of Adams Street below.

When she reached the top of the stairs, she took a deep breath, then knocked.

He was usually home during the day. He and his friends supposedly owned a company that provided lawn mowing and snow removal services, but it was obvious they didn't do much landscaping, which meant the business was likely just a front for whatever illegal stuff they actually did to make money. She'd never question him about any of it though. The less she knew, the better.

The door swung open, and Sean appeared in the doorway. "Hey, sis."

"Hey. I thought you'd be more surprised to see me in town."

"I already knew you were here."

"How?"

"It's a small town. People talk."

"Oh. Of course." She awaited an invitation inside, but after several moments of silence, one hadn't been extended. "Can I come in?"

He wiped his eyes. "Yeah. Why not?"

Why not, indeed. She was just his only sister who he hadn't seen in months and hadn't even talked to in several weeks. Why would he invite her into his home?

He stepped aside and motioned for her to enter. A stench of stale cigarettes and boy-stink hit as she stepped inside his apartment. The place was cluttered with discarded clothing, and dirty dishes towered out of the sink. The place was even worse than she'd remembered it.

"Have a seat." He motioned toward the ratty couch. "You want a beer?"

"No, thanks."

"Water or pop or something?"

She sat on the edge of the cushion, where it seemed the cleanest. "I'm fine, thank you."

He walked to the refrigerator and got himself a bottle of beer. Popping it open, he sat on a stool by the kitchen counter. "So? Ma send you?"

An involuntary snort-laugh escaped. They both knew that was the only reason she'd be there. "Of course she did."

He nodded. "Another dinner invite?"

"That's the plan."

"Tonight?"

"No. Tomorrow night. At seven. Donnie's coming too."

Sean nodded, then sipped his beer. "How is he?"

"He's good. He's liking school. And he's in a band now. They're actually really good."

"Oh yeah? Last I heard he was looking to start a new

band. I hadn't heard it'd come together though. That's awesome. He's a talented little dude. I'm happy for him."

"Yeah? Then you should come to dinner tomorrow. You can tell him all of that yourself."

Sean smirked. "How's everything with you?"

A change of subject was expected, so she allowed it. "Life is good. Work is going okay too. David and I got a new place in Oak Park."

He finished a gulp of beer. "I uh... I think you got a new job since we last talked, didn't you? What d'ya do these days?"

"I mow lawns and stuff."

He chuckled. "There's good money in that."

"That's what I hear." She smirked. "No, I work for a nonprofit called Lifeswork. We help people get jobs. Particularly people who've been out of the workforce for a while or who are experiencing homelessness."

He nodded. "That's cool."

She looked around the place. Beer bottles littered the coffee table and the end table, along with wrappers from fast food places. "Does Brooke live here?"

"Naw. She's got her own place."

Reagan nodded. It made sense. No girl would want to spend too much time in such a bachelor hell-hole. "She's invited to dinner too. Ma specifically said that."

"I think she has to work tomorrow night."

Reagan nodded. "Is she still a server at that Mexican restaurant?"

"No. She works in retail now. Fashion Junction downtown."

"That trendy chain place that took over the old Gleason's hardware store?"

"That's the one. I guess the pay is decent, and she gets a discount."

"That's good." Reagan looked around the place again, beginning to feel like she'd already overstayed her welcome. "So? Dinner tomorrow?"

"I don't think so, sis."

"Please come. It would mean the world to Ma."

"And what about Dad?"

"He misses you. You know that."

"You sure about that? Things didn't exactly end on good terms the last time we spoke."

She shrugged. "How long ago was that? Two years ago?"

"Not quite that long." He took a gulp of beer. "And we've spoken since then, on the phone, mostly. Shit is still weird though."

"Just come to dinner, Seanie. One, maybe two hours, and then you're done."

"I dunno. Doesn't seem like a good idea."

"Please. It would mean *everything* to Ma, and you can catch up with Donnie too."

He nodded as he stared at the floor. "I dunno. Maybe."

"Please, Sean. If it turns into a shit-show, you can leave early. But I honestly think things will be fine. Dad misses you, despite whatever you believe, and Ma wants the whole family together again *so* badly. She's really hurting. If you saw how sad she looks every time she requests a family dinner, there's no way you'd be able to say no."

"I get all that, but things never go like you think they will."

"Then at least you know what to expect, right? Please come over. Just this once. Just try one more time. Please?"

He drew in a deep breath and exhaled it slowly. "You really think this is a good idea?"

She nodded. "I do."

"Okay. What time again?"

"Seven, or earlier. Ma would be impressed if you brought flowers or something." She was pushing it now.

"Yeah? Okay. I can do that."

"She'll be overjoyed." She stood up and hugged her brother. "Thank you."

"Yeah. Sure thing."

"I mean it. This will make her *so* happy." She stepped toward the door. "Okay, I'll leave you alone now."

He followed her to the doorway. On the stairs, she paused as a wave of satisfaction washed over her. She'd done it. She'd actually gotten him to agree to a family dinner. Although, it was still twenty-four hours away, so there was no telling if he'd show up or not.

sean

Sean parked on the street along the curb. A spot that offered a quick getaway, should it be needed.

The house looked good, basically the same as it always did. Although Dad had obviously painted the trim and mended the porch railing recently.

He stepped onto the porch and let the cool fall breeze pass over him as he stared at the doorbell, unable to make his finger press it. Glancing at the flowers he'd gotten on the way over, he contemplated his options. He'd come this far—put this much effort into the night already—it seemed stupid to turn back now. Ma would love the mixed bouquet he'd gotten, even though it was the least expensive bouquet sold in the Hy-Vee floral department. The point was, he'd already bought flowers, so he might as well ring the doorbell and give them to her.

Alternatively, he could just turn around, get back in his car, and toss the flowers in a trash can somewhere.

Before he reached a decision, the door swung open to reveal Reagan on the other side. "Having second thoughts?"

He chuckled. "Something like that."

She glanced at the flowers. "You *can* take a hint. Brooke must love that about you." She chuckled, stepped aside. "Come in. Ma and I are still cooking. Dad and Donnie are watching TV."

Stepping into the house he passed the staircase and spotted his dad and brother in the living room, sipping beers and watching a football game. Dad rose from his chair, seemingly happy to see him. A torrent of memories flooded Sean's mind. The fights. The yelling. Sean at seventeen, storming across the front lawn with Dad screaming at him, telling him he would never be welcome in the house again. The brief reunions, and then more fights.

"Hey, pops."

"It's great to see you." Dad extended his hand.

Sean met his hand and shook it, but Dad pulled him closer, wrapped an arm around him, patted him on the back.

"You look good, son."

"Thanks. You too."

Donnie stood, hugged Sean.

Pulling away from the embrace, Donnie pointed at the flowers. "Those for me? Don't you know that I prefer chocolates."

Sean shoved him. "Shut up, dipshit."

Donnie punched him in the arm. "Mama's boy."

Dad chuckled. "Can I get you a beer, Seanie?"

"That'd be awesome. Thanks."

Reagan nodded her head toward the kitchen, a not-so-subtle request that he go say hello to Ma.

Sean took that hint too and proceeded his father into the kitchen. "Hey, Ma."

She greeted him with a hug, spoke with excitement as she called out his name.

"I got these for you." He held the flowers outward toward her.

"They're lovely." She took them from him, sniffed them. "You didn't have to bring me anything though. I'm just thrilled that you're here."

Dad slid past them to get to the fridge. "She's not just saying that. She's so focused on your visit that she forgot to get beer when she was at the store. I had to drag my tired bones out and get it myself." He grabbed a case of Old Style from the fridge, plopped it on the counter, and kissed Ma. "Can you believe that?"

Ma slapped his arm. "Poor baby."

Dad tore open the box and handed a can to Sean. "It's for the best though. This way, I could be sure we're good and stocked. There's two more of these out in the garage fridge, just to be safe."

He offered Reagan a can.

She shrugged. "Why not?"

He set two more on the counter, then offered Ma one. Her face contorted, so he returned the can to the box, and the box to the fridge.

Ma set something in the microwave and pressed a few buttons. "We'll be ready to eat in about fifteen minutes. Why don't you go back to your game. I'll let you know when it's ready."

Dad chuckled. "In other words: get the hell out of my way."

She smiled. "I was trying to say it nicer though."

Sean returned to the living room and sat down on the couch beside Donnie. Dad handed Donnie a beer, then returned to his favorite chair.

Sean watched Donnie crack the can open. "Are you old enough to be drinking beer?"

"Shut up, ass-monkey. I'm months away from being legal." He pointed to their dad. "Besides, he gave it to me. You saw."

Reagan leaned against the wall by the kitchen and cracked her can open. “So, Dad’s an enabler? Is that what you’re saying?”

Dad chuckled. “Are you friends with him on Facebook? Seems like he drinks plenty of beer with or without my influence.”

Reagan looked at Donnie and shook her head slowly. “You need to fix your privacy settings, baby brother. Block certain people from certain aspects of your college life.”

Donnie shrugged. “I got no secrets.”

Ma stepped into the room, looked at Reagan. “Let’s circle back to this privacy setting thing. Have you been blocking parts of your life from your loving parents?”

Reagan shook her head. “Not from you guys. Never.”

Everyone laughed and Sean watched the family with the same amazement he felt when he saw families like them on television. If the seventeen years he’d spent in the aging house on Monroe Street had featured this version of his family, he might have stuck around a little longer. It wasn’t the version he’d known though. The version he remembered was one that trusted the opinion of teachers and doctors more than what their own son told them. Who forced him to take medications to treat ADHD, anxiety, and depression. Who talked about his brain’s “imbalance” like it was something that made him inferior to the other models of children available on the market. Like he was broken and that they needed to fix him because they couldn’t afford to upgrade to a newer version.

It all came back to him. The reasons he’d hated growing up in the house. The reasons he hated going to school. The reasons he hated coming home. Why he hated his parents, and now he was trapped there with them yet again, expected to eat dinner with them all while pretending none of the awful bullshit from back then happened.

He stood. "I gotta hit the can."

Reagan was waiting in the hallway when he finished in the bathroom.

Sean startled when he opened the door. "Jesus. Do you always creep on people when they're taking a piss?"

"Are you okay?"

"I'm fine." He started down the hall, but she blocked his path and showed no signs of budging.

"What happened back there? In the living room."

"What d'ya mean?"

"We were all having a good time, laughing, being a normal family, and then your mood flipped like a switch, and you stormed away. What's going on?"

"I didn't storm away. I had to pee."

"What's wrong, Seanie? What can I do to help? It means so much to Ma that you're here—and Daddy's being super cool. What can I do to make things okay for you?"

"I'm fine. Let's just eat and get this over with."

"Please, Seanie. Just let me in on what's bugging you. I'll help if I can."

"You can't help. And no one did anything wrong. It's just..." He released a breath that'd been trapped inside him for too long. "You can't fix any of it, so stop trying, okay?"

"At least tell me what's bugging you. Please?"

He exhaled another deep breath. "Just, you know... A lot of old, bad memories come back whenever I'm in this house."

She nodded like she understood, but she couldn't possibly understand, not really. She'd grown up in an alternative version of the same house. Like one of those Choose Your Own Adventure books where you got to pick what happened next—their stories started out the same, and remained the same up to a certain point, but ultimately played out on different pages of the same book. Reagan's adventure took her to a world where she got good grades and passed tests with ease. Meanwhile, Sean struggled. Reagan became their parents' favorite kid, while Sean became a burden—something broken that they didn't have the money or expertise to repair.

Reagan pulled him in for a hug. "I love you, Seanie. I know you hated growing up here, and I'm sorry about that. I need you to believe me when I say I'll do whatever I can to make tonight better for you."

Pulling away from the embrace, he nodded. "If you think you're up to the challenge."

"Does that mean you're planning on staying for dinner? Ma made meatloaf. You love her meatloaf."

"Meatloaf? What about you? I thought we'd be eating tofu steaks or something."

She rolled her eyes. "I made myself some delicious spinach and cheese stuffed portobellos. You're welcome to have some though."

"That sounds awful."

"Suit yourself." She shrugged. "Does that mean you're staying?"

"Yeah. I'll stay."

The streets seemed empty, aside from the occasional car passing by on the way to somewhere other than the isolated city of Mendota. The tiny warehouse sat tucked away on the edge of downtown, situated between a propane dealer and the offices of some kind of construction company—an area of the city that didn't get much traffic late at night on a Saturday.

A decent score awaited them inside. They'd spent a couple hours earlier in the day at the mall in Peru, wandering the rows of tables covered with trading cards, bobble heads, autographed mini football helmets. Tons of crap people were apparently willing to hand over wads of cash just so they could brag to their friends that they owned some arbitrary piece of sports history, often with an equally arbitrary signature from some once-great sports figure.

Careful not to draw attention to themselves, they pretended to shop, blended into the crowd. Covertly they kept an eye on how much business the guy did. Impressively, in the hour or so they'd watched him, he'd taken in at least two grand in cash. Even if that had been his busiest hour of the six-hour day, he likely pulled in more than a thousand bucks an hour on average, which meant plenty of cash sat unguarded inside the warehouse.

They'd brought Jack's pickup in case they needed to load the safe into the bed, but it seemed unlikely. Everything Sean found out about the safe indicated that it wouldn't take much to get inside of it, and once they popped the door open, they could just carry out the cash in their pockets. Sean drove his car as well, just in case they needed a separate vehicle for a getaway. The job was small and should be quick, so it didn't make sense to make it more complicated by using stolen cars, or even stolen plates. If something went south and they had to leave Jack's truck behind, they'd simply report it stolen later.

At a dollar store, in a clearance bin, they'd found a few goofy masks left over from Halloween a few weeks ago. Sean selected some kind of werewolf, Travis chose a mummy, and Jack bought a truly creepy bloodied clown. The specifics didn't really matter though. The masks concealed their faces in case a camera captured them, and that was the important thing.

They arrived early and Jack parked his truck at the Amtrak station where it could sit as long as they needed it to without looking conspicuous—just another vehicle left by someone traveling the rails. The three of them sat in Sean's car, parked on the street near a restaurant that had closed hours ago. It served a good purpose too because if anyone asked what they were doing there, they'd say they were searching Google for a place to eat that was still open.

Sitting in the car, smoking cigarettes and trading stories, they watched the warehouse, just to make sure no one was still inside the building. After fifteen minutes without a sign of anyone around, Sean felt confident they could get to work.

"All right. Let's do this." Sean raised the driver's seat from its reclined position and turned to Travis in the seat beside him. "Go get into position."

Travis nodded. "You still want me on the roof?"

"Yeah, and once you cut the internet to the building, go ahead and give the camera above the door a good kick. No sense in leaving any risk that it captures us at all. Let us know over the radio if you see anyone coming."

"Cool, cool. You sure you don't need any help with the alarm?"

"Naw. Jack and me will make sure the sensors are blocked, then we'll attack the safe."

Travis nodded but didn't get out of the car. "Can I go inside instead?"

"What?"

"I wanna hit the safe. You two always do that shit. I want a crack at it."

Sean sat in silence. Travis wasn't wrong. He and Jack were always the ones that went into buildings, and with good reason: Sean wanted to keep an eye on Jack. He couldn't say that to Travis though, especially with Jack in the back seat.

Aside from needing to monitor Jack's activities, he also didn't trust that Jack would act as an effective lookout. It was a truly important job, one that kept everyone out of trouble, and out of handcuffs. Important things to any job that couldn't be entrusted to Jack's volatile decision making.

Sean shook his head. "Next time, all right? Let's stick to what we've planned for this job."

Jack patted Sean on the shoulder from the back seat. "It's cool, bro. I'll take the roof. Travis can go in with you."

Travis seemed pleased with the revised plan, but Sean wasn't happy.

Sean turned in his seat to face Jack. "The internet absolutely has to get disabled. Everything we've got planned hinges on the internet being out."

"Relax, bro." Jack held up the bolt cutters. "I know how to cut a fucking cable."

It wasn't that simple. The man on the roof was also responsible for paying close attention to everything—every headlight in the distance, every sound, no matter how far away. Sean wasn't convinced Jack was up to all that the task required. "It's not just about the internet. We need to make sure that the—"

"I know, bro. The camera." Jack sounded annoyed. "I'll punt that fucking thing six blocks. Don't worry about it."

Travis opened the door. "Awesome. Let's get this done."

Before Sean could protest further, Travis hopped out of the car. Jack followed and soon disappeared into the alleyway on the side of the building. From there, a ladder would take him to the roof. Things were in motion and now, Sean could only hope that Jack wasn't too high or too distracted to keep everyone safe. It was an obvious mistake to task Jack with the most important role, but hopefully it wouldn't be a catastrophic error.

Jack never had been one to focus on the details. When they were in high school, Jack worked at a fast-food joint called Rocky's, and after a few months, he'd managed to get the combination to the safe by covertly looking over managers' shoulders as they opened it. Hitting Rocky's was their first big job—the first one that required deep planning—the first where the stakes were high enough that if anything went wrong, they'd be looking at serious time in juvie, or worse, since they were old enough at the time to possibly be convicted as adults.

At closing time, before the Rocky's crew exited the building for the night, Jack set his coat down on a prep table in the back room. As the manager led them to the door, Jack announced that he'd left his coat behind. While retrieving it, he unlocked the rear door.

Sean, Travis, and Jack waited about an hour after close, then set out for the restaurant on foot. With a two-way radio in hand, Travis took up a lookout spot in a secluded corner of the parking lot. In addition to keeping an eye out for cops, he'd also been tasked with breaking a window once the job was done. With a broken front window, the whole thing would look like a random break-in and not an inside job.

The place had cameras, but they only recorded locally onto a DVR that sat unsecured on a desk by the safe. The plan was super simple: enter through the unlocked back door, steal the DVR to eliminate any chance of video evidence, open the safe, and make off with the deposit bags from each cash register.

It went well.

Until it didn't.

Sean and Jack strolled through the unlocked door with ease and locked it behind them to further obscure evidence that someone who worked there had left it unlocked. They headed straight for the office and Sean unplugged the DVR, shoved it into a backpack to take with them so they could destroy it later. Jack knelt and punched the code into the safe's keypad, which popped open without issue. But as Jack pulled the deposit bags out of the safe, Sean noticed a problem. A big one that none of them had thought of. On the wall was a keypad with a backlit display. Scrolling across the screen was: ALERT......ALERT......ALERT.

Sean slapped Jack on the back to get his attention and shouted, "Fuck, dude! We tripped an alarm."

Jack raised his head, looked around in confusion. "What? I don't hear anything."

"It must be silent. Trust me, we've gotta get outta here! Now!"

"Shit. Okay. Just let me get the cash."

"Leave it, dude. We gotta go."

"It won't take me long."

Sean grabbed a two-way radio and shouted orders to Travis on the other end and said, "Break the window! Break it now!"

The radio crackled. "What?"

"Break it! Break the fucking window now, then get the hell out of here!"

More crackling. "O—Okay."

Jack popped up. "I got the money."

“Let’s fucking go then!”

Sean hurried toward the back door, and as he and Jack stumbled outside, the unmistakable sound of shattering glass echoed into the night.

He turned the corner and ran east on Lincoln. From the corner of his eye, he saw Jack beside him. “Dude! What the fuck? You’re supposed to go down Rockford. We can’t go the same fucking direction.”

“Shit. Okay,” Jack said before turning right at the next street.

Sean kept going, running full speed, so fast that he tripped over his own feet. He stumbled into Stout Park where he collapsed on a bench, completely out of breath. His chest pounded, his lungs depleted of air. Sliding to the ground, he sprawled out across the sidewalk, focused on getting oxygen into his lungs. In the distance of the calm evening, he heard the familiar sound of a train horn just across the Fox River, most likely the train was picking up a load of silica sand over in the town of Wedron. What he didn’t hear was sirens. It didn’t make sense. The cops had to be on their way.

They later learned that Rocky’s hadn’t paid the alarm company in months. They’d never been in danger of it alerting cops to the robbery, but it was a close call. Too close. If the cops had come while they were still inside, they would have been trapped, and they’d have been fucked.

It was the last time Sean let Jack plan a job on his own, but even with more planning, it didn’t mean Sean trusted that Jack could take care of important details.

The radio crackled, shattering Sean’s reverie. Jack’s voice cut through the static. “We’re all set.”

Sean raised the radio to his mouth. “The internet’s out?”

"Yes." Jack sounded annoyed.

Travis and Sean crossed the street and headed toward the front door. Sean double checked that Jack had gotten rid of the camera, and to his amazement, he had. Sean nodded his chin toward Travis who then pulled the jamming transmitter from his pocket and turned it on. They'd rigged it to constantly broadcast radio interference at 433 megahertz, which would create enough interference to block the wireless alarm sensors from communicating with the base station.

Sean jammed a Halligan bar into the door frame near the deadbolt. Travis wedged one in next to the latch. With minimal pressure, the old door popped open.

No alarm sounded. The jammer worked.

They entered and rounded a corner to a small office, just off the open warehouse area where stacks of boxes lined the wall, likely filled with sport cards and other useless tchotchkes. Against the back wall of the office stood the crappy safe. It wasn't bolted to the floor, or even to the wall, and with one good shove, Sean sent it tumbling to its side on the concrete floor below.

Travis wedged his Halligan between the safe's door and its frame, Sean followed, placing his a little lower. Taking turns, they pried and lifted until the entire door bent so much the latches no longer connected to the frame. Inside sat a few credit cards, a passport, and keys to something. Ignoring all of that, Sean reached for the three vinyl bank bags. Unzipping one, he peered inside. Cash. Lots of it. In the second, more cash. In the third, more cash and some rolls of coins.

"This is it." He shined a flashlight into the safe to make sure they hadn't neglected anything else good. Flat against the back wall sat a small box that contained about a dozen sports cards. Each one was probably worth a fucking fortune, but also too difficult to unload and too easy to trace.

Sean tossed them back into the safe. “Let’s go.”

Travis nodded, followed him outside.

The building’s bent and busted front door refused to stay shut on its own, so Sean grabbed a large rock from the side of the building and propped it closed. Travis released the jammer, returning the alarm to regular use. The door might blow open in the night and set off the alarm, but they’d be back in Laytons Grove by then, divvying up the stacks of cash.

mary

Without waiting for the engine to warm, Mary put her SUV in gear and headed toward her parents' house. It was nearly two in the afternoon, and she was supposed to be at their house forty-five minutes ago, but she'd gotten stuck at the police station trying to wrap up some work, hoping to find a good enough stopping point to pause and step away for the day to enjoy Thanksgiving with her family.

As she made her way across town, she worked on excuses to give her mother—searching for something that would ease the anger caused by her tardiness. She was sure her mother was mad, even if she wasn't one to show anger.

Mary arrived to find the driveway filled with cars, so she parked on the street. Balancing her famous cornbread dressing on her arm, she pulled the screen door open and hurried inside the packed house. Aunts and uncles, grandmas and grandpas, family friends, and so many cousins that she couldn't easily remember all their names.

Michael was in the kitchen helping Mom with the evening's big feast. It was an odd setting for him because he didn't really cook and every other guy in the house was in the den watching football with Papa.

Notably absent from those gathered in the house were Mary's girls. She'd hoped Ashley and Emma would be in the kitchen with their grandmother learning to cook a big meal from a master who'd done it more times than anyone could count, but instead, they were in the basement playing with some of their cousins.

Mary set her things down and gave her mom a hug.

Following the short embrace, Mom handed her a knife and a sprig of rosemary. "Chop this, please."

She obliged, though she knew it wasn't providing a great deal of assistance to a seasoned chef like Mom.

Michael stood on the other side of the kitchen island, cutting up potatoes. When he finished, he held the pan up for her to inspect, just like he'd done as a child. "How's that?"

Mom nodded. "That looks great."

An accidental noise exited Mary's mouth. Sort of a snort mixed with a sigh.

"What?" Michael glared at her.

She shook her head and returned her attention to the rosemary. "Nothing." It was unbelievable that a grown man needed praise from his mommy for cutting some potatoes into cubes.

"Clearly there's something you wanted to say."

"I just cleared my throat, Mikie. That's all."

Mom interjected before Michael could respond. "Someone needs to clean those green beans."

Michael glanced at his watch. "Sorry, Mom, but I have to go pick Kim up."

Another involuntary snort-sigh escaped Mary's lips.

Again he glared at her. "What?"

"Kim? As in Kimberly Walsh?"

"Yeah." He shrugged. "So what?"

"Nothing."

"What?"

"I was just clarifying." Mary grabbed the bag of green beans and started snapping off the stems.

"Clearly you have some issue with her."

Mary didn't actually know Kim, but she'd been friends with her older sister Lisa throughout high school. Kim was the Walshs' middle child, and it showed. She sought attention from anyone who'd give it to her, and when it came to the boys at school, she'd do just about anything to get their attention.

Michael stared. "What's the problem?"

"Nothing, Mikie."

"Say whatever you've got to say."

"It's just..." She sighed. "I just didn't know you were like, dating her or whatever. That's all."

"Yeah, well, we've been seeing each other for a few months. Is that a problem for you?"

She sighed as she set the knife down. She'd been willing to let it go, but if he insisted on hashing things out right now, she wasn't opposed. "Didn't you two already date like a year ago?"

"I don't know that I'd say we were dating then. We went out a few times. That's all."

"Okay."

"What? What's your problem?"

"Nothing. Forget I said anything."

He clearly had his own view of his time with Kim, but Mary remembered things differently. Kim had gotten him to take her to some very nice restaurants, buy her some very expensive gifts, and once Michael had fallen under her spell, she abruptly announced she was getting back together with an old boyfriend.

"Fine." Michael rolled his eyes. "You don't like her. I get it."

"I didn't say that, Mikie."

"What then? What's your issue with her?"

"It's not even with her. It's just... I don't want to see you get hurt again, that's all."

"She didn't hurt me."

"Well, she wasn't very fair to you last time, as I recall."

"In what way was she unfair? Because she moved in with Gary? We weren't exclusive or anything, and I knew from the start that she'd been reconnecting with him."

While Michael may have known Kim and Gary had reconnected, he was nonetheless crushed when Kim ultimately chose Gary over him. Not to mention that the entire time she and Michael were dating—or whatever he wanted to call it—Kim constantly had her eye on every other man, always on the hunt for something better.

Michael shoved the pan of potatoes toward the center of the island. "Look, all of that was forever ago anyway."

"Sure, in a world where eight months counts as forever." She probably should have dropped the entire thing, but it bothered her too much. Kim had led him on, spent his money, and then left him heartbroken. She didn't want to see it happen again.

Michael turned and left the kitchen but stopped. "My point is, all of that was a long time ago, and Gary turned out to be a drunk who couldn't hold down a job. Kim has changed since all that too."

Mary sighed again. The idea that Kim had changed was laughable. Maybe she'd made some small adjustments in her life, but the fact remained that any man dating Kim Walsh was going to need to earn a sizable paycheck because she required a constant flow of shiny items to maintain her interest. "I hope things are different. I really do."

"They are."

"Okay. All I want is for you to be careful. Maybe ask yourself why she came back to you and make sure it's for the right reasons."

"Thanks so much for your concern."

"It's genuine concern, Mikie."

"Last I checked, this was *my* life that I'm living."

"It is. I know that it is, and I'm sorry if I upset you, but please be careful, okay? That's all I'm really asking here. I know a bad relationship when I see one."

"Oh, so Kim and I are in a bad relationship? You don't even know her, or anything about her." He started to walk away but paused again. "So what? You knew her in high school, big deal. No one's the same as they were in high school. You know nothing about her or who she is now, or anything about our relationship. You don't get to compare us to you and Aaron. I'm sorry he turned out to be a dick. I'm sorry he's not here for Emma and Ashley. That sucks, but don't assume everyone's relationship is a disaster just because the *one* relationship you've had in your entire fucking life didn't work out."

Mom smacked the counter with her palm. "Stop it! Both of you."

Mary had nearly forgotten she was in the room. "Sorry, Mom."

Michael grabbed his coat from the back of a dining room chair. "If you'll excuse me, I have to go get Kim now."

Mary rolled her eyes at his theatrics but followed him to the front door to apologize, but by the time she got to the door, he was already outside, getting into his car.

She returned to the kitchen to find Mom glaring at her with the same disappointed look she'd been giving her since she and Michael were kids.

“Sorry, Mom. I just don’t want him getting hurt again. He was devastated when Kim went back to Gary. It’s like he’s forgotten how mopey and sad he was after that.”

“Maybe he has, but he’s a thirty-two-year-old man. He’s more than old enough to make his own decisions, so you can understand why he doesn’t like others trying to dictate his choices.”

“But he’s headed toward devastation again, don’t you think?”

“We don’t know that, and it’s not our place to assume it.”

“Don’t you think we owe it to him to help, if we can?”

Mom smiled wryly. “When your father and I tried to prevent you from experiencing heartbreak with Aaron, how did you respond?”

Mary chuckled because no words came to mind.

Mom’s smile widened. “You see my point, don’t you? Though we tried to stop it from happening, it was something you had to learn on your own, and we don’t know for sure that Michael is headed for devastation. I think we all need to give Kim a chance. It’s not fair to condemn her for what happened in the past, and it’s especially not fair to condemn her for what *might* happen in the future.”

As usual, she was right. The more her mom and dad tried to stop her from seeing Aaron, the more she wanted to see him. She snuck out of the house to see him. She lied about going to friends’ houses so she had a cover story to go see him. No one could have said anything to her that would’ve made her stop spending every moment with him.

She was drawn to Aaron, perhaps because he was older than she was. While she was still in high school, he’d gotten a job as a mechanic at a garage downtown. He made good money, but still, her parents hated him. At one point, Papa forbade her from seeing him, which, of course, only made him seem sexier. By the end of senior year, she was pregnant.

Aaron proposed soon after and her parents acquiesced that he would become part of the family. A few months after the wedding, they welcomed Ashley into the world. Emma wasn't far behind, but soon after her birth, Aaron decided that having a family was too much responsibility and he left town.

Mom spoke, forcing Mary to return to reality.

Mary hadn't heard her mother's words though. "Sorry, what?"

"I asked if that was something you needed to deal with?" She pointed at Mary's cell phone on the counter, its screen glowing with a new text message.

"Oh. Probably."

It was her boss. He apologized for interrupting her holiday but asked her to meet him out front because he needed to speak with her, so Mary hurried outside, leaving her jacket behind.

Flanigan paced back and forth on the sidewalk in front of the house. "Sorry. I know you're trying to enjoy some time with your family."

"It's fine. What's up?"

"I just learned about two overnight burglaries, both out of town. I thought you'd want them on your radar. They seem to jibe with other cases you're working. Neither of these seem as well planned or as sophisticated as some of the other ones you're looking into, but I thought you'd want to know all the same."

"Definitely. You got details for me?"

He nodded. "First one happened around midnight at a pawn shop over in Spring Valley. Brute force entry through the front door. Owner said most of the high-priced items were locked in safes overnight, but the thieves still got away with some guitars, computers, and a few rare coins."

"Any surveillance footage?"

"Cameras in the area didn't get anything. The building's internet was cut, rendering their cameras useless. They had a hardwired system too, but the suspects took the DVRs."

"Any other evidence or suspects?"

"Nothing." He shook his head. "The second one happened around three in the morning in Princeton. A smoke shop. They rammed a stolen truck through the front doors. Stole cigarettes, vape pens and cartridges, other small merchandise. Also hit the cash register, and it looks like they tried, unsuccessfully, to gain access to a safe."

"Dare I ask about surveillance footage from this one?"

He shook his head. "Seems the building's internet was cut just before the truck crashed through the windows."

"We know anything about the truck?"

"It's the only link to the first burglary. Ninety-seven Ford Ranger reported stolen out of Spring Valley, but the report didn't come in till this afternoon. Princeton PD tracked down the owner in Spring Valley. Some local guy, who's known for drinking a little too much, said he'd driven himself to a local tavern, but he didn't remember how he got home. Said he tends to leave his keys in the visor though, and Princeton PD found the truck crashed partially inside the business, engine running, keys in the ignition."

"Has the owner been cleared as a suspect?"

"Princeton PD says nothing ties him to it. A neighbor saw him stumble home around one in the morning."

"Do we think the same guys who hit the Spring Valley pawn shop stole the truck while in town, then hit the vape shop in Princeton?"

"It's what, fifteen, sixteen miles in between the two? My guess is that's exactly what happened, but that's just a theory at this point. I'll update you with anything we learn."

Mary's attention shifted to the black Audi pulling into the driveway. Michael stepped out of the driver's seat. Kim exited the passenger side with a leather Marc Jacobs bag draped over a shoulder, her body clad in a black dress, black boots up to her knees. Her perfectly straight blond hair sat tucked behind her ears, which were adorned with diamond studs.

The two shuffled into the house, barely acknowledging Flanigan or Mary.

Flanigan nodded toward the door. "I won't keep you any longer. Just thought you'd want to know about these crimes."

She thanked him, saw him to his squad, then stared at the house where she'd spend the next several hours eating Thanksgiving dinner while pretending to get along with Kim, pretending that her need for an expensive wardrobe wasn't the real reason behind Michael's plans to expand the family business.

sean

The sound of a hair dryer droned from behind the partially closed bathroom door and Sean slid out of bed to investigate. He pushed the door open to reveal Brooke standing at the counter with a towel wrapped around her body. She smiled at him in the mirror as she waved the dryer wildly across her dark hair.

Sean stepped behind her, slid his hand under the towel, caressed her smooth ass.

She smacked his hand as she switched off the hair dryer. “If that’s what you wanted, you should have woken up earlier.”

She turned, kissed him.

He again slid his hand up the towel. “We got time, right?”

“Sure.” She tightened the towel around her breasts. “I’m off at eight.”

“C’mon, blow off work and come back to bed.”

She brushed his hair out of his eyes with her fingers. “It’s Black Friday.”

“So?”

“So, if I don’t show up today, my boss’ll kill me.”

“Fuck him.”

“Her.” She smiled. “And I like Hannah. I’m not going to abandon her on a day like this. That’s shitty.”

"Fine. Leave me for Hannah." He chuckled. "She'd better be hot as hell."

"Oh, she is." Brooke smiled, kissed him with a quick peck. "You have my permission to think about us together while you're here alone all day."

She returned to the mirror and combed out her hair. The image of Brooke with another girl filled his mind, even though he didn't know what Hannah looked like.

He shook the thought from his head, went to the living room, grabbed his phone. Jack still hadn't called or texted. He was supposed to join them at Brooke's place last night for Thanksgiving dinner, but he never showed, never texted. The last time they'd spoken, Jack sounded high as fuck, which probably explained why he'd been absent last night.

It was nothing new. Every time they pulled a lucrative job, Jack spent most of his cut partying. He was free to do whatever he wanted—it was his money, his life—but they had other jobs in the works too, so he'd need to sober up long enough to plan them and then do them.

Brooke emerged from the other room fully dressed for work in a gray sweater, tight jeans, and her favorite white Adidas Superstars. "Hey. Me and some of the crew are going out after work. You should join us."

"Yeah? Okay. Let me know when and where."

"Cool." She paused. "What are you going to do today?"

"Thought I'd go visit my parents."

Her eyes narrowed. "Seriously?"

"My mom was pretty bummed that I didn't come for Thanksgiving, so I figure the least I can do is swing by for a few."

"Well holy shit."

"What?"

"I'm just surprised, that's all."

He shrugged. "Last time wasn't too bad, but we'll see. I don't plan to stay long."

"Okay." She leaned in and kissed him. "I gotta go."

He didn't text before showing up. Ma always insisted he was welcome at any time, and this way, he had until he rang the doorbell to back out of the whole thing.

The neighborhood was quiet. At the end of the street, Mr. Wroblewski was busy hanging Christmas decorations, and across the street, the Zeller's youngest grandkid rode his bike in circles in the driveway. Things never changed much on Monroe Street.

Sean took a deep breath and pushed the button. No turning back now.

He stared at the sign on the door—white paint on dark-stained wood that spelled out MCKENNA in block lettering with an American flag to the left and an Irish flag to the right. Ma loved the thing. She'd had it made by someone at a craft fair inside Douglas Elementary School. He remembered the day because he and the guys had used the craft fair as cover while they did some recon work as part of a job where they stole cash from the school's offices. Funds collected from a fundraising event.

The door creaked open, jolting him back to reality.

Ma stood before him, smiling.

"Hey, Ma."

"Well, this is a great surprise! Please, come in."

"Sorry I didn't call or anything."

"Nonsense. You're welcome anytime. No call necessary." She hugged him. "I was just making some tea. Can I pour you a cup? Or get you anything else?"

"Uh, just some water, I guess."

She walked toward the kitchen. He followed, examined the place he once called home. It was quiet, empty.

"Where's Dad? I thought he'd be off all weekend."

"He's out with a friend." She grabbed a glass from the cupboard by the sink and filled it from the tap. "You remember Bill Fitzgerald, don't you? Your father worked with him at Johnson-Power."

Sean sat down at the table where the cat greeted him by brushing against his leg. "Yeah, I remember him. Nice guy."

"Well, he's in town visiting. Your father met him for a beer."

"Cool." Sean pet Baxter on the head.

She set the water in front of him. "I'm not sure when he'll be back."

Sean took a sip of water. Maybe it was for the best. Things were better between him and his dad, but still not great.

Ma poured water from a kettle into a mug and joined him at the table. "How about you? How are things with you?"

"Things are okay." He sipped the water. "Sorry I couldn't make it for Thanksgiving."

She patted his hand. "It's okay, dear. You had plans, yes?"

He nodded. "Brooke and me had dinner at her place. Her roommate cooked a whole big meal, and we had some friends over."

"That sounds lovely." She stared at her mug, plunged a teabag in and out of the water. "Perhaps you could come here for Christmas?"

"Uh, maybe." He didn't have plans, and he hadn't come prepared with a lie to get out of Christmas with the entire family. "I'll have to see what Brooke is planning."

"She is more than welcome here too. You know that, don't you?"

Sean nodded, stared at the table. He may as well say what he came to say, and the fact that his father wasn't around might make things easier. "So, hey... Reagan was saying there was some kind of issue with Dad's job. That they were laying off a bunch of people or something?"

"Yes." She stared into her tea. "It's all a little too familiar, you know? Like we've been here before." She sighed softly. "I think things will be okay though."

"They are doing layoffs though?"

"A few. Your father says they had to cut some positions to save money, but he seems to think what they've done will be enough."

"How are things otherwise though? Reagan implied you were having some financial troubles."

She shook her head. "Nothing you or Reagan should be concerned with."

"I can help, you know? And I want to." Sean reached into the interior pocket of his jacket, pulled out an envelope, set it between them. "I don't know how much you need, but this is two grand. I can do more, if this isn't enough."

She exhaled a long, deep breath. "I appreciate that, dear, but... We can't take this."

"It's not what you think. It's legit money, from my yard business."

And it was, sort of. While Valley Lawn Care & Snow Removal existed mostly so Sean and his crew could report income on their tax returns, the company did have a few legitimate clients who paid them with legitimate cash too. Besides, what did it matter where the money came from? They needed help and he was able to offer that help.

Ma stared into her tea. "It's less about where the money came from and more about the fact that your father doesn't accept help well. Maybe it won't matter anyway. He's been applying for new jobs, and he's got an interview with a place down in Ottawa next week."

"Yeah? Okay. That's good news."

She nodded in agreement. "He'd even get to join the union and everything."

"Awesome, that'd be cool."

She turned to look at the clock. "I'm afraid I'll need to get ready soon. I'm helping out at the store today."

"The thrift store?"

She nodded. "I'm back, just a few hours a week."

Years ago, after Donnie left for college, Ma took a job at Fido & Friends, a second-hand shop that acted as the fundraising arm for the Laytons Grove Humane Society. Supposedly, she did it because she liked to get out of the house a bit, but it seemed like she returned to work there every time money was tight.

"Cool. I won't keep you." He pushed the envelope closer to her. "Why not take this for now? I'm sure you could use it for something."

She shook her head. "You know your father. He'd never let us spend your money."

"Then consider it a loan, if that helps. Use it for whatever you need, just to get you through."

She patted his hand, looked him in the eye. "I do appreciate it, Seanie, but I can't take this."

Sean sighed, reached out, pulled the envelope closer to his body. "The offer stands, if you change your mind."

"Thank you. You're a sweet boy."

He slid his chair back. "Well, I have some things I need to take care of, so I'll get out of here."

"No, please, stay. I didn't tell you about my job to chase you off. It won't take me long to get ready. I just have to change shirts."

He agreed to stay and when she disappeared into the bedroom to change into her Fido & Friends polo shirt, he wandered the house, inspected the family photos displayed throughout the main level as if he were a stranger who was visiting for the first time. It was a good lens to view things through. Any visitor would see a happy family. A near-perfect family. Smiling kids, doting parents. No signs of the torment he felt living in the house. The doctors and specialists they dragged him to. The pills they forced him to take as they attempted to fix the things they'd deemed were wrong with him. No visitor would see the life he'd lived back then, the one where Tommy made it so he didn't want to go to school, and his parents made it so he didn't want to come home. Instead, visitors saw snapshots of family vacations. Multiple awards and certificates with REAGAN MCKENNA printed across the middle, accolades given to his brilliant sister for science fair achievements, academic achievements, and sports achievements. Visitors also saw photos and album covers featuring the great bass player Donovan McKenna.

Nothing in the house touted the achievements of Sean, the only one in the family who'd found a way to support himself. They wouldn't even accept his help.

Over the years, Ma had created an official family motto: Family First. She'd ingrained the idea into all their heads from childhood. The phrase was repeated often and found throughout the house. It was needle pointed on a pillow in the living room. Stenciled on a wall in the hallway. It was even painted on a sign that hung by the front door, strategically placed so that everyone would see it as they left the house each day—a reminder as they walked out into the world that no matter what they encountered that day, their family was always waiting for them at home.

He spotted Ma's purse on the sofa. With a quick glance down the hall to ensure she was still in the bedroom, he peeled the top flap open and slid the envelope inside.

mary

Downtown Laytons Grove looked like a Hallmark movie this time of year, with its Christmas tree in the park aglow with multicolored bulbs, the windows of storefronts filled with holiday displays, and garland hanging from the lampposts.

Mary had watched it all come together piecemeal over the past few weeks as she drove to witness interviews or shifts at Morelli's. Some of the decor had gone up in the days before Thanksgiving, but now, the holiday season had fully arrived. Shoppers were out in force already too, going store to store as they hunted for bargains and for the perfect gifts for everyone on their list.

For most people, giving was front and center in their minds, but that giving spirit wasn't with everyone in town. Some were busy taking, and they were becoming increasingly aggressive about it too.

Overnight, the owner of an auto parts store near downtown became the latest victim of the Grinch. Without any witnesses or working security cameras in the area, Mary had little to work with, but then she got a call from a detective in Ottawa, about ten miles south of Laytons Grove. The detective said they'd recently had a very similar break-in at a hardware store on the northern edge of town, and so it seemed worth her time to drive down there this afternoon to see what evidence they'd collected.

The short drive gave her a bit of time alone to contemplate the situation. She'd gleaned from the initial incident reports that the Ottawa break-in had been more lucrative for the thieves than the Laytons Grove one had been. They'd gotten away with about two-hundred dollars in cash from a register, and they'd managed to carry out about three grand worth of tools as well. Though a successful caper, it still wasn't clear if the break-in had been committed by the same thieves who'd hit the auto parts store in Laytons Grove.

Her initial gut feeling was that they weren't linked, and she didn't necessarily think the Ottawa one was connected to any of the recent smash-and-grab crimes in the area either because the patterns of the burglaries didn't align. Some of the cases that'd made it to her desk had a level of sophistication not seen in others.

For instance, when thieves targeted a food truck business back in November, the entry into the warehouse was brutish, with the perpetrators simply prying the front door open. However, despite the brutish entry, the crime most certainly wasn't random. The thieves likely knew about the large amounts of cash inside the building ahead of time, and they seemed to know where it was stored, and their entry and exit were quick, indicating they'd been well prepared.

On the other hand, when criminals struck a pawn shop in Spring Valley, they got away with very little because everything of value had been locked in safes. That discrepancy indicated that whoever carried out that break-in hadn't done their homework. Even so, the thieves rendered surveillance cameras useless by cutting the internet to the building, and by stealing the DVR that contained surveillance footage, so they'd clearly gone into it with some level of planning. But hours later, someone hit a smoke shop in Princeton, and the lack of sophistication in that burglary seemed almost laughable—a stolen vehicle rammed through the entrance, a failed attempt to open a safe, and nothing of much value taken from the shop. The only link she could see was that the thieves had avoided being captured by surveillance cameras because they'd cut the internet to the building.

The fact that the vehicle used had been stolen in the same city where the pawn shop had been hit seemed to point to a commonality between the two, and the internet being cut in both cases all but solidified that theory. It was still possible, however, that none of the recent burglaries were linked in any way at all. Perhaps the Illinois Valley was under siege by multiple groups of criminals with varying levels of skills and sophistication.

Messy or planned, all the recent break-ins had one unifying factor in common: the methods used were primitive and forceful, and it seemed they'd been carried out by impatient thieves. At least compared to some more sophisticated burglaries that had stumped LGPD investigators in recent years.

She pulled into a parking spot on the side of the Ottawa PD station, and once inside, Detective McEmery led her to a computer to show her some video they'd collected. Although the thieves had disabled the cameras at the hardware store—cameras mounted outside a business across the street had captured some of the incident.

McEmery loaded a flash drive into a computer and typed away, the clunk of the keyboard echoing in the small room.

He stepped aside and turned to face her. "I've gotta warn ya, the video's pretty poor quality, but at least it's something."

Mary sat down in front of the computer as the grainy video appeared on the monitor. It showed two male subjects of average height and thin builds approaching the front of the hardware store. Without preamble, one jerked his arm back and tossed something at the window, smashing it. Then both males ran inside the building.

McEmery paused the video. "They broke the window with a brick. We recovered it from the scene." He shook his head. "I've watched this two dozen times, but unfortunately, it doesn't show what they do once they gain entry. Looks like one of the males' heads to the cash register while the other male begins grabbing tools. Beyond that, I can't see what happens, but maybe you'll catch something I didn't."

He unpaused the video and Mary leaned in closer. Following minimal movement inside the building, one of the males exited with an armful of what appeared to be hand tools, which he tossed in the bed of a small pickup truck parked just out of view of the camera. The license plate was partially in view of the camera, but even if it'd been in full view, the image quality was far too bad to capture the plate number.

"Can you pause it?"

McEmery obliged.

She looked up at him. "I don't suppose you have any info on this truck?"

McEmery shook his head. "Seems to be an older F-150. We couldn't find anything distinguishing about it though. I've tried six ways to Sunday to get a look at the plate, even a partial number, but I've had no luck. Maybe another agency has some better software that could pull it, but we haven't sought assistance from any outside agencies so far."

"I take it no one's reported an F-150 stolen lately?"

He shook his head. "Not yet at least. I s'pose it's possible they just ain't noticed yet."

"Any recent suspicious vehicle reports or anything involving a pickup like that?"

He shook his head. "Not that I've found."

"Have area pawn shops been alerted to look for anyone trying to sell the tools?"

McEmery nodded. "We've also got folks monitoring eBay, Craigslists, and Facebook. Places like that. On top of that, we've alerted a CI we work with. He's a fence, so if someone with a bunch of tools comes to him, he knows to call us."

A criminal informant was worth a shot. Whoever took the tools was going to want to sell them, and if they were lucky, the thieves would go to McEmery's CI to do it.

On the way back to Laytons Grove PD headquarters, Mary stopped at the store to check in with Papa. Michael was supposed to work the afternoon shift, so she was prepared to fill in if he failed to show yet again.

Papa handed change to a customer and closed the drawer, thanking her.

Mary waited until the woman exited, then joined him at the counter. "How are things, Papa?"

"Oh, it's been pretty slow today, even for a Monday."

"Well, I'm glad I caught you. I wasn't sure if you'd still be here or not."

"Few minutes later and you might have missed me."

Mary turned her attention to the office at the back of the store. "Is Michael here?"

"He'll be here soon."

"So he's late?"

"Shoulda been here about ten minutes ago."

Michael was the store's least reliable worker. If he wasn't a part owner, they'd have fired him months ago.

Mary set her things on a shelf under the counter. "Why don't you go home, Papa? I'll take over until he gets here."

"Oh, I'm in no rush."

"I'll bet Mom's got dinner cooking though. You should go. Spend some time at home. I can handle things here."

"That isn't necessary."

After a couple minutes of back-and-forth pleas, Papa finally agreed to go home, leaving Mary alone with the store. Plenty needed done around the place—things that Michael should have already done.

She started with restocking the canned goods aisle, then she restocked the stir sticks at the coffee station and straightened the cups at the drink station.

A chime rang out. She looked up to see Michael casually strolling into the store.

Exhaling a sigh, and part of her anger, she walked over to him. "Glad you could make it."

His eyes squinted. "I was supposed to close tonight, right?"

"Yes." She checked the clock on the wall. "You were supposed to be here nearly a half hour ago."

"That's a bit of an exaggeration. I'm like twenty minutes late. Chill out."

"Twenty-eight minutes, but that's not really the point. Late is late. That's what we tell the staff, right? If you were an employee, I'd be writing you up right now."

"But unlike our employees, I was doing work for this store. That's what made me late, so feel free to climb down from that fucking pedestal now."

"What work were you doing?"

"I was in Joliet talking to a lawyer."

"A lawyer? What about?"

He tossed his bag under the counter. "The expansion."

"What expansion? No one's agreed to any of that."

"No, but it doesn't hurt to have some stuff in place."

"In place for what, Mikie?"

"For when we move forward with things."

"You mean *if* we move forward."

"C'mon, are you telling me you really don't want to see this place grow? To see our family's brand grow?"

"What I want is for this place to be around for several years to come. To provide for our family, maybe even provide for Ashley and Emma's families, if they're interested in taking over the place. But for any of that to happen, Morelli's needs to stay in business."

"We've been over all of this before. That's *exactly* what I'm trying to do here! I'm trying to secure this store's survival."

"Yeah, we've covered all of this, but it's like you didn't hear a word Papa or me said, and yet again, I must ask you: how is buying some decrepit building out by Starved Rock going to financially strengthen the family business?"

"It's just the first step, but that building isn't what I'm talking about. I was meeting with a lawyer to get his opinion on what the best model is."

"Model?"

"Yeah, you know, do we sell franchises, or do we take on investors and open company-owned stores? Right now, I'm leaning toward franchising but with an option that we can buy out the franchisee within a certain amount of time. That would allow us to open dozens of stores in the next few years, and in ten years or so, we could buy back the most successful ones. I think that once we've got fifteen or so profitable stores, we could even go public."

"Go public?" Mary exhaled sharply. "Like, the stock market?"

"Yeah, exactly."

"Have you literally lost your mind? We're not running the next Google or whatever here. This is a goddamned convenience store, Mikie."

"You don't have to be a tech company to sell stock to the public. Plenty of store chains are publicly listed companies. Casey's General Stores, TravelCenters of America, Murphy USA. Why not add Morelli's to that list? But all that's a bit down the road anyways. Right now, I think we need to focus on franchises. License our name and concept."

"Our concept? What concept? It's a gas station that sells food items, I don't think we can claim ownership of that idea. Besides, who in the hell would buy a Morelli's franchise?"

"Lots of people." He walked to the coffee pots and poured himself a large. "People in the towns all around us—people who've shopped here and know what we're about." He shook two sugar packets, tore them open, dumped them in. "It's simple really: we license them the company name, set them up with our distributors, and they run the place. It's their store but it has our name above the door. It's all about brand building."

She sighed. "Again, Mikie, I don't see why anyone would want to do that."

"I'm telling you, they will. Trust me."

"If someone wants to run a gas station, why wouldn't they just buy an existing one, or start a new one from scratch? And why wouldn't they name it something they choose?"

"Because buying a Morelli's franchise is a good deal for them. With a franchise, they're their own boss, but they get to benefit from our experience. They get to order from our vendors." He blew on the coffee, then sipped it. "And it's good for us too. They pay us licensing fees, so we make money off each store. And like I just said, if we structure the contracts right, we can buy back any of the stores we want. They get a nice return on their investment while we take over a fully functioning store that's turnkey. Do that a dozen times, and we've got a huge footprint in the area—stores we own but that were built on someone else's dime."

"Okay, well, back here in Realityville, USA, Morelli's Convenience is just one store, and there are months where it's a massive struggle to keep the lights on *and* make payroll. Isn't it *just* as likely that every one of these theoretical franchised stores will fail and drag our name down in the process?"

Michael shook his head and wandered away from her.

He was mad. She'd seen it thousands of times, but he was also being ridiculous.

The door chimed. She glanced across the store and saw a tall man with dark hair dressed in a suit and tie. He didn't look like the typical customer, and he didn't seem to be shopping for anything. Instead, he stood by the counter checking the time on his flashy watch. She pegged him for a businessman passing through town on his way to Chicago and that he needed directions to I-80.

Mary walked to the front of the store. "Can I help you?"

"Hi." He flashed a phony smile. "I'm looking for the owner."

"I'm the owner. What can I do for you?"

His eyes narrowed. "Sorry. I'm looking for Mr. Michael Morelli." He handed her a business card. "My name's Luis."

She studied the card with a brightly colored logo for Prairie Land Oil Corp. in the top left corner. In the center of the card, printed in black ink: LUIS RIVERA, VICE PRESIDENT OF ACQUISITIONS.

Mr. VP of Acquisitions stared at his phone. "I believe I had a meeting with Michael this evening, unless I've mixed up my days."

Before she could respond, Michael hurried toward him and shook his hand. "Luis, good to meet you in person. Thanks for making the drive, and for accommodating my schedule."

"No problem. No problem at all."

"I trust you had no trouble finding us?"

Mr. VP shook his head. "Not in the least."

"See? What'd I tell you? We've got a great location here."

Michael chuckled.

Mr. VP chuckled.

Both men smiled phony smiles.

Michael motioned his arm toward the back of the store. "This way, please."

Mr. VP walked toward the back of the store with Michael beside him.

Mary called for her brother.

He stopped. "What?"

"Could I speak to you for a moment?"

Mr. VP turned around to see what the trouble was.

Michael sighed. "I'm sorry, Luis. Why don't you head back to my office, and I'll be in shortly. Help yourself to a cup of coffee along the way, if you'd like."

Mr. VP looked at Mary, then at Michael. "Will do. Take your time."

Michael glared at her. "What's up, sis?"

She couldn't remember the last time he'd called her that, if he ever had. "Are you just assuming that I have nowhere to be? I was watching the store for Papa until *you* got here. I hadn't planned to stick around while you hold random business meetings. Also, Prairie Land Oil? What the hell is this about?"

"It's just an informal meeting."

"An informal meeting about what?"

He shrugged. "Just weighing all of our options."

"Selling the store to Prairie Land Oil is an option?"

"It's a *possibility*, but not the only one. I also want to talk to him about co-branding, or maybe even us buying a Prairie Land license."

"You're talking to him about selling the store?"

Michael shrugged. "Maybe. Like I just said, I'm looking at all the options. I just want to hear what the guy has to say. Do you know about Prairie Land Oil?"

"Um, yeah, they're our main competition in town, so I'm familiar."

"No, I mean, like, do you know their story? It's remarkable. Hugh Cohan started the company in the late nineties with just one store in Evansville, Indiana. Within four years, he owned two more stations in Indiana, and by two-thousand-five, he'd expanded into Missouri and Illinois with seven more stores."

She waited for some kind of point to accompany his ramblings. It never arrived. "So what?"

"So, today they're a massive company with stores in nearly every state. They build and acquire stores in small towns, like Laytons Grove. They only operate in small towns. That's the beauty of their business plan. Just this year they've purchased a station in Spring Valley, another in Peru, two over in Morris, and one in Coal City."

"Good for them, Mikie. What the hell does that have to do with us?"

"Look, Luis is interested in Morelli's, so I thought I'd hear him out. That's all. Maybe it's not worth selling, maybe it is. Or maybe I can pick up a few things from this guy about expanding the business. Things we can use in the expansion of Morelli's."

"Are you seriously standing here telling me that you're considering selling Papa's store? Isn't that something you should talk to Papa about?"

"I will. When the time's right."

"Mikie, the time will never be right, because this store is not yours to sell. Anything like that would be a family decision."

Michael shifted his weight and glanced toward the back office. "I just want to hear this guy's pitch. Can you cover the store for like fifteen minutes? We'll talk when he leaves, okay?"

Yes, we will, she thought.

Michael stepped behind the counter and reached into his bag. "Here, in the meantime, check this out." He handed her a folder with a full color picture of a Prairie Land Oil station on the cover. "Read through it. There's a ton of good info in here."

"Maybe there is, but again, Morelli's isn't for sale, so none of this matters."

"Just let me talk to the guy. Please? Fifteen minutes."

Mary glanced at the clock, noting the time. "You've got ten minutes."

"Thank you. You and I will talk about all this stuff later." Michael spun on his heels and marched toward the office.

Mary tossed the folder on the counter and flipped it open. Stuffed into the interior pocket on the left were several glossy pages with pictures of Prairie Land stations and smiling employees. The next few pages provided stats about acquisitions the company had made of small stations across the country.

The other pocket contained details on purchasing a license to use Prairie Land's marks and products to convert your existing store into a Prairie Land Oil station. The company would provide signage, uniforms, promotional materials—all they had to do was "focus on running your business," or so the packet proclaimed. Of course, none of that came for free. You were required to pay a hefty franchise fee every quarter, and the fine print contained dozens of things you'd have to agree to—things that stripped more management decisions from your hands. The entire thing seemed fraught with problems, and it seemed less like they'd be running their business and more like they'd be paying Prairie Land Oil a bunch of money for the pleasure to run a Prairie Land Oil station.

The door chimed. A man walked in and requested a pack of cigarettes. Mary tossed the folder under the counter to focus on the customer. She'd seen what she needed to see anyway. No matter what Michael thought—no matter what Mr. VP had to say, they weren't selling the family store to Prairie Land Oil, they weren't buying a Prairie Land franchise, and they weren't going to expand the current store, especially without approval from Papa.

reagan

David had something planned for tonight, but he wouldn't say what it was. All he'd told Reagan was that he'd pick her up at seven, which seemed unnecessary since they lived together.

From the sofa, she checked her watch, then peered out the window. No sign of him yet.

He'd insisted on taking her out tonight, and when she texted him to get a little more detail, he said that tonight they were going to celebrate her birthday, even though her actual birthday was several days away. When she asked what she should wear, he replied, "Anything will do. You always look great." Though a sweet thing to say, it was a typical guy answer that didn't particularly help her plan an outfit, so she pressed him further. After some badgering, he finally said that she'd need "something nice, but not fancy." Still not particularly helpful.

She knew where they were going though: the Monogram, a super-fancy restaurant in downtown Chicago. It wasn't a guess, and figuring it out hadn't required a deep investigation because a few days ago, David had borrowed her laptop to check his email, and when she sat down to use it afterward, the Monogram's website was open in a browser tab.

It made sense that he'd take her there because he'd taken her there for her birthday a few years ago, when they were still in college and had just started dating. Though the name was a bit weird, the place was very upscale, with dark woods, fancy linens, and an impeccably dressed wait staff. The restaurant operated from a historic building once used as an old garment warehouse and was later home to a well-respected tailor who made custom suits for Chicago's most notorious politicians and mobsters alike. When the space was converted into a restaurant, the only thing left inside was an antique Singer embroidery machine used to stitch monograms into clothing, and from that, the restaurant got its name.

Her first visit to the Monogram coincided with her first big date with David. She was so nervous that night, partly because dating David was still so new, and partly because she'd never eaten in such a fancy place before. It wasn't unusual for David though. He came from a world where dining at places like that was normal, even if he'd left that life behind him when he moved to Chicago from the Pacific Northwest where his family still lived—and where his father hoped he'd return to join him as a commercial real estate developer.

It was over dinner at the Monogram that Reagan first learned about the discord between David and his father, and she learned that he had no desire to follow in his father's footsteps.

"You don't want to go into real estate development?" she'd asked.

"Sorta the opposite. He cuts trees down to make way for shopping centers, and I want to plant trees and hug them."

It was the exact moment that Reagan fell in love with David. He could have returned to Oregon, joined his father, and probably made a fortune. The kind of money most people only dream of—but it was the kind of job that would have kept David from doing what he really wanted to do, which was help other people. It was what he did now at his current job by helping them with things like filing workers' compensation claims or even organizing unions.

Again she peeked out the window, but there still was no sign of David.

She'd ultimately settled on a classic little black dress and low heels. The Monogram was a tad fancier than that, but the outfit was the fanciest thing in her closet, so it would have to do.

With another check of her watch and another peek outside, she still saw no sign of David.

He'd been working a lot this week, including today, despite it being the weekend, but he'd also given the impression that it would only be a couple hours, so now she was starting to worry.

A knock at the door shattered her reverie. She cautiously peeked through the peephole in the door and found David standing on the porch wearing a suit and tie and holding a bouquet of red roses.

She opened the door and stared at him. "What are you doing?"

"I'm here to pick you up for your date, my lady."

"You have a key. You live here. Why are you knocking?"

"Why, I must say, you look lovely, my lady."

She rolled her eyes. "Will you stop being weird?" Her face warmed at the thought of the neighbors watching the spectacle.

“Sorry, my lady.” He made a grand motion with his arm. “But your carriage awaits.”

She shifted her gaze past his outstretched arm and to the street where a black limousine sat double parked in front of their building. “That’s not for us, is it?”

“No. It is for *you*, my lady.”

She slapped him on the shoulder. “Stop being weird. Is that really ours?”

He laughed. “Well, I didn’t buy it or anything, but yes, it’s ours for the evening.”

“You’ve got to be kidding me!”

“Not at all. You deserve it.” He leaned in to kiss her. “Happy birthday.”

“It’s not my birthday.”

“Close enough.” He bent his arm and extended his elbow toward her. “Shall we?”

She threaded her arm through his. “You didn’t go to work today, did you?”

He chuckled. “Not at all. I’m afraid that was a ruse, my lady. I had a few final loose ends to tie up.”

As they approached the limo, the driver opened the rear door for her.

She stopped to face David. “You lied to me? On my birthday?”

“It’s not your birthday.”

David retrieved a chilled bottle of Champagne and poured her a glass. Outside the window of the limo, Reagan watched as portions of the Eisenhower Expressway blew by in a blur. It’d been an amazing evening already—wearing nice clothes while seated on the comfy leather seats of a limousine, sipping from a crystal flute. It was a life most anyone could get used to, but she couldn't stop thinking about how fast it would be over, or how undeserving she was. Even if today had been her *actual* birthday, turning twenty-four didn't warrant this level of lavishness.

She turned to David and smiled. "Thank you for all of this."

"Of course."

"This is lovely, but it certainly wasn't necessary."

"Nonsense. The restaurant is a good twenty miles from home. You didn't think I would make you get all dressed up to take a bus or a train, did you?"

She couldn't remember exactly where the Monogram was but knew it was somewhere in the northern part of the Loop. As they approached the city though, the limo turned onto Lake Shore Drive and headed south, the opposite direction of the Monogram.

She leaned over and gazed out the window. "Where are we going?"

"Dinner." David took a sip of Champagne.

"I know that, but where?"

He smiled. "A place you'll like."

His vagueness would have been annoying if not for his dimples, which eased any slight annoyance she felt boiling.

The driver made a turn onto 53rd Street and Reagan began to recognize her surroundings, Hyde Park, home to their alma mater, but several miles from the Monogram.

She stared at him. "Where are we going?"

"Din—"

"Dinner, I know, but where at?"

"Well, I hope you don't mind pizza."

"I don't mind at all. Pizza from where?"

A wry smile filled his face. "A delicious place."

She didn't want to get too hopeful, or too cocky since she'd been so wrong about the Monogram, but she thought she knew where they were going.

A smile slid uncontrollably onto her face. "Are we going to Gino's?"

"You know the place?" His crooked smile gave him away. He was messing with her.

"You know I know it, but how do *you* know about it?"

"What? I used to go there all the time in college."

"Oh yeah, with who? Your *other* girlfriend?"

"Huh." He nodded. "Yeah. Come to think of it, shit. I guess it might have been her."

"Better not have been." She slapped him on the arm. "Stop messing with me. How'd you know about Gino's?"

"Oh, well... Your mom *may* have mentioned it to me, and she *may* have mentioned how much you love it and how much it means to you."

"Did she, now? When did this alleged mentioning happen?"

"I guess it happened around the time I called her and asked her for ideas of where I could take you to dinner." He smiled. "You do like this place, right?"

"I freakin' love it!"

Gino's was a funky pizzeria that her parents had been going to for years. They first found it while on one of their first dates. They'd gone to Chicago to see a performance of *Much Ado About Nothing* but found themselves extremely bored and left before the show ended. That's when they stumbled into Gino's for the first time. By the time they'd gotten married, Gino's had become *their* spot. It soon became the family's spot too. The place they went nearly every time they were in Chicago.

The limo stopped in front of the restaurant and before she'd even had a chance to set down her glass, the driver opened the door.

It'd been a few years since she'd last been there, but Gino's hadn't changed much. It was a tiny space, especially for a restaurant, with about a dozen tables in the main room and a few more in the room in the back. The tables were painted white, and the simple wood chairs were painted either red or green—a subtle attempt to remind visitors of the Italian flag.

The wallpapered walls were blanketed with framed black and white photos, mostly photos of buildings in Rome. A few color photos of the Italian countryside were mixed in too. The place was perfect. Just the right amount of tacky and cozy.

An employee greeted them and took them to the little table near the kitchen. It was the most secluded spot in the restaurant, with a short wall around one side of it that blocked off the kitchen entrance. It was Reagan's favorite table, and an indication that David must have arranged for them to sit there.

Reagan pushed her plate toward the center of the table. "I can't eat another bite."

They'd ordered a large veggie, and Gino's larges were large by any measurement you used.

David chuckled. "You sure?"

She nodded. "I've already eaten too much."

"Huh."

"What?"

"Well, I was going to order a tiramisu for dessert, but that's cool. I can eat the whole thing myself."

"Oh, I have room for that."

He snort-laughed. "Of course you do."

"I just meant I couldn't eat another bite of pizza."

"Uh-huh. I get it." David smiled and reached for the dessert menu, but his jacket sleeve caught the edge of his fork, sending it to the ground. "Oops." He slid out of his chair to retrieve it, but didn't return.

She leaned around the edge of the table to see what was taking so long and found him on one knee, holding a ring toward her.

"Reagan Shea McKenna, would you do me the honor of spending eternity with me?"

sean

It'd been two days since Sean last heard from Jack, and now he couldn't get hold of Travis either. He'd texted Travis about fifteen minutes ago, and with no response, Sean called him. It was just about noon, so he should be awake by now.

The call went straight to voicemail.

He hung up and tried Jack's phone. The phone rang twice, then went to voicemail, a good indication that Jack had seen his name on the screen and rejected the call.

Sean hung up and texted him, demanding that he call him back.

After waiting a few minutes, Sean called Jack again. This time, he accepted the call.

Sean waited for him to speak, but after several seconds of a shuffling noise on the other end, Sean spoke. "Hey, what the hell's going on, man?"

"Uh, hey." The voice didn't belong to Jack. "Jack's not available."

"Who's this?"

"Uh, hey. It's Matt."

"Matt who?"

"Matt Winston."

"Who?"

"I'm a friend of Jack's."

A vague memory of Matt took shape in his mind. Jack and Matt had worked together briefly for a moving company. Sean had met him once or twice, but he wasn't someone who was around very often. Jack only hung out with him when Matt had meth or coke.

"Well, where is Jack?"

"I think he's at the house."

"What house? His mom's place?"

"Uh, no. That little place over on Seventh Street."

"I have no idea what house you're talking about."

"Oh, well, uh... It's just a house that we've been staying at."

"Why do you have his phone if you're not with him?"

"He left it behind, so I grabbed it."

"I need to talk to him. Where is this house at?"

"It's on Seventh, uh, just west of Missouri Avenue."

"This place have an address?"

"I'm not sure what the address is, but it's a little gray house on Seventh. There's some busted furniture in the driveway and some boards on the windows."

Sean tried to get more information from Matt, but he seemed too high to be of much help. He told him to have Jack call him if he saw him, then headed to his car.

Plopping into the seat, he turned the key. The engine struggled, choked. The fucking thing had been acting up for a couple weeks. He needed to have someone look at it, but with all the shit going on, he hadn't had a chance. He slammed his head into the headrest, released a deep breath. Something was off with Jack. Sure, sometimes he went on mini-benders where several days could go by without Sean hearing from him, but this felt different. It was like he'd disappeared, or like he was hiding from someone. He'd never mentioned anything about moving into a new place, or anything about hanging out with Matt.

Sean turned the key again. The engine sputtered but choked to life, and so he backed out of the parking lot and headed toward Seventh Street.

The house Matt described was most likely a flophouse, and that probably meant Jack had crashed there to sleep off whatever he and Matt used to get high last night. It wasn't uncommon for Jack to smoke or snort most of what he earned. He also wasn't the type to set money aside for things like rental deposits, and though he lived rent free with his mom, she only put up with so much and usually kicked him out once she reached her limit for bullshit. She usually took him back after a few days, but during those stints where he had no place to call home, Jack often gravitated to dudes like Matt, and together they'd find some shitty place where they could crash for a few days and get high.

Turning onto Missouri Avenue, he spotted Jack's truck parked on the street near a gray house with a sunken roof, peeling paint, and plywood covering most of the windows. The driveway was littered with broken furniture and discarded items from the house, just like Matt described.

He parked behind Jack's truck and walked to the door cautiously. Jack probably wasn't the only person inside, and startling meth-heads was never a good idea.

The front door had been boarded shut, so he balled up a fist and banged on the plywood, calling Jack's name as he did.

No one responded, so he rapped on the wood again. "Jack? You in there?"

A corner of the plywood had been peeled away from the door frame, so Sean pulled on it to create enough space to slip inside the house. The place was dark, light limited to any sunlight that sneaked past the boarded windows. A wave of body odor, piss, and shit slid into his nostrils. A glance into the hallway bathroom revealed a toilet overflowing with human waste, the house apparently deprived of the running water needed to flush it away.

He called for his friend. "Jack? You here? It's Sean."

Standing in the hallway, he listened as someone mumbled some words from one of the rooms at the end of the hall. Sean followed the noise to a doorless bedroom where Jack lay face down on an old mattress.

Sean nudged it with the toe of his shoe. "Hey, shithead. Wake up."

Jack mumbled as he rolled over onto his back. A broken meth pipe sat on the soiled carpet beside him, small pieces of burned foil stuck to his chest.

Sean kicked the mattress. "Jack?"

His eyes opened slightly, fluttered. "What?"

"What the fuck is going on?"

"With what?"

"With anything. I haven't heard shit from you in days."

"My phone—" He slapped his hand around, searching for his cell phone. "I don't know where my phone is."

"Matt has it."

He moaned. "Oh. Okay."

"Have you heard from Travis? He's not returning my texts either."

More mumbling, flopping. "Shit, bro."

"When's the last time you heard from him?"

"I—" He rolled over, tried to sit up, but laid back down on the mattress. "Shit, dude. We got a problem."

"What kind of problem?"

"You didn't hear?"

"Hear what?"

Jack whipped his eyes with the back of his hand. "Travis, man... He got pinched, bro."

"What the fuck are you talking about? He was arrested?"

Jack sat upright, rested his elbows on his knees, buried his face in his palms. "He's so fucked, bro."

"Dude, what are you talking about? What'd he get picked up for? Did he have a warrant or something?"

Jack shook his head. "No, bro. The watches."

Sean's face warmed with anger. "What fucking watches?"

"The Movados an' shit."

"The watches from the job we *all* agreed not to do?"

He nodded, fidgeted with things around him, probably looking for a pipe that wasn't broken.

Sean kicked the mattress. "What the fuck? You guys did the job anyway?"

Jack's eyes met his. "We were gonna cut you in, bro. Ten percent, you know, because you're a partner and all."

"I don't give a shit about that. We agreed to pass on that one because it was too risky."

"Well, I don't know what to tell you."

"For starters, tell me what the fuck happened to Travis."

"Like I said, bro. He got pinched. They're charging him with the whole fucking thing, and a bunch of other shit too. Like, high-level felony shit."

"Why? What the fuck happened? Did you get caught at the shipping yard?"

"No, bro. All of that went fine. Shit went south when we tried to offload the watches."

"Jesus Christ." Sean ran his fingers over his face, tried to calm his rage. "That's *exactly* why I said we shouldn't do the job. Goddamnit, man. Selling shit like that is so fucking risky."

"I'm sorry, bro."

Sean exhaled a deep breath, soothed his anger. "What the fuck happened?"

"I dunno, dude. The guy... I guess he was working with the cops."

"What fucking guy, Jack? A fence? Who did you sell them to?"

"Just this dude that Matt knows."

Sean exhaled sharply, turned to lap the small room, stepping away from the urge to kick the shit out of his oldest friend. Years ago, all three of them agreed to never involve outsiders in any job they did, a simple pact that had proven effective in keeping everyone out of handcuffs.

Sean knelt, faced Jack. "What the fuck? Why is Matt arranging meets for jobs?"

"He knew a guy, man. A guy who was supposed to get us sixty percent of retail on the entire haul."

"And that didn't sound a little too good to be true?"

"Fuck, dude. I dunno. Matt vouched for the guy."

"Why the fuck is Matt involved at all? He shouldn't even know what jobs you're doing, let alone be the one setting meets with fences."

"Matt's cool, dude. I trust him."

"What else does he know?"

"What do you mean?"

"Does he know about jobs we're looking at? Does he know about things we've done?"

"No, dude. I just ran into him a while back, and we... We did a few jobs together. Nothing major. Nothing you'd have wanted to do."

Sean stood, took a lap to calm himself. "Fuck, man. Are you kidding me? What kinds of jobs?"

"Small shit, bro. Don't worry about it."

"What kinds of jobs, Jack? I have a right to know."

"Nothing big. We hit a pawn shop, and a vape store, both out of town."

"How can you be sure you didn't leave a trail back to you, or to me?"

"Man, fuck you." Jack stood, faced him. "I know what I'm doing. I know how to cover tracks. None of this involves you, so don't fucking worry about it."

"Jesus, man. Any job you pull anywhere in the Illinois Valley involves me. Every time a place is hit, cops start poking around, and they start looking for clues that link to other shit. If they find enough evidence at one scene, they might be able to piece together everything we've ever done, and if they do that, they can get a jury to convict us on all of it."

"Dude, we're good. We used a stolen truck. We took out the cameras. We wore masks. No one's gonna link it to me, or to Matt, or to you, so chill the fuck out."

"Dude! They've got Travis, remember him? Where is he?"

"The jail in Ottawa. I guess the dude he met with down there was working with cops or some shit. All I know is he went to meet with the dude, and like, that was it. Next thing I hear, they got him in custody."

Sean sighed. "How many fucking jobs have you and Matt done?"

"Man, fuck you. It doesn't matter. It doesn't involve you. I ain't like you, bro. I don't live like you. I spend what I make, so I need to get more, and to get cash more often, you know? You take forever to plan shit, and we do like one small-ass job every couple months. I need more than that, dude."

"You're right, I do take forever to plan this shit, because the planning is what keeps us out of prison." Sean turned away, paced the perimeter of the room. "Don't you get it? If the cops trace any of these jobs to you, they're going to start looking at me and Travis. And now that Travis is in custody, they have a reason to look at all three of us. Travis and I have shoplifting convictions together. All three of us own a business together. How long do you think it's going to take the cops to figure that shit out? To start connecting those dots? How long until they start looking at every job we've done in the past few years, looking for evidence that links us to them?"

"Dude, you know Travis. He ain't gonna tell the cops shit."

"He doesn't have to. The cops, they're going to dig into his life, figure out who he knows, who he hangs out with. That list will become their list of suspects."

"Well, sorry, bro."

"You're sorry?" Sean fought the urge to hit him. "What else have you and Matt hit?"

"Don't worry about it. It doesn't concern you."

Sean got in Jack's face. "The fuck it doesn't. I just fucking explained how all of this concerns me, so what have you guys hit?"

"Jesus, bro. Nothing much. A place in Spring Valley, and one in Princeton."

"Nothing in town?"

His head drooped. "Just one place, but it was mostly Matt. I just drove us out of there."

"What place?"

"Some auto parts store."

"Nowicki's? On Adams?"

He nodded. "Yeah."

"Fucking Christ, man. That's right by my fucking apartment. What the hell were you thinking?"

"I told you, man, I didn't have shit to do with it. Matt decided to hit the place, and I drove him."

"How much thought went into his decision? Any at all?"

"Dude, whatever. It's done, and that's the only place in town we've hit."

"What about the watches? That was in town, wasn't it?"

He shook his head. "Matt wasn't part of that one. He just arranged the meet with the fence."

"Jesus, man. He was still involved though, and his involvement got Travis arrested."

"Fine, dude. Whatever. I get it. I fucked up."

Sean exhaled sharply. "What does Matt know about you, me, and Travis?"

"Nothing, dude."

"Nothing at all?"

"I mean, he knows what we do, but I haven't given him any details."

"So, you worked with the guy for a few months forever ago, and then you happen to bump into him, and then you decide to trust with something as big as fencing stolen goods? Are you fucking retarded?"

"Fuck you, man. How was I supposed to know the dude in Ottawa was a snitch? You can't pin this shit on me."

Sean stepped into Jack's face again. "Don't do the job at all. That would have protected all of us. Simply not doing the fucking job like we'd agreed on would have prevented all of it. That's all you had to do. Leave it the fuck alone."

Jack shoved him. "Bullshit, man. *You* decided the job was too risky. We still wanted to do it, so we did, and guess what, bro? It went fucking great."

"Oh? It went great? Really? Travis is in jail, asshole. So no, it didn't go great. That's what I hate about moving merch, man. You can't sell shit right away. You've got to sit on it for months before you shop it to fences. Did you really think that cops weren't out there looking for a bunch of high-end watches just days after they were jacked from a truck?"

"It's fucked up, bro. I know that. Shit didn't go like we'd thought."

"Fuck!" Sean's voice echoed throughout the empty house. "Okay, whatever. That ship has fucking sailed. What can we do for Travis? Do we need to get him a lawyer or something?"

"His parents are already hiring some tough-ass lawyer. Shit'll be all right, bro."

"Oh, will it? How do you think tough-ass lawyers win cases like this? The cut plea deals with the DA, that's how. Do you know what's usually part of those deals? Agreement to cooperate with investigations into accomplices."

"Travis ain't gonna say shit to no one about us, bro. You know that."

"I guess we'd both better hope that's true." Sean turned toward the doorway, kicking a piece of a broken pipe out of his path. "Quality fucking place you've got here, man. Really nice. When you're taking your morning shit in a toilet that won't flush, maybe spend some time thinking of ways to fix your life so you can enjoy it until we all go to prison."

Sliding past the plywood and onto the front porch, Sean took a deep breath, slowing the urge to vomit. He opened his car door and flumped into the driver's seat.

Right now, at this very moment, Travis could be talking to his lawyer. He could be telling him about all the shit the three of them had done. Even if Travis wasn't talking about them, the cops were probably investigating every break-in, burglary, and probably even every bicycle theft that'd happened anywhere in the Illinois Valley in the past several months. The more they investigated, the more they'd realize Travis didn't pull jobs alone. And even if all of this were to blow over—and by some miracle it didn't send him and Jack to jail too—they couldn't pull any new jobs while all this hung over their heads. Every cop in LaSalle County, and probably several surrounding counties, was on heightened alert for any kind of theft or break-in or theft. Even if he were to go it alone, any job he did now came at an increased risk. Cops could be steps ahead of him, maybe doing surveillance, or deeper forensics afterward. They could even be watching him right now, and by visiting Jack at a flophouse, Sean could have just provided the confirmation needed for them to connect him and Jack to every job they'd pulled.

reagan

Reagan directed her fiancé to turn left onto Forsythe Avenue, then right on Sixth Street. He followed her directions without protest, and before long, they pulled onto Peoria Street and parked in front of St. Thomas where she'd spent nearly every Sunday of her youth.

David chuckled.

She turned in the seat to face him. "What?"

"Nothing." A smirk filled his face.

"What are you smiling about then?"

"Oh, just picturing you as a Catholic school girl, that's all."

"Shut up." She slapped his shoulder.

"You don't happen to still have your uniform, do you?"

She rolled her eyes, not wanting to answer. A few pieces of her old uniforms were still in boxes in her parents' attic, but he didn't need to know that. "Anyway... Isn't this church beautiful?"

He leaned toward her to get a better view of the Gothic Revival structure. "It is beautiful, but it's also a little... Formal."

"I think it's gorgeous."

"Is this where you went to school too?"

"No." She shook her head. "I mean, yes, St. Thomas ran the school, but the classrooms are over there." She pointed to the squat building behind the church. "I was only there until the start of high school though."

"Ahh. Is that eh... Is that when your dad got laid off?"

She nodded. "Yeah. The unexpected loss of income meant they couldn't afford private school anymore. Sean and Donnie were perfectly happy to switch to public school, but I really liked it here."

"I'm sorry. I can tell by your face that it still causes you pain."

"It's okay. Everything happens for a reason, right? If I'd finished school here, maybe I'd have gotten into Harvard or something and we'd never have met." She extended her hand and glanced at the engagement ring on her finger, the sunlight dancing on the edges of the diamond. "Maybe I'd be wearing the ring of some tennis pro with a sweater wrapped around his neck."

He chuckled. "Oh? Is that secretly your type?"

"Why not? Summers on Martha's Vineyard, lunch with the ladies every afternoon, and a mother-in-law named Buffy. We could have a couple of kids too. A boy and girl. The boy would play water polo, and the girl would be a ballerina."

He laughed, a sound of genuine enjoyment. "Do these pretentious fantasy children have names?"

She contemplated it for a moment. "Our son is named Thane."

He snort-laughed. "Okay. What's your daughter's name?"

"Veruca."

"As in Salt?"

She shrugged. "Hey, if it's good enough for Roald Dahl, it's good enough for me and my husband, Raphael."

He tossed his head back as a ruckus laugh escaped his lips. "Raphael? I thought you married a tennis pro, not a painter."

"Oh, he's got the body of an athlete, but yeah, he paints. He's very cultured."

"I can see you've put a lot of thought into this. I guess it's a good thing you settled for UChicago, and for me."

She leaned across the center console and kissed him. "I think I did damn well for myself."

"I hope I make you happy."

"Very much so."

"If it helps, I could probably talk my parents into buying a vacation home on Martha's Vineyard, if that's really important to you."

"We'll see." She laughed, then pointed up the road. "For now, let's continue our tour of the exotic land known as Laytons Grove. Go up to the stop sign and take a left."

David obliged and put the car in drive.

She hadn't lied to him. As difficult as things got after Johnson-Power closed, things had worked out for the best, even though she had to navigate plenty of bumps in the road. The transition from private school to public school had been the roughest. Aside from the lack of academic challenges at Lincoln High, she'd never really fit in with the other kids there, and the Catholic school uniform that David was so excited about had played an early role in that difficult transition. Within days of starting school at Lincoln High, a boy had gotten hold of a St. Thomas yearbook and photocopied a page that featured Reagan in the school's uniform. He printed dozens of copies and before long, it seemed that every guy at her new school had a copy of it. She and her friends found them everywhere—hanging in bathrooms, littering the floors of the hallways, and even taped to the inside of several guys' lockers.

That incident, and plenty others, pushed her to find a college far away from Laytons Grove, but she also wanted to major in environmental studies and the University of Chicago offered a great program. When she landed a scholarship, the dream became financially possible, so when she was accepted, she jumped at the chance, even if it seemed a bit too close to these things she wanted distance from.

David's voice shattered her deep reverie. "Where do I turn?"

It took her a moment to reset in reality. "Um, turn right onto Main Street. The next light up there."

Reagan felt happy about the path life had put her on, and she was most happy about the events that led her to David. Everything about their time together confirmed that everything else happened for *that* reason.

As they drove along Main Street, Reagan pointed out the many beautiful brick and stone buildings in the old business district, then she directed him through downtown, around the town Christmas tree, into the tree-lined neighborhood streets, back to Main, and over to Peoria Street where the Alice Theatre stood.

David parked in front, as directed.

Reagan rolled down the window so he could see it better. "This is The Alice."

"The old theater you've raved about?"

She rolled her eyes. It was so much more than an *old theater*. "It opened in 1926, initially as a vaudeville palace, then it showed silent movies later on, and by the thirties, it began showing talking pictures."

"Talking pictures? What are you, like a hundred years old?"

"That's what they called them back then." She slapped his arm with the back of her hand. "Anyway... The place ended up closing in the early sixties and it sat vacant for decades before an investor reopened it as a modern movie theater. That was sometime in the eighties, but it was still showing movies when I was a little girl."

He reached over, gripped her hand. "You really love it here, don't you?"

"Nearly every movie I've ever seen in a theater was inside this place. With my family, with my friends, even my first date was here. I'm very happy it didn't get torn down."

"No, not just the theater. I mean, this town. You love this town, don't you?"

Tears formed in her eyes. It was a stupid and unexpected reaction, but he was right. She did love Laytons Grove. After spending her entire life trying to leave it, that decision made no sense now.

She squeezed his hand. "I do love it here. I didn't realize how much until recently, but spending time here, seeing all these great places in person again... It's a special place."

She discreetly wiped the tears from her eyes and, in an effort to change the subject to something that didn't make her want to ugly cry, she directed him down Main Street and over to Rockford Avenue to the little park where she learned to ride a bike.

She pointed toward the western edge of the small park. "They've reseeded since then, but there used to be a little dirt path worn in the grass over there. It was the perfect spot to learn to ride without training wheels because whenever you fell, you were surrounded by grass."

He smiled. It seemed obligatory. She was boring him, she could tell. She was sure he'd sighed as he shifted the car into park, like he wasn't having fun.

"Sorry, we can go back to my parents' place now."

"What? No, it's cool. I was honestly just thinking how cool it is that you remember all of that. I don't really remember learning to ride a bike at all."

"Are you sure?"

"Sure that I don't remember?" He chuckled. "Yeah, I'm very sure."

"No, that you don't mind seeing all these places. Are you sure I'm not boring you?"

"Not even a little bit. I love seeing where you grew up."

"I heard you sigh."

"I did not sigh."

She studied his face, looking for signs that he was lying. "I've probably shown you all of this stuff before anyway, haven't I?"

He shrugged. "I've seen a couple of the things, yeah, but before today, I didn't know you learned to ride a bike in a park."

"And you probably didn't *need* to know that either, did you? I mean, basically every kid learns to ride a bike, eventually."

He smiled. "I don't suppose I *need* to know it, but I'm glad I do. I like learning things about you, and I think it's really cool that after all this time, there are still things to learn."

"Yeah? In that case, go up the street and turn left on Joliet Avenue. I'm gonna show you where I took piano lessons."

"You play piano?"

"No." She laughed. "I said I took lessons. And by lessons, I mean two of them, just enough to qualify as a plural."

He obeyed and drove a few blocks, then turned when directed.

David reached over and patted her leg. "So look... I confess. You did hear me sigh, but not because I'm bored. It was because I'm wondering if you're stalling, you know, because you're afraid to tell your parents our news."

She wanted to deny it, but she couldn't. "I guess maybe a little."

"Do you really think they'll be anything but happy?"

"I think they'll be over the freakin' moon."

"Then why are we stalling?"

She gazed out the window at her favorite town, then released a long, deep breath. "I guess I like that it's just kind of *our* news right now. Something no one else knows about."

"I can understand that. I feel it too. Nothing says we have to tell them today."

She turned to him and smiled. "No. I'm ready. It's amazing news, and it should be shared."

She found Ma in the kitchen, already prepping for tonight's meal. David took a seat in the living room as Reagan joined Ma by the sink.

Ma turned her head to look at Reagan. "Did you two have fun sightseeing?"

"We did." Reagan nodded, fighting back more tears. If Ma knew how sentimental she felt right now, she'd for sure start pushing for her to move back to town. "Pretty sure I've shown him all the same things ten times before. He was a good sport though."

"He loves you, so I'm sure he doesn't mind seeing a few of the sights more than once."

Reagan nodded. She didn't mind discussing her visit to town, but she was far more concerned with how things with her parents were going. "Can I ask a slightly personal question?"

"I suppose, dear."

"How are things here? With Dad's work and all."

Ma set a pan on the rack to dry and turned to face her. "We're doing well, dear."

She nodded, but realized she'd have to be more direct. "I read in the *Telegraph* that Midland Ceramics was planning another round of layoffs. Is Dad's job at risk."

"We don't know, dear. It's kind of out of our hands, but I've been working some good hours at Fido & Friends, and your father's been looking for a new job."

"How did his interview at the place in Ottawa go?"

She shook her head. "He hasn't heard back, and it's been a good while. But he's applied to about three other places. We'll be okay."

"David and I could probably help out, if you needed."

"Things will work out, dear. God has a plan for us, and he'll see to it that we're taken care of."

Reagan nodded in agreement, even if she didn't necessarily agree with the sentiment. The situation was far too reminiscent of the early days, the weeks and months before Johnson-Power Glassworks shut down, and when that happened, it wasn't God who helped. It was family.

Ma reached for a pan in the cupboard but struggled to grab it. Reagan stepped forward to help, but before she could, David blew by her and grabbed it. "I got that, Mrs. McKenna."

Reagan glanced toward the living room, half expecting to see a David doppelgänger still in the chair. "I thought you were in the other room."

"I was, but it seemed unfair since your mom is in here working hard on our dinner."

Ma stepped aside to allow him to reach the cupboard. "David, I've told you many times, you don't have to call me Mrs. McKenna. You can call me *Ma*."

He pulled the pan down and set it on the counter. "Okay, Ma, here you go."

"Thank you." She smiled as she moved some sliced veggies from a cutting board to the pan. "Reagan said you two had a good time seeing the town, even though you've seen all the same things before."

"Probably not *all* the same things." He chuckled. "But I don't mind seeing things again. I love this little town."

"Oh? Good." Ma began washing some potatoes in the sink. "You know, there are some very nice homes for sale right now."

Reagan chuckled to herself. It was a predictable response from a mother. "Ma, all he said was that he loved the town."

Ma smiled, a wide grin that filled her face. "And all I said was that there are some really nice homes on the market right now. In fact, they just listed that old Victorian on Stout and Madison. The one you always said would make a lovely bed-and-breakfast. Remember?"

"I remember saying it would make a great B and B, but I don't recall saying I wanted to buy it or that I wanted to run a B and B."

Ma turned and smiled at her. "Could be a nice business for a young couple. That's all I'm saying."

David peered over Ma's shoulder at the potatoes. "What are we doing with those?"

He was trying to change the subject, and Reagan loved him for it.

Ma moved the potatoes to the counter. "We'll do these au gratin. Just as soon as I have a chance to slice them."

David grabbed a chef's knife from the block. "I can slice them for you." He set a potato on the cutting board and positioned the knife above it. "I assume you'd prefer equal slices, so they cook evenly?"

Ma smiled. "I'm not too particular, dear."

Reagan's eyes narrowed as she watched him. "I didn't know you knew how to slice anything with a knife."

He laughed. "See. There are things you can still learn about me too."

"I guess there are. You don't have to help though. I can do that."

"It's already being done."

The stairs creaked and Reagan turned to see who was coming down them, expecting it to be her father. Instead, it was Sean.

She turned to face him. "What are you doing here?"

"I'm just as thrilled you're here."

"You know what I mean." She rolled her eyes. "Have you been here long?"

Ma set the cleaned vegetables on a cutting board. "He came over to help me with the television upstairs. Netflix wasn't loading on it."

Reagan returned her gaze to Sean. "Cool. Did you fix it?"

He nodded. "And now I'm going to take a break." He held up a pack of cigarettes out of Ma's view, even though she surely knew he smoked.

Reagan understood though. Being back in the old house had a way of making you revert to your teen years.

Reagan hugged him. "I'm glad you're here. Are you staying for dinner?"

Ma interjected. "I bribed him with a home-cooked meal in exchange for a working TV."

A smile filled Reagan's face. It was good to see them getting along again.

Sean nodded his head toward the door. "Anyway, break time."

She grabbed her coat and followed him onto the front porch.

He leaned against one of the support posts and lit a cigarette.

Reagan sidled up next to him. "I'm really glad you're coming around here more often. It means everything to that wonderful woman in there."

He nodded as he exhaled a drag. "It's starting to feel more natural. Me and the old man are still kinda avoiding each other though."

"It'll get easier. Give it time." She stared down at the porch for a moment. "He never meant the stuff he said that day, you know right? The day you left home. He was upset with you for ditching all the medication. They want you here, and you are welcome here."

Sean smiled as he exhaled another drag. "I didn't ditch it. I sold all of those fucking pills. Made a nice profit off some dipshits at school. That's what he's pissed about."

"Whatever the semantics of it, he didn't really mean that he never wanted you back in this house. Both of them are happy when you come over."

He took a drag and nodded. "I guess."

They stood in silence, and she stared at her shoes, unsure what else to say to convince him that their family was stronger with him. She'd watched their parents fight for years, ever since Sean first started having problems in school, somewhere around the fourth grade. All families fought though. She never expected it would grow into the problems it did—grow into something as serious as Sean leaving home and not returning for years.

She watched as he took another drag from the cigarette. "I thought you were going to stop that nasty habit."

He nodded as he exhaled a cloud of smoke into the cold evening air. "I've tried. A couple of times. Even tried to replace cigarettes with vaping. It's not the same, no matter what anyone says."

"Should I lecture you about what you're doing to your lungs, or how you're cutting your life shorter with each drag?"

"I hear that a lot, that it cuts years off my life, but it's the years at the *end* of my life, right? It's not like they come from my twenties."

She rolled her eyes. "Fine, then should I lecture you about the lengthy list of health problems it causes? Run through all the ways you could die painfully and slowly?"

"No, I'm good."

"What about the harm you cause to others through secondhand smoke?"

He nodded. "You make a good point. You shouldn't be standing near me." He pushed her gently, creating space between them.

She chuckled. "I'll be fine, doofus."

"Maybe, but the secondhand smoke probably isn't good for my niece or nephew."

Her face flushed and her hand involuntary moved to caress her stomach. "How did... You, um... You know that I'm pregnant?"

"Yeah, I know."

"How?"

"Dave told me." Sean smirked, happy that he'd shocked her. "Relax. I won't say anything before you guys tell everybody tonight."

"Why did David tell you that?"

Sean shrugged as he took a drag.

"Okay, when did he tell you?"

"A while back, when he was looking for a place to propose to you."

"You knew about *that* too?"

Sean nodded and puffed on his cigarette. "Yup."

"Well, thank you for not ruining our surprises."

"I'm a vault. Information stored here never leaves."

Sean stared out across the lawn. He seemed off. Sad or something.

Reagan bundled her coat tighter and leaned against the railing. "You doing okay?"

Sean shrugged again. "How do you mean?"

"I mean, we don't talk much these days, so what are you up to? How's life? Those sorts of things."

"You want to know what I've been up to?" He chuckled. "Work. Brooke. Sleep. That basically covers it."

She nodded, accepting that she'd asked a vague question and deserved a vague answer. "It seems like something's bothering you. Everything okay?"

He stubbed the cigarette out on the railing, then flicked it toward the street. "I guess."

"You guess? That sounds like a 'no' to me."

He sighed. "Travis got arrested."

"Holy shit! What for?"

Sean shrugged. "Some stupid thing he did with Jack."

"What kind of stupid thing?"

"I don't really know the details."

It was an obvious lie, but there was no point in pushing it any further, with him being a vault and all. "Do you still hang out with Jack?"

"Yeah."

"I mean, I know you two... I know that you, like, own a business together or whatever the hell you call it, but I didn't know you hung out together aside from that."

"Well, we do."

Again, pushing further was only going to upset him, so it was best to stick to the key questions on her mind. "Why wasn't Jack arrested during whatever it was they did?"

Sean shrugged again. "Not sure. Luck, maybe?"

She'd hit another wall with him. It was time to change the subject, at least a little. "How is Jack doing these days?"

"He's living with this dude Matt. They're both busy gettin' high way too much."

She nodded. It made sense. Jack had struggled with addiction most of his life. "Meth?"

"Yeah, at the least."

"And you still hang out with him?"

He sighed. "Yeah. We covered that already."

She wanted to say a lot more, but they'd been down that road a number of times and each time it had ended with Sean and her not speaking for long periods. At the same time, she was scared for him. "You haven't done any of that shit, have you?"

"Meth?"

"Yeah. Or whatever else he's into."

Sean shook his head. "Not really."

"What does 'not really' mean? That sounds like you have."

He sighed again. "Like, I've tried it before. Years ago, but I hated it, okay, Mom?" He chuckled.

She nodded, accepting that her maternal instincts had already sprouted. She also recognized that she'd pushed about as far as she could, bent him as much as she could without causing him to snap. "Sorry, I don't mean to sound like a bad PSA commercial or whatever, but I am glad you didn't go down that road."

"Yeah. If nothing else, it keeps me feeling like I'm better than Jack, I guess." He took in a deep breath, then released it slowly as he watched the water vapors trail out of his mouth. "Anyway, what about you? What's new in your life? You know, aside from being engaged and pregnant. Is the new apartment working out for you guys?"

"For now."

Sean shoved his hands deep in his pockets. "You don't plan to stay there?"

"Initially we planned on staying for years, but a lot has changed in our lives since we signed the lease, and truthfully, I wouldn't mind moving home."

"Seriously? You mean, like, to *this* town?"

She nodded. It felt good to say it out loud. She'd been thinking about it for so long that it was calming to say the words *to* someone. "This is a good place."

He shrugged. "I guess. I mean, I don't hate it here, but it seems like Chicago would be a way cooler place to live."

"Maybe it is, until you start thinking about raising a family."

"Makes sense."

"Not something you've thought about, little brother?"

"Not even a tiny bit."

"No? Is Brooke not *the one*?"

He shrugged. "I have no idea. She's cool and we have fun. Neither of us have pushed for anything beyond that really."

"Have you said, 'I love you' to each other?"

He nodded his head.

She smiled. "You have? And? Did you mean it? Do you love her?"

He snort-laughed. "I wouldn't have said it if I didn't mean it. I mean, I'm not really sure what love is, but I like her, and I care about her. Is that the same thing?"

"Do you feel like you'd be sad if she was no longer around? And not just sad, but like crushed? Lost?"

He nodded. "Yeah, in a way."

"Do you feel like your life is made better by her being part of it?"

"She's basically my best friend, and yeah, life is better when she's around."

"Damn, little brother. You *might* just be in love."

He blushed a little. "Okay, shut up."

"Fine, fine. I'll drop it. As long as you promise to invite me to the wedding."

"Yeah, you got it." He unzipped his jacket and walked toward the door. "I'm going away from you now."

She smiled, content in knowing she'd made him uncomfortable.

He paused before stepping inside. "You coming?"

"In a minute."

He shrugged and stepped into the house as she gazed out across the front yard and down Monroe Street. She felt at home there. At ease. Like she belonged there. Later tonight, after they'd told her parents about the pending birth of their granddaughter, maybe she'd find the courage to tell David that she wanted to move back to Laytons Grove.

mary

With the sun rising in the distance, Mary met Detective Kilmartin at the small auto parts store at the intersection of Adams and Joliet, just a few blocks north of Morelli's Convenience. It'd been more than twenty-four hours since the store was broken into, and Kilmartin and other LGPD investigators had already collected plenty of evidence from the scene, but she wanted to see the crime scene for herself in hopes she could suss out any clues that indicated the burglary was connected to other recent crimes in the area.

At the front of the store, she found the front window boarded and some remnants of broken glass on the sidewalk below. All indications were that the thieves had gained entry through those windows. Around the back of the building, she found the steel frame surrounding the back entry door bent, the door slightly mangled. The door's latch still held it securely shut though, which indicated the suspects had attempted to gain access to the building through the door but instead settled for smashing the front windows. The quicker but louder option.

The thieves again used pry bars inside the business where they'd forced open both cash registers, damaging them beyond repair. The store's owner, Dan Nowicki, said he didn't keep cash in the registers overnight though and that the cost to replace the damaged registers was higher than the total amount of cash stored on the premises at any point.

The thieves also kicked in an interior office door, as well as another door that led to a room where the safe was located, cracking the doors and shattering the surrounding wooden frames. In all, Mr. Nowicki estimated the damage to the interior and exterior of the building to be more than eight grand.

The safe sustained some damage as well, but it was minimal, limited to some scratches around the door and slight damage to the dial. It appeared the thieves failed to gain access to the safe itself because when Mr. Nowicki opened it in front of investigators, the contents were untouched. In fact, the thieves hadn't gotten away with much of anything. According to Mr. Nowicki, they'd taken a few boxes of brake pads, some headlight bulbs, and a fuel filter that only fit a few Buick sedans. They did, however, manage to grab a couple socket wrench sets and a digital torque wrench, which Mr. Nowicki valued at about two hundred dollars.

Mary and Kilmartin entered the business to inspect the layout of the store. All the car parts sat on metal shelves behind a counter that held the two cash registers. The markings on the car part boxes didn't provide much detail on the contents, so without knowledge of the store's inventory, or without using the computer system to look up part numbers, a thief could only grab boxed parts blindly. A weird sort of lottery where some boxes would contain expensive parts and others inexpensive parts, or parts that may not fit a wide variety of vehicles. In this case, it seemed the thieves had ended up with inexpensive parts that were likely in a dumpster somewhere by now.

Kilmartin tucked his thumbs into his belt as he surveyed the mess left behind. "This can't be related to all of the other break-ins."

Mary nodded in agreement. "No. This feels clumsy, unplanned. They caused thousands of dollars in damages but only got away with a few hundred in goods. Lately, we've been seeing the opposite: limited damage with several grand in cash missing."

"What are you thinking? Crime of opportunity?"

"Something like that. Nothing here indicates that they had knowledge of the business' internal practices. If it'd been an inside job, the suspects would probably have known that no money was kept in the registers overnight, or at least, they would've had an idea of what parts and tools to take. As it is, it seems they lacked knowledge of what car parts are valuable, and the tools, well, that seems to have been a last-minute decision as they exited the building."

"What's your feeling on motive? Drug addicts looking for some quick items to sell?"

"I'm not sure if it's that simple."

"Because of the pry bars used?"

She nodded. "It could be drug related, sure, but the tools used indicate that at least some planning went into this. Aside from the use of burglary tools, it seems they arrived with a plan for how to get inside, even if that plan failed and they settled for shattering a window."

Mary walked toward the busted cash registers to inspect them closer. The marks left by the pry bars indicated the thieves had made multiple attempts to access the contents of the drawers, likely because they weren't familiar enough with the equipment to know its weak points. All signs that this hadn't been a sophisticated burglary.

Mary pushed the open drawer of one of the registers closed. "My theory is the suspect, or more likely multiple individuals, came looking for the cash. When they didn't find any in the registers, they went searching for the safe. But once they found that it was bolted to the floor and harder to get into than they'd anticipated, they grabbed what they could easily carry and ran away."

Kilmartin nodded in agreement. "What about the fact they're not on camera? Think that was dumb luck, or did they take steps to ensure they wouldn't be?"

"Given everything I've seen so far, I'm leaning toward luck." She took a lap around the showroom floor and inspected the store's camera placement. Its four cameras fed to a monitor in the back office, but unfortunately, there was no recording mechanism. While it was possible the thieves knew that, it was just as possible they'd gotten lucky.

Mary gazed out the store's untouched window, toward the business across the street. "Do you know if we've asked the businesses around here if their cameras happened to capture anything?"

Kilmartin nodded. "Responding officers checked, but one needed corporate approval before releasing footage to us. Supposed to hear something later today."

"Good. Maybe they captured a getaway vehicle or something else of use."

Mary stopped for lunch at Mazzarella's Deli where she ordered an Italian sub and then settled in at a table by a window that overlooked Main Street. Pulling out her notebook, she reviewed what she had so far. Nothing added up. A string of burglaries all over the Illinois Valley, some sophisticated, others primitive smash-and-grab jobs.

Meanwhile, Ottawa PD had a kid in custody who'd tried to sell dozens of expensive watches. The watches had been reported stolen out of Laytons Grove in a daring burglary in broad daylight. The thieves behind the heist showed a moderate level of sophistication and planning. They were skilled enough to strike a shipping dock at the right time by sneaking onto the property, apparently after distracting the workers there with a deliberately set fire. Yet, despite the skill level required to swipe tens of thousands of dollars' worth of jewelry in the middle of the day, they'd been dumb enough to try to sell them just hours later.

The string of burglaries at other places seemed unrelated to the watch heist though. She also wasn't sure of any connections to the store break-ins. Where the auto supply shop thieves smashed out a window to gain entry, other break-ins had been carried out with precision. And despite similarities in all the recent cases, her gut told her that at least two different crews were at work.

The squeak of the overhead speaker jolted her. Her order was ready.

Shoving her work aside, Mary walked to the counter, collected the awaiting tray, and returned to her work.

A few bites into her sandwich, Flanigan called to say that uniformed officers had detained a male subject around 16:00 today. They'd responded to a call at a garage on Main and LaSalle after a mechanic there called LGPD to say he'd been approached by a man wanting to sell him a torque wrench and some other tools.

The caller provided a description of the male subject and said he'd gotten into a late-model silver in color Chevrolet Cruze with a second male subject behind the wheel. Approximately fifteen minutes later, an LGPD officer spotted the silver Chevy at a fast-food restaurant on Chicago Avenue. The officer initiated a traffic stop but only located one individual inside the vehicle—nineteen-year-old Nicholas Shevlin—the registered owner of the Chevy. The officer also spotted tools and auto parts on the floor of the vehicle.

Mary glanced at her notes on the table. "Do you happen to have a list of the tools found?"

Flanigan chuckled slightly. "Way ahead of ya. We've checked them against the missing inventory from Nowicki's Auto Parts, and we've got some matches. I've got something else you'll wanna hear too."

"I'm listening." She hated Flanigan's flair for the dramatic.

"We got a hold of some surveillance footage from a tattoo shop across from Nowicki's. One of the cameras captured low-resolution footage of three male subjects climbing into a silver four-door car, possibly a Chevy Cruze, around the time of the break-in. The men appeared to toss several items into the back seat before driving away."

Before Flanigan even finished, Mary had wrapped her sandwich in a napkin and was headed to her SUV. She wanted to interview the man they had in custody.

At a table in an LGPD interview room sat nineteen-year-old Nicholas Shevlin. Legally, he was an adult, but everything about him made him seem like a child. He had a babyface and was short, skinny, and twitchy. He seemed terrified and was likely coming down from the effects of some narcotic.

She stared at him from across the table. "Mr. Shevlin, did you break into the auto parts store?"

He wouldn't look at her, but he nodded in the affirmative.

"Why did you break in?"

He rubbed his left arm with his hand, scrubbing at it like he was showering. "I dunno."

"You don't know? It was what? Just a whim? Something to do?"

He shook his head.

"Were you looking for money?"

He nodded. "We thought there'd be some in the drawers."

"We? Who else was with you?"

"I can't say."

"Because you don't want to tell me their names?"

He nodded. "It doesn't matter what their names are."

"What if I told you I already know their names? Uniformed officers arrested two individuals moments ago." She was bluffing; a technique that proved useful in situations like this. "They're being questioned right now. What do you think they're saying about your role in all of this?"

None of it was true. No other arrests had been made, and she didn't know the identities of any other thieves, but Mr. Shevlin had no way of knowing that.

He scratched his arm. "Shit, I dunno. It wasn't my idea though. Matt's the one who wanted to hit the place."

"What's Matt's last name again?"

He shook his head vigorously. "I ain't saying."

The kid had wised up. It'd be harder to get information on his accomplices now, so Mary moved on. "So after you guys broke in, you tried to break open the cash register drawers, correct?"

He nodded and scrubbed his arm.

Mary pretended to write in a notebook. "Were you surprised to find the drawers empty?" It was good to mix in some of what she did know to draw out the things she didn't know.

He nodded. "We thought there'd be lots of cash in there."

"So you took some tools instead? And some car parts?"

Again he nodded. "Yeah."

"Specific parts? Or whatever you could grab."

"Just, you know... Some stuff that looked good."

"How did you gain access to the building?"

"Huh?"

"How did you break into the store?"

"Oh, uh, I hit the window."

"With what?"

"A crowbar. One like firefighters use."

"And was this after you'd already attempted to enter through the back door?"

He nodded and scrubbed.

Mary pretended to write. "Did you plan ahead of time what you'd do to get in?"

"No."

"So again, this was just a whim? Something to kill some time?"

"Yeah. I mean, no. Like, we talked it over a little bit, then went and got some stuff."

"Like the crowbar?"

He nodded.

"Where'd you get the crowbar?"

"From... It doesn't matter."

"Did one of the other two men provide it?"

"I don't know."

He obviously knew but didn't want to incriminate anyone, so she moved on. "Why this particular business? Why'd you steal from this place?"

"We just... Like, for the money, you know? We needed it."

"What did you need it for?"

"Because, man... I've got, like, a problem. We—we've got a problem."

"A drug problem?"

He nodded. "Well, yeah, but we've got a bigger problem with this other guy."

"What other guy?"

"Just some dude named TJ."

"TJ? Who's that?"

"Just some guy. A dealer, I guess. But like, once we started owing him, he made us start selling for him too."

"What's TJ's last name?"

He shook his head vigorously. "I got no idea. People just call him TJ or whatever."

"So you were looking to steal some money to pay TJ back?"

"Basically. I mean, to get high too, but yeah, we need to pay TJ 'cause I'm afraid of what he'll do if we don't get him squared."

"Why is that? Has TJ threatened you?"

"No. I mean, yeah, like, in a way."

"What way is that?"

"I mean, like everyone knows what he's like. What he's done to people."

"What has he done to people? Give me some examples."

"I dunno. Like, he supposedly burned those two guys to death and shit."

Mary's interest was piqued. She assumed he was talking about the two men whose bodies showed up in a ditch a few weeks back, but when it came to convicting criminals in court, there was no room for assumptions. She needed specifics.

Mary leaned closer to him. "What two guys? Do you know their names?"

He shook his head. "No. I didn't know them at all, but like, it was on the news. You guys found their bodies on Seventy-One burned alive and shit."

"And TJ is the one who burned them?"

"That's what I heard. That's what he been sayin'. I ain't looking to have that happen to me, you know what I'm saying?"

"Is that why he killed them? They owed him money?"

"Basically, yeah. He makes loans, and then he fronts product for you to sell, and if you don't sell it—or if you wind up smoking it—then you end up burned in a ditch like those two fools."

"Do you know where TJ lives?"

He shook his head.

She leaned away from him. "How can I get in touch with TJ?"

He shrugged. "No idea."

"Do you have TJ's phone number, perhaps?"

He fidgeted in his chair, then sighed sharply. "No."

"We're in the process of getting a warrant to search your phone. When we do, we're not going to find a phone number for TJ in there? Or messages to and from him?"

He fidgeted more but stayed silent.

Mary decided to leave the room for a bit and give Mr. Shevlin a little time to consider his options. If he were truly afraid of TJ, he probably didn't want to end up back on the streets where TJ could get to him. If instead, he decided to help them arrest TJ, then he'd be that much safer. Maybe with a little time alone to consider those things, he would be more willing to talk, and more willing to provide the names of his two accomplices in the burglary at Nowicki's Auto Parts.

sean

Flipping through channels, Sean found nothing interesting to watch. Saturday afternoon TV offered only college football or old cop shows, and cops were the last thing he wanted to think about.

Travis was out of jail at least, but the judge placed him on house arrest with an ankle monitor. Sean got to see him briefly, but they weren't able to talk long. Travis looked like shit though, and so far, he was taking all of the heat for the shit Jack got him into, and Travis swore he wouldn't mention Jack's name to anyone.

Sean believed him, but that wasn't what concerned him most. He was a lot more worried that as the cops built a case against Travis, in the process they'd figure out that Jack was involved in the theft of the watches. Once that happened, it would only be a matter of time before they figured out all the links between all three of them. In the worst case, they'd assume Sean took part in the thing with the watches, but in the best-case scenario, they'd figure out that Sean was linked to Jack and Travis in a number of ways and then start watching his every move.

Travis seemed unsure about his lawyer too, who was apparently just some family friend his dad had known for years. The dude told Travis he was sure he could get some of the charges dropped because of how some of the evidence had been obtained. Travis seemed uneasy about all of it though, and with good reason. Lawyers were salesmen, so of course they'd tell their clients all the good things they could do. The reality though was that if the guy failed to deliver on those promises, Travis was facing some serious time behind bars.

The sound of a key in the front door brought Sean's daydreaming to an end. The door swung open, and the room filled with sunlight. Brooke stepped into the living room, her hair pulled into a ponytail.

He stood to greet her with a kiss. "Hey."

"Hey. Sorry I didn't text first."

"It's fine. You're always welcome here."

"I can't stay long. I close tonight. Just wanted to grab my water bottle." She disappeared into the bedroom and reappeared moments later with the pink Hydro Flask in her hand. "What are you up to today?"

"Just chilling, watching some TV. Nothing good's on though."

She rested her hand on his chest, traced the collar of his shirt with her finger. "I would have come over sooner if I knew you were around."

He kissed her lightly on the lips. "Yeah? Well, maybe you can swing by after work?"

"I promised my sister I'd help with her baby shower stuff after work."

"Blow off work then."

She smiled. "Yeah? What would we do?"

Sean turned to look at the bedroom, then shrugged. "Fun things."

Her smile widened. "Most any other day I'd take that offer, but if I don't go in, Hannah would be alone for hours. I can't do that to her. Not on a Saturday night."

"You're seriously ditching me for work again?"

"No, I'm ditching you for Hannah, technically. Remember, we've discussed how I like her more than you."

He couldn't help but smile at her sarcastic sense of humor. "Hey, do you like working there?"

"The Junction?" She shrugged. "It's not bad, I guess. It's better than most jobs I've had, and Hannah's a cool boss. The discount is decent too."

"Are they hiring?"

"Only like every day and all the time."

"Yeah? Think they'd hire me?"

She snort-laughed, but her expression soon turned genuine. "Are you being serious?"

"It's just a thought."

"You actually want to work at the Junction?"

He shrugged. "Maybe. I guess I'm curious about it."

She scanned him up and down. "Don't take this the wrong way, babe, but you don't dress like someone who's up to date with what Fashion Junction sells."

He chuckled. "I can fake it though."

"What's up? Is your business not doing well?"

He paced the living room floor. He'd always avoided talking about what he and the guys did for a living—sticking to the lawn care story like he did with everyone—but he also knew she wasn't stupid. Brooke knew what he did, even if they'd never discussed it specifically. "Travis got arrested."

"Oh, shit! What for?"

"I don't know all the details, but some dumb-ass plan of Jack's. It went south—because of course it did—and now Travis is on the hook for all of it."

"Is he in jail?"

"House arrest, but that's just till trial. Who knows what will happen when it's all settled."

"That's crazy." Her face was tight, full of concern. "Is it... Could they come for you because of it?"

Sean shook his head. "I had nothing to do with any of it."

Her watch chimed and she glanced at it. "Shit. I'm going to be late. Can we talk about this later? Tomorrow maybe?"

He nodded. "Yeah. Sure."

"I'm sorry. I really want to talk about this, but I have to get to work, and I don't know how late I'll be with my sister."

"Tomorrow's fine."

She kissed him, slid her hand gently down his arm, like she was soothing a child who'd fallen off his bike. "We'll definitely talk later. I'm sorry that I can't stick around right now."

"It's cool. Come over tomorrow, whenever. I'll be around."

She nodded, stepped toward the door. "I'll um... I'll ask Hannah about hiring you, if you really are interested."

He nodded, kissed her goodbye. By the time the door closed he'd already regretted saying anything about the Junction, but things were out of control and Jack's recklessness had cut off his ability to earn. He'd need to get money from somewhere, but he'd figure it out somehow, because the more he thought about things, the more he realized that no matter what, he wasn't going to go work at the fucking Fashion Junction.

After another pointless trip through all the channels, he decided to watch a movie instead. About thirty minutes into *Batman Begins*, his phone chimed. A text from Jack wanting to know what he was doing.

He tossed his phone onto the cushion beside him. Jack was probably just as bored as he was, and under different circumstances, they'd get together, drink some beers, smoke some weed. But he couldn't hang out with Jack right now. The guy had sent Travis into a storm, and the entire time, stood on the safety of the shore, unwilling to help in any way. It was unfair that Jack walked away unscathed, free to do anything he wanted, while Travis was stuck inside his parents' house with an ankle monitor reporting all his movements. It was also likely that detectives were watching Jack, or maybe even Sean, or more likely, both of them.

Again his phone chimed.

Jack again, this time offering to grab a sixer on his way over.

Sean stared at the screen for a moment, then typed. SORRY, DUDE. BROOKE'S HERE. WE'RE IN FOR THE NIGHT.

Jack didn't respond, so Sean unpaused the movie.

His phone rang.

He sighed, considered letting it go to voicemail, but gave in. "Hey, man. Sorry. We're gonna chill here tonight though."

"That's cool, bro." Jack's voice was rough, scratchy. "Um... Are you sure we couldn't talk real quick though? Just for a few?"

Sean searched for a lie, but nothing came to him quickly. "Yeah, okay. What's up?"

"Not on the phone. I *really* need to talk to you, bro. Like, *tonight*! Please, man?"

His words carried an urgency that Sean had never heard from him before.

Sean sighed again. "Yeah. Okay. You can drop by if you need to."

“Thanks, bro. I’ll be like ten, maybe fifteen minutes.”

“I’ll be here.”

When the movie ended, Sean searched for something else to watch. Jack should have been by more than an hour ago, but he hadn’t shown up, called, or even texted.

Finally deciding to just move onto the next film in the trilogy, Sean grabbed the disc for *The Dark Knight* and popped it into the Blu-ray player. In the middle of the opening bank robbery scene, a knock at the door.

Sean paused the movie, walked to the door, peered through the peephole. Jack paced back and forth in the small landing at the top of the stares, blowing into his bare hands to keep them warm.

Sean took a deep breath, opened the door. “You made it.”

“Of course, bro.”

“Took quite a while.”

“Did it?” Jack glanced at his phone. “Shit. Sorry.”

He looked terrible. Skinny and dirty, with greasy hair and scabs on his face, probably from wounds he’d created by picking at his skin while high.

Sean let him in, grabbed him a beer from the fridge.

“Thanks.” He took the beer, stared at the label. “Sorry I’m so late, bro. I didn’t realize that took so long.”

Sean cracked open a beer of his own, sat on a stool. “So... What’d you need to talk about?”

He set the beer down. “Well, um....” He nervously rubbed his bony arm, looked toward the bedroom. “Is Brooke here?”

“Naw. She ran to Sullivans to get some stuff for breakfast tomorrow.”

"Okay, cool. I, uh, I really need your help with something, bro. Something I'm doing tonight. Well, like, before sunrise."

Sean shook his head. "I'm not interested."

"You haven't even heard what it is yet. Just hear me out."

"I'm taking a break, man."

"What? Why?"

"There's a lot of shit going on right now and it's not a good time to do anything. We've gotta let some shit blow over before we even *consider* doing any jobs."

"C'mon, bro. This ain't like that other shit, and you don't have to do anything major. I just need a lookout. A pair of eyes to keep watch. That's all."

"I can't, not right now, and you shouldn't either. Who knows what they've got on us? They could be watching everything we do. Everywhere we go."

"Travis didn't tell 'em shit, bro. I know he didn't. I talked to him."

"I know. I talked to him too, but that's not what I'm talking about. You, me, we're linked to Travis in a bunch of ways. Cops around here know a lot of shit's been taken lately and they're probably trying to figure out who's behind all of it. Hell, there might be cops sitting outside right now keeping tabs on us as we speak."

"I doubt that, bro."

Sean shrugged. "But we don't know for sure, do we? Until we can be sure it's safe, we can't do shit."

"C'mon, bro, this will be quick. I'll give you a twenty percent cut."

"Is that the same deal Travis got? Maybe he could help you—oh, wait, no. He's got an ankle monitor strapped to his leg because of the last thing he helped you with."

"Hey, that shit wasn't on me, a'ight?"

"Who's fault was it? Matt's?"

"Yeah, sorta."

"Oh yeah? Are you sure it wasn't Travis' fault? I mean, he shoulda known the guy he met with was a snitch, right?"

"Of course not, bro. He couldn't have known that."

"That's my point. There's one person who's to blame, and that's you. But you refuse to accept that, or to take responsibility for how things went down."

"Fuck, dude. I get that, but... I dunno. The whole thing was fucked up, all right?"

"The 'whole thing' was a job that you pushed for. One that Travis didn't even want to do."

"Bullshit! Is that what he's saying? Fuck that, bro. He was all in on the idea."

"Fine, Jack. Whatever. That's not even the point. All I'm saying is, I ain't doing this next thing, whatever it is."

"Bro, c'mon. This'll be an easy one. I'll give you a bigger cut."

Sean stared at the counter, sighed. "The cut isn't the problem, Jack."

"Whatever, bro. C'mon. I've got everything lined up here. Just listen to me. You know James Trundle, right?"

"I don't think so."

"No, you do. He went to school with us. He was a few years behind us. He's Adam Trundle's brother."

"I don't remember these people, Jack."

"Okay, fine." He waved his hands wildly. "Whatever. The thing is, James works at the Morelli's gas station. He told me that the keypad on the safe broke a couple of days ago, and as of right now, they can't lock it. They've just been putting the deposits in there and closing the door without a lock."

Sean sighed, traced the mouth of the beer bottle with his thumb. "I don't care, dude. I'm taking a break. Letting shit blow over."

"You sure? Seriously, the cash is just sitting there, bro. All I have to do is get inside, and all that money's mine. Ours, if you help me."

"This one is not for me, sorry."

"How is this not for you? It's the kind of job you're always saying we should look for. Cash. Easy. Fast entry with a quick exit, and nothing to fence. All I'm asking you to do is make sure that no one's coming. I'll up your cut to twenty-five percent."

Sean sighed again. "Again, dude, it's not about the cut. I'm taking a break."

"Seriously? One job goes bad—one that you weren't even a part of—and you're done forever?"

"I'm not saying it's forever. All I'm saying is I'm going to lay low for a while, let some of the heat blow over. Okay?"

"You can take a break after tonight, bro. C'mon, I've done my homework on this. I've scouted out the back door. It's old and it won't take much to pry it open, and since it's in the alley, no one's going to see me."

"I'm sure they have cameras, and probably higher end stuff than most of the jobs we've done."

"Just one camera in the alley, but a little spray-paint on the lens and it's done. Inside, they've got a few, but they're all focused on the shopping area and the cash registers. You know the hallway to the bathrooms and the back office? There are no cameras back there at all. No one's gonna see me."

"What about an alarm?"

He nodded. “Old school. No cellular or Wi-Fi. If triggered, it calls the monitoring company over a landline, so if I cut the phone line beforehand, it can’t call anyone.”

“What about the alarm itself? You just gonna do a smash and grab with a siren blaring?”

“That’s where I’d like your help, bro. There’s one door sensor on the back door. It’s basic and pretty old. I think we can defeat it by sliding a little magnet up to it, you know, to trick the sensor into thinking the door is closed, even once I pry it open?”

“Yeah, dude. I know all about how door sensors work.”

“I know you do. That’s why I need your help. You’re a fucking pro with that shit, and you’ll do it right, so I don’t accidentally trip the alarm.”

“So now I’ve gone from being a lookout to actively helping you bypass an alarm system?”

“I’ll cut you in for thirty percent.”

Sean sighed and laughed at the same time. Jack wasn’t taking the risks seriously enough.

Sean set his beer on the counter, stood, looked Jack in the eyes. “It’s not the right time for any of us to do a job. Any job.”

“C’mon, man.”

“Dude, for fuck sakes. Morelli’s daughter is a cop.”

“So what? She ain’t gonna be there.”

“She’ll certainly be involved in investigating what happened. She’s probably already one of the cops looking into every single thing we’ve done in the last few years.”

“C’mon, bro. You don’t know for sure that *any* cop is looking into our shit.”

“I can almost guarantee they are. I’d bet anything that they’re looking over every recent theft, trying to find links, or patterns, or evidence left behind. If they find the slightest fucking thing that links one of us to a job, they'll come after all three of us, so we can't do any jobs right now."

"You're too paranoid, bro. That's not gonna happen. C'mon. This town barely has a police force. You think they're gonna spend that much time on us? C'mon, I did my homework on this one."

"Dude! It's just too fucking risky. There are just too many things that could go wrong. And Morelli's? C'mon, man. Don't you think the old man is going to have his daughter use all the resources of the police department to figure out who robbed them? Don't you think she'll do anything she can to bring us down? Jesus, man. It'd probably be safer to rob a fucking bank."

"Bro, c'mon. Please. I gotta do this." Jack's words carried a surprising amount of urgency.

"Why? Why is *this* job so goddamned important to you?"

Jack rubbed his neck, gazed at the floor. "It's the perfect time, bro. The safe ain't working, and they've got cash from the entire weekend just sitting there. All of Friday's take, all of Saturday's. All the cash from their two busiest days of the week, and it's just sitting there waiting for me."

"So what? There will be other jobs like it in the future, ones where cops aren't related to the businesses' owner. Just chill the fuck out and wait for shit to calm down."

"I can't wait."

"Why not? What the fuck is going on? Why does it have to be right now?"

Jack didn't speak. He walked to the window, peered down onto Adams Street.

Sean tried again. "What the fuck is going on, man? Why tonight?"

Jack released a slow sigh. "I'm in pretty deep to my guy, and he wants his money, like right now."

"What guy? A dealer? Who is it?"

"This dude TJ."

"Christ, man. That's your problem?" Sean reached into his pocket, pulled out what cash he had—about a hundred and twenty bucks. "How much do you need?"

Jack ran both his hands over his eyes, wiping them. "A lot."

"How much is a lot?"

"Twenty."

"Grand?"

Jack turned toward him, nodded.

"Fuck." Sean sighed sharply. "You've done twenty grand worth of dope?"

"No."

"Then how the fuck do you owe that much?"

"I got into debt with him, bro."

"How? How can you possibly owe that much?"

He sighed, stared out the window. "I got behind on what I owed, so I started slinging for him. It went okay, for a while, but I started dipping into it for my own use, you know? I didn't think it mattered because I was still selling tons, but then, like, I dunno. People stopped buying. I guess there's some others in town slinging fentanyl now, and so like, people aren't that into crank. Anyway, homie wants his cash, and I've gotta get it to him."

"Jesus Christ, man. I can probably pull together about eleven grand, *maybe* twelve, but I don't have anywhere near twenty."

"I figured. That's why I need to do this."

"Why? What happens if you don't pay?"

Jack glared at him. "You know what happens."

"You really think this guy's going to kill you? If he does, then he never gets his money. No, fuck that. Let's put together what we can and give it to him. We'll work something out to pay the rest later."

Jack sat down in the chair, sunk his face into his hands. "TJ's not gonna go for some payment plan bullshit. You know those two dudes they found burned alive? TJ did that shit." He looked at Sean. "I'm fucking scared, bro."

"Then dip out."

"Leave town?"

"Yeah. Why not? Take the cash we've got now and get the fuck out of here."

"I'm not running, bro. I'm not a little bitch." He stood again. "Are you going to help me or not?"

"That's what I'm trying to do, Jack. If you really think this dude will kill you over this, then getting out of town is your best option."

"No, what you're doing is offering a bunch of hypothetical bullshit. Let's just go hit Morelli's, get TJ his cash, and be done with this."

"I seriously doubt there's twenty grand sitting in an unlocked safe at Morelli's."

"So you're not gonna help me?"

"Fuck, dude. What I'm saying is that even if I did help with this, it's not going to solve your problem."

"Whatever." Jack stopped toward the door, flung it open. "Be a dick about it. Just forget about all the shit I helped you with over the years." He stepped out the door but paused on the landing. "Remember when we met at school? You had no friends, and I was there for you. I helped you with your shit. I took care of you. That mean nothin' at all?"

"Look, dude, that meant the fucking world to me. It still does." Sean leaned against the doorframe. "You need some help, man. More than I have to offer. Get out of town and we'll find you a treatment program. We'll figure the TJ shit out after that."

"Don't give me that rehab shit, and don't pretend that you're bailing on this because of what happened to Travis. You've changed, bro. You used to love this kind of shit."

"Fine, dude. It's me. I changed."

"Fuck you, asshole." Jack flipped him off, then stomped down the stairwell.

Sean stared at the ceiling for what felt like hours, unable to sleep. Every time he heard a noise on the street below, he wondered if Jack was in trouble. Every time he heard sirens, he leapt out of bed to look out the window, half expecting to see LGPD squad cars surrounding the Morelli's station a few blocks down the street.

Sean sat up, scooted to the edge of his bed. Jack would surely go through with his stupid plan, and he would manage to fuck it up somehow. Sean should have agreed to help. At the very least, he should have walked through Jack's plan with him. Jack tended to ignore problems, and he wasn't good at planning for the things that could possibly go wrong. Sean could have at least helped identify those potential problems and maybe come up with ways out of them.

Jack wasn't thinking about cameras at nearby businesses, or the possibility that the alarm had a tamper alert that might sound if the system detected the loss of the phone line. And these were just a couple things that could go wrong *tonight*. The coming days were filled with at least a dozen other possible problems he'd likely overlooked. What if someone were able to give a suspect description to cops later? What did Jack plan to do with the checks and bank slips that would certainly be in the deposit bags? If he were to get caught with those, they'd provide proof that he'd done the burglary. Had he considered *any* of that?

Sean grabbed his phone and called Jack. It was just after three in the morning. Maybe he hadn't done the job yet, maybe there was time to stop him.

The call went to voicemail.

He awoke just after six, after managing to doze off to sleep here and there. Glancing out the window, the streets below were calm, empty. No cop cars or flashing lights, though it had started to snow a little.

Sean got dressed, and at the door, he grabbed his coat and car keys. Hurrying down the stairs, he hopped into his car and slid the key into the ignition. The starter whirred, but the engine sat in silence. The problems with the car had worsened with the colder weather. If the fucking thing would just turn over, he'd head to the abandoned house on Seventh. Maybe Jack was still there, and maybe he'd listen to him. This time, instead of attacking the mechanics of Jack's plan and insulting him in the process, he'd appeal to his sense of dignity. Show him that he'd hit the bottom, and that with support from his family and friends, he could get the help he needed. Sean was sure they could pool enough cash to get Jack out of trouble, if they could just have a few days.

Sean turned the key again, but the car only sputtered. He flung the door open and went back into his apartment. Jack's mom often attended the early service at First Presbyterian, so she'd probably be awake. With the overnight snow and cold weather, she also might have allowed Jack to stay at her place last night.

She answered quickly but was reluctant to talk about her son. "He's not allowed to stay here anymore, but he did come by last night."

"What time?"

"Midnight or so. Bastard stole some shit from the shed. Some tools. Probably gonna sell 'em for more drugs, you know?"

Sean knew what the tools were for, and while Jack might sell them later, he planned to use them to help pry his way into Morelli's. "Look, he owes someone quite a bit of money. I'm willing to help him out, but I don't have nearly enough. Is there a chance you could pitch in too?"

"Honey, that's a very sweet thing for you to offer, but you should know by now that there's no helpin' my boy. He'll spend anything you give him on crystal, and that's just the cold truth."

"He seems really scared though. I think he's ready to get help."

"Like I say, honey, I've seen it before. I know you've been friends since forever, so you've seen this before too. I know I've seen it too much, that's for sure. Too much, and too often."

"I'm just afraid he's going to do something really stupid if we don't help him. So, if I can find him, would you agree to help pay off his debt to this guy?"

The line was silent for a moment. "Honey, I just can't. I'm sorry. I think it's sweet you care for him but be careful. He'll bleed you until you're dry, if you let him. Now, I'm sorry, but I gotta get going."

Sean's face warmed. It was unbelievable that his own mother could dismiss him so quickly. No wonder Jack was in such bad shape.

He put his coat back on and headed down the stairs again. The snow had picked up and the streets were empty. Climbing into his car, he gave the engine another chance to cooperate, but it didn't even attempt to start, so he set out on foot towards Morelli's. Maybe the back door would be wide open, indicating Jack managed to get away with the whole thing. Or maybe it'd be untouched, indicating Jack abandoned the stupid idea.

Turning onto Peoria Street, Morelli's entered his view ahead. Someone dressed in black stood on the side of the building, but ducked into the alleyway behind the store before Sean could definitively ID the person as Jack. It had to be him though.

Sean jogged toward the store. When he got to Washington Street, he spotted a black Audi in the parking lot—Michael Morelli's car. The place was closed, but that didn't mean the building was empty.

Sean picked up speed, switched to a full run. Jack would have the door pried open any minute now and he had no way to know that Michael would be standing on the other side of it.

Stepping onto the street, Sean nearly fell when his foot hit a patch of ice. His only hope now was to get there before Michael saw Jack, maybe distract Michael enough to give Jack a chance to flee.

Running past Michael's car, Sean reached for the front door. Through the glass, he spotted Michael standing by the drink refrigerators. He could just make out Jack near the back room, his face covered with a mask. Sean recognized his hoodie though. It was the same one he had on last night.

The two seemed to be talking, but Jack was holding a fucking gun. Sean yanked the door open, rushed inside.

A chime rang out, alerting his presence. Jack jerked, turned toward him and a loud pop echoed throughout the store.

reagan

Reagan spotted her parents in the third pew from the front and she and David joined them. David scooting in first to sit beside Ma, Reagan slid in beside him. Ma smiled at them but sat with her hands folded in her lap, patiently waiting for Father Paul to begin mass. Reagan could sense her mother's annoyance. She and David were late, at least by Ma's standards.

Ma always liked to arrive early. As she saw it, early was on time, and on time was late. Church had always been important to her, but as kids, Reagan and her brothers usually caused the entire family to arrive late—late by anyone's standards.

It wasn't a conscious effort. Though Sean and Donnie never wanted to go to church, and they'd sometimes stall, most weeks the family was delayed because someone had lost a shoe, or their tie, or someone would have to go back in the house to retrieve something precious to them. Still, they always made it to St. Thomas, even if it took longer than Ma was comfortable with. No matter what though, they'd eventually stagger through the big wooden doors, sometimes to judgmental looks by fellow churchgoers who'd gotten there much earlier.

Reagan glanced to her right and caught her father looking at his phone. The Bears played at noon, hours from now, but he was no doubt already planning what he'd grill before kickoff.

Shifting her gaze to the pew in front of them, she smiled at Mary Morelli as she and her girls took a seat, right next to Mary's parents. Reagan squeezed David's hand. He looked uncomfortable. He hadn't grown up going to church and she wasn't oblivious to how overwhelming the formalness of it all could be. She squeezed his hand again, a nonverbal way to thank him for coming with her. He turned his head and smiled at her, a hopeful sign that he was doing okay with everything. She gave him a slight smile, then returned her focus to the front of the sanctuary. The mood in the room had changed though. The ambient volume rose—people mumbled. Those seated in the pews in front of her turned around to look at the back of the sanctuary. Reagan turned to look as well as the volume of the chatter rose again, then the sound of sirens outside cut through the murmuring in the sanctuary.

A few people stood and turned toward the doors just as a woman approached the pew in front of Reagan. She motioned for the Morellis to follow her, and Mary slid out of the pew. The woman leaned close to Mary and said something to her. Though the chatter in the room concealed most of the conversation, Reagan heard the words "shooting" and "across the street." At almost the same time, several in the sanctuary gasped. Mary whispered something to her father, and both of her parents stood and made their way to the aisle. Mary walked quickly toward the doors—almost jogging—and her parents followed.

The whispers and chatter in the sanctuary grew louder, phones chimed and beeped. More people stood from their seats and several headed toward the sound of sirens in the street.

A man in the pew behind Reagan whispered something to her father and the color faded from his face. He stood and stumbled into the aisle. Ma followed.

Reagan nudged David, then grabbed his hand, pulled him toward the end of the pew.

Outside, sirens still blared. From the doorway, Reagan spotted an ambulance pulling up to Morelli's, just across the street from the church.

Reagan hurried to catch up to her father. "What's going on?"

"It's... It's hard to say."

"What did that man say to you?"

"He, uh... Someone thinks that something happened to Sean. That maybe he's been hurt."

"Hurt in what way?"

Dad didn't answer.

She pulled David out the front doors and onto the sidewalk. Across the street, police cars and ambulances surrounded Morelli's as two paramedics exited the store with someone on a stretcher.

Ma gasped. "Is that Seanie?"

Reagan shook her head. "I can't see."

Reagan crossed Peoria Street with David and her parents following closely behind her.

Ma gasped again. "It is Sean."

Dad charged forward.

Ma and Reagan followed.

An officer blocked their path just as they reached the edge of the Morelli's parking lot. "You can't go any further."

Dad didn't stop. "That's my son."

The officer spun on his heels and hurried to catch up to her father, reaching a hand for Dad's shoulder, the officer yanked Dad back. "Sir, this is an active crime scene. You will be arrested if you proceed further."

Reagan peered around the cop toward Sean. His clothes were bloodied, his left leg heavily bandaging. He seemed to be alert and talking to paramedics though.

Dad shouted over the officer's body. "Seanie? Are you all right?"

Sean didn't respond and the paramedics loaded the stretcher into the back of an ambulance.

Dad shouted toward the paramedics. "Is my son okay?"

A woman closed the ambulance doors, then walked toward them. "Are you his parents?"

"Yes." Dad nodded vigorously. "What's going on? Is he okay?"

"We're transporting him to Laytons Grove Community."

"Why? What happened?"

"He suffered a gunshot wound to his left leg, but right now, he's conscious and breathing."

Ma gasped again. "Who shot him?"

The paramedic fidgeted with a glove on her hand and removed it. "I'm sorry. I don't have that information, ma'am."

Ma wiped tears from her eyes. "Is he okay?"

"He'll likely need surgery, but all of that will be determined at the ER. Do you have transportation to get to the hospital?"

Dave stepped forward. "I'll drive them."

The woman nodded. "I'm very sorry. I'd tell you more if I could."

Reagan's gaze shifted to the front doors of the store. Two more paramedics wheeled out another stretcher and Mary Morelli ran toward it, grabbed the hand of the man on it, her brother, Michael.

Reagan sat in the waiting room, nervously twirling her phone in her hands. Donnie sat beside Ma, in the corner of the room beneath a large TV mounted to the wall. Brooke sat across from them, alternating between staring at the TV and staring at her phone. Dad, meanwhile, paced the floor, walking from one end of the room to the other.

David put his arm around her and stroked her hair, an obvious but futile attempt to calm her. She ignored it and stared at the television on the wall. It was tuned to CNN. The anchor provided updates to all kinds of things happening in the world, but the one thing Reagan most wanted an update about wasn't going to come from CNN, and no one from the hospital's staff had told them anything in nearly an hour. Last they'd heard, Sean's vital signs were normal, except for an elevated pulse and blood pressure. The bullet had apparently entered his upper thigh and exited without damaging anything vital, which the doctor assured them was a positive thing. However, the doctor also said he was concerned about the wound's close proximity to Sean's knee joint. More scans were needed though to fully assess the situation. Depending on what they found, orthopedic surgeries could be needed, and no matter what, Sean faced a long recovery, perhaps a year or more before he was back to normal.

Reagan shifted her attention to her phone, spinning it clockwise in her left palm, then transferring it to her right to spin it counterclockwise. It was a nice distraction, one that faded quickly, so she returned her gaze to the TV.

Dad continued to pace in front of her.

The big blue door along the wall swung open and she hopped to her feet.

Dad hurried toward the woman in gray scrubs. "Is he out of surgery?"

The woman nodded. "He's been relocated to a private room. You may see him now, if you'd like."

Everyone gathered their coats and hats and hurried down the hallway to Sean's room.

Reagan stepped through the door first, but someone was already in the room with him. A tall man wearing a button-down shirt and tie with a handgun strapped to his belt.

Dad spoke first. "Excuse me. Can I help you?"

The man turned to Dad and extended his hand toward him. "Hello. I'm Sergeant Flanigan with LGPD's detective bureau."

Dad shook his hand. "Frank McKenna. This is my wife, Kathy, and my family."

Unperturbed by the man's presence, Brooke joined Sean at his bedside, clasping his hand in hers. Reagan followed her and sat down beside her brother. "Are you okay?"

Sean nodded.

Dad stepped closer to the detective. "If you'll excuse us, we'd like to visit with Sean."

The detective nodded. "I understand, Mr. McKenna, but your son was a witness to one crime, and the victim of another. I have some questions for him, and it's best to get his statement when things are fresh in his mind."

"With all due respect, I think he should be resting, not answering questions."

Sean spoke, his voice weaker than usual, raspy. "It's okay. Let's just get it over with."

The detective turned to face Sean. "I'll be as quick as I can." He flipped a page in a notebook. "What time did you arrive at Morelli's Convenience this morning?"

"I don't know."

"Do you have an estimate?"

"Seven-thirty or so, I guess."

"What were you doing there this morning?"

"I needed some cigarettes."

"Are you aware the establishment doesn't open until ten a.m. on Sundays?"

Sean shrugged. "I had no idea. There were cars out front, and the door wasn't locked, so I assumed they were open."

The detective nodded as he wrote in the notebook. "Do you typically buy your cigarettes there?"

"Sometimes."

"Why were you seeking cigarettes at that hour of the morning?"

"I ran out, so I went to buy some more."

"Are you an early riser most days, Mr. McKenna?"

Sean shrugged. "Depends."

"On what?"

"What I have to do that day."

The detective nodded as he wrote in his notebook. "What do you do for a living?"

"Lawn care, snow removal. Lots of different things."

Brooke met the detective's gaze. "I'm trying to get him a job where I work, Fashion Junction."

Sean patted her arm. "I don't work there now though. I just do lawn care."

The detective again wrote in his notebook. "Are you scheduled to work today? If so, you may need to call your boss." The detective pointed toward Sean's leg with his pen.

"I'm off today."

"That's good." The detective nodded. "Do you always get up early on your days off?"

"Sometimes."

"How about today? What had you out of bed early today?"

"I wasn't sleeping well, so I went to get some smokes. Figured maybe I was having nicotine withdrawal or something."

"You told one of my officers that after you walked into the store, you saw a man in a ski mask near the back of the building, is that correct?"

"I'm not sure it was a ski mask. Just, you know, a mask that was covering his face."

"That man then shot you, is that correct?"

"I don't know what happened. I just heard a pop. I didn't even think it was a gunshot. I didn't know what was going on. All of it happened super quick."

"Did you see a gun in the suspect's hand?"

Sean shook his head. "No. I couldn't really see what was going on. I just walked in and then I heard the pop."

"What happened next?"

"I don't know. It was loud, my ears were ringing. My leg felt weird. Kinda burned, then it went numb, and I collapsed. Next thing I knew, a bunch of paramedics were standing over me, cutting my clothes off, asking me a bunch of questions."

"What did the man in the ski mask do after shooting you?"

"I have no idea."

"You didn't see him after he fired the shot?"

"It was all kind of a blur. I honestly didn't see him once I collapsed."

"Did you see the masked man leave the premises?"

Sean shook his head.

The detective consulted his notebook. "Do you think he left out the front, or the back?"

"I have no idea."

Sean wasn't being honest, Reagan knew that, but she couldn't figure out why. He was much smarter than he was pretending to be, and more aware of things around him. Just a few years ago, he'd been riding his skateboard when a car nearly hit him, and as he dodged the car, he tumbled onto the pavement and hit his head. Even though he'd briefly lost consciousness and suffered a concussion, he was still able to give a description of the car, including part of the license plate number. He had to know more about what happened inside Morelli's than he was saying.

The detective flipped through some pages of his notebook. "When did you learn that Mr. Morelli had been injured?"

"Not until you guys got there. I heard a cop say it over the radio."

The detective nodded as he wrote in the notebook. "Mr. McKenna, at any point, did you and the gunman exchange words?"

"Nope. Not at all."

"You don't recall him saying anything to you?"

Sean shook his head.

The detective flipped through more pages of the notebook, reviewing notes on other pages. "He didn't say a thing to you? Not one word?"

"I don't think so. I don't really remember what happened. Seriously, it was all a blur."

Reagan studied his face. He was clearly lying. The only good reason for him to lie was because he knew the person who'd shot him.

She stood and faced the detective. "Are you saying this masked guy is the one who shot my brother?"

The man nodded. "Seems so, ma'am." He turned back toward Sean. "I know you're in some pain, but you're a fortunate man, Mr. McKenna. That gunshot could have killed you. You got lucky. Must be the Irish blood in your veins."

Reagan walked around the bed to face the detective. "The shooter was a man?"

The detective nodded. "Yes, ma'am. Based on witness descriptions: adult male, slender build, about five-foot-eight, possibly in his late twenties or early thirties, dressed in all black."

The description sounded familiar. Very familiar.

She turned to Sean. "Was it Jack?"

Sean shook his head. "What? No. Why would Jack shoot me?"

"Why does he do *anything* that he does?"

"It wasn't him. I'd never seen this guy before."

"Why do you always defend him? He let your best friend go to jail, and now this. When will it be enough that you stop defending him?"

"It wasn't Jack, okay?"

More lies. But why? Why was Jack worth protecting? It didn't make sense. "Just tell the truth, Sean. Jack did this, didn't he?"

David grabbed her arm. "C'mon, sweetie. Let's get some fresh air."

"Don't do that. Don't shush me." Reagan jerked her arm away. "I want the guy who did this to be held accountable for his actions."

"I know, but stress isn't good for you or the baby."

She turned to David. "Would you stop that? It's really annoying."

The detective interrupted, turned around to fully face her. "I'm sorry. I didn't mean to stir things up." He flipped to another page in his notebook. "This Jack... Do you know his last name?"

Reagan nodded emphatically. "Hoffman. Jack Hoffman."

mary

Mary slid the key into the new lock on the back door and stepped inside. Aside from rekeying the door, the locksmith had also repaired the damage to the frame, and he'd even added a steel plate to prevent it from being pried open again in the future. The inside of the store was still a mess though. She'd been at the hospital most of the day—sitting with her parents as they awaited the results of a variety of tests—so cleaning up the store had been a low priority.

So far, the doctors didn't see anything that concerned them too much, but they were keeping Michael overnight for observation. He said he'd confronted the suspect as he walked out of the office and attempted to grab the man, but as Michael reached out, he slipped on the wet floor and fell, hitting his head on the hard linoleum.

Things could have been much worse, and Mary was thankful that her brother was okay, but she also couldn't shake the terrifying idea that this could have happened while Papa was at work. It was scary that it happened at all, but at least Michael was young and in good health. Chances were good he'd recover fully, but if it'd happened to Papa, a fall like that could have killed him.

She didn't need to be at the store, but checking on it provided a good distraction for her mind—a way to keep herself from joining the investigation into who the masked gunman was. As much as she wanted to dig into leads, Flanigan had removed her from the case, insisting that it would be a conflict of interest for her to have *anything* to do with it. There was no conflict though. She wanted the same thing any cop wanted: to see the person who'd committed the crime off the streets and in prison.

Unfortunately, Michael wasn't able to provide many details about the robbery, or the suspect, and she hadn't been in the room when Flanigan interviewed her brother.

Mom made it clear that she wasn't to question Michael about any of it either, or "interrogate him," as she'd put it. So far, Mary had followed orders from Flanigan and her mother, but she also hadn't had an opportunity to talk to Michael alone. If, hypothetically, she was able to question him, one of the first things she'd ask was why he'd been at the store so early on a Sunday morning. It didn't make sense. He wasn't scheduled to work. Amber usually covered Sundays by herself, with a little overlap from a second part-time employee during the post-church rush. Michael didn't need to be there at all, and besides that, he rarely came in on weekends.

Mary stepped into the main aisle and surveyed the damage. A rather large blood stain remained by the front doors where the McKenna kid had been shot. She'd never expected to see something like it at Morelli's, but here it was. Laytons Grove had always been a safe community, but undeniably, things were getting worse, and more violent. The fact that an act of violence had happened within the walls of a place she'd grown up—a second home where she'd often done her homework in the back office as Papa sat at his desk and did the books—made it all the more unsettling. Three generations of the Morelli family had spent most of their waking hours in the little building on the corner of Main Street and Peoria Avenue, and being there had always felt as safe as being inside her home. Seeing the remnants of violence on the floor of that safe space was as surreal as it was disturbing.

While there'd been a huge influx of break-ins across the Illinois Valley in recent years, none had turned violent. Of all the recent burglaries she'd investigated, no one had even been confronted by the thieves, and they certainly hadn't been shot or even threatened with a firearm. And while armed robberies weren't unheard of in the area, the Laytons Grove Police Department hadn't had reports of one within the city's limits in more than two years.

Mary grabbed the mop bucket and rolled it to the front of the store to attempt to remove the blood stains from the floor. After several passes with the mop, she'd succeeded in reducing the discoloration of the linoleum but removing it fully would likely require the help of a professional floor crew. Realistically, the stain would have to be removed before they could reopen. None of the townspeople should have to look at the reminder of what happened.

Mary rolled the bucket down the hall to the supply closet, then stepped into the office. It appeared that Flanigan had moved some things around during his investigation, but the room looked mostly like it did last night at close. It didn't seem like the suspect had spent much time there at all. The safe door sat closed, but it was still unlocked due to the broken keypad. The locksmith said he couldn't work on safes, so she needed to schedule an appointment with someone who specialized in them. One more thing to do before reopening.

The suspect had clearly been inside the safe though. He'd grabbed one bank bag before fleeing the store. It was the bag from Friday, so he got away with about seven hundred in cash. He'd somehow missed Saturday's bag though, which would have gotten him at least double what he left with.

On the desk, the ledger book lay open to December. The book wasn't open last night, that much she remembered. She moved Michael's bag from the office chair to the desk, then sat down to inspect the ledger. Some of the entries seemed fresh, so maybe Michael had come in to work on the books. That made sense.

Mary reclined in the chair, closed her eyes, and took some deep breaths. All day people had been asking how long the store would be closed, but she didn't have an answer for them. Hell, she wasn't even sure she wanted the store to reopen. Maybe Michael had a point. Maybe selling to Prairie Land Oil was the best option at this point. Cash out, let Papa retire.

Exhaling one more long breath, she opened her eyes, stood up, grabbed Michael's bag, and tossed it back into the chair. Sticking out of the top was a ledger book. One identical to the open one on the desk.

She freed the ledger from the bag and opened it, spreading it across the desk above the other one. She assumed it belonged to the music app company that Michael had invested in, but it was laid out just like the store's books, and the top page was labeled with the store's name, just like the one on the desk.

She flipped to December and started comparing the numbers to the ones in the ledger on the desk. They were different. The ones from his bag were higher—quite a bit higher.

Returning to Michael's bag, she searched the pockets. Stuffed in a front pocket, she found a stack of the store's deposit slips—ones that had been filled out by Mary,

James, and Amber. Ones that should have gone to the bank with the nightly deposits but for some reason were in Michael's bag instead.

She grabbed the key from the desk drawer and unlocked the filing cabinet. After a quick search of the files, she pulled the folder containing last week's deposit records. Comparing the numbers from each night's closing paperwork to the deposit slips, the numbers were off by a lot, sometimes by as much as a few hundred bucks.

She stared at the glaring evidence in front of her. He'd been skimming and then cooking the books to cover it. But why? And how long had he been doing it?

sean

The doctors finally allowed him to leave the hospital, but he had to use crutches and was under strict orders to not put any weight on his left leg for the foreseeable future. The nurse who'd given him the instructions seemed to think it was an easy thing to abide by, but she didn't seem to consider that going home required that he climb a steep flight of stairs to his second-story apartment. Before Sean had a chance to fully contemplate the ramifications, Ma stepped in and decided that he would stay at the family house for now.

It didn't seem like a particularly helpful solution though since his old room was located at the top of an even steeper flight of stairs, but Ma had an answer for that too: she'd simply rearrange the furniture in the living room, and then he could sleep on the couch.

Dad helped him through the front door, and before he had a moment to decide which room to go to, Ma directed him toward the sofa, insisting that he lie down.

"Stretch out there and rest. Your father and Donovan will rearrange things." Ma turned to Dad. "You don't mind, do you?"

He shook his head while a smirk crept onto his face, seemingly aware that he didn't have much more of a say in the matter than Sean did.

None of this was going to work as a long-term solution. Sean needed to put an end to it. "Am I just supposed to sleep here for the next several months? Where is everyone else going to sit, or watch TV?"

Ma fluffed a pillow and placed it behind him. "Let's not think too far ahead. One day at a time."

Reagan came down the stairs, laughed. "Look at mommy's little boy." Her voice was singsongy and filled with mockery. "You all good and comfy, mama's boy?"

Sean rolled his eyes. "Why are you here? You don't live here, remember?"

She shrugged. "I have a bedroom here."

"It's a guest room these days."

"I'll always have a room here, won't I Ma?" She kissed Ma on the cheek.

"Of course you will, dear. All my children will. You know that."

Sean rolled his eyes again, then returned his gaze to Reagan. "Anyway... You guys hitting the road soon?"

She shook her head. "Nope. Just the opposite. We'll be staying in town for a few more days."

"Why?"

She sat on the couch, nestled beside him. "To make sure my beloved little brother has everything he needs." She leaned over, kissed him on the cheek.

"Get off me." He pushed her away. "So, what's the plan? You're sticking around just to annoy the crap out of me?"

She nodded emphatically. "Pretty much."

"Thanks, sis."

"I know you'd do the same for me." She stood. "Now, Ma and I are going to get a start on dinner. Maybe whip up something you hate."

"That's easy. I'll hate any of the tofu shit you cook."

She shot him a fake smile, then headed toward the kitchen.

Dad sat down in his favorite chair, his ass toward the edge of the cushion, not fully set. "Can I get ya anything?"

"The remote, I guess."

He grabbed the remote from the table and handed it to Sean. "I'm glad you're okay."

"Me too. I'm already looking forward to ditching the crutches though."

Dad reached behind his back and produced an envelope from his pocket, tossed it onto Sean's stomach. "I think this is yours."

Sean peeled back the flap and peeked inside at the cash he'd given Ma. Seemed like all of it was there. "It was meant to help you and Ma."

Dad nodded, settled into the chair fully. "I appreciate the gesture, but we'll be okay."

"It's legit money, Dad. It's from the lawn company."

"Maybe it is, but that's not really even the issue. You don't have to take care of us. That's my job, and I'm working on it. Things are going to be fine."

"What about the layoffs?"

Dad's eyes widened, obviously surprised Sean knew as much as he did.

He thought about the question briefly, then shook his head. "I won't have to worry much longer about what happens at Midland. I'm getting out before they have a chance to cut me."

"Seriously? Getting out how?"

"Your old man's got himself a fancy new job." He chuckled. "Millennium Manufacturing, down on Jefferson. I start in two weeks. Full benefits, union shop. The whole works."

"Holy shit! For real?"

"For real." He nodded. "I was going to make a big announcement after church, but then you went and stole my thunder."

Sean snort-laughed. "Sorry about that. If I'd known about your big news, I'd have scheduled my shooting for another day."

Dad smiled awkwardly, as though he wasn't ready to joke about it just yet. "Well, at any rate, I do appreciate you wanting to help the family out, but we don't need it. We're going to be just fine."

"Is it that you really don't need it, or that you're just really bad at taking help from anyone?"

He nodded like he accepted the criticism. "In this case, both I guess." He pointed to the envelope. "That money, and where it came from... Look, Seanie, I don't care. Not really. Sure, there are moral issues there, but I'll leave them to you and whatever god you pray to. And sure, I'm not about to brag to my friends about what you do for a living, but I guess, ultimately, all I care about is that you're alive and well. That became very apparent to me today."

"And I am alive and well, Dad."

"Sure, this time it turned out okay, thanks to God, or luck, or whatever. For years you've skirted by on those things, but that streak almost ended at Morelli's. I don't know what happened, or why you were there, and this isn't me asking. All I'm saying is that you nearly died, and no matter what, the things you do, they all lead to jail or death, Seanie. I don't want either of those for you. And look, I get it. I know I'm to blame. You grew up here feeling like your mom and me were the enemy—that we treated you like you were stupid or something, and I'm sorry for that. You're not stupid, and you've got some gifts.

So please take your gifts and do something safer." He stood. "That's it. That's my dad speech."

Sean nodded, unsure what to say. "Okay. I hear you. But what happened at Morelli's... I wasn't there for the reasons I think you're imagining."

"No?" Dad rubbed the scruff on his face. "So, what? You really were there just to buy cigarettes?"

Sean nodded.

"What on earth made you go for cigarettes at that hour of the morning?"

Sean shrugged. "I don't know. I was awake, I was out of cigarettes, so I just figured I'd go get some."

"I really wish you'd stop smoking. That'll kill you too."

"I've tried to quit."

Dad nodded. "It's hard, believe me, I know."

"How'd you quit?"

"Patches and gum." He chuckled. "And your mother making me smoke outside in the winter." He sat down on the edge of the coffee table, faced Sean. "I can't tell you how glad I am to have you here. I don't just mean in this house, although I'm happy for that too. You scared me."

"Sorry. I had no idca anything like that would happen."

"Be more careful from now on, yeah?"

Sean nodded. "Yeah, okay."

It took forever for everyone else in the house to go to bed, but once he was sure he was alone, Sean grabbed his phone and pulled up Jack's number from the contacts list. He hadn't responded to any texts all day and Sean didn't know if he still had his phone with him, or if it'd been switched off, or if the service had been canceled. He didn't even know if Jack was still in the area. Hopefully he'd gotten out of town by now.

He dialed Jack's number, but it didn't ring at all, went instantly to voicemail. At least it confirmed that Jack still had cell service. Maybe the battery had died.

If Jack hadn't left town, he was most likely laying low at the vacant house on Seventh. Under normal circumstances, Sean would just hop in his car, drive over there, talk to him in person. Even if these were normal circumstances though, he wasn't sure what he wanted to say to Jack. He simply wanted to know that he was okay.

He hoped he was wrong about things, hoped that Jack wasn't at the house. Hopefully he'd gotten out of town. Aside from TJ, every cop in the Illinois Valley was probably searching for him, maybe even every cop in the state. What happened at Morelli's was fucked up, but Jack didn't deserve to be locked up for years because of it. He needed help. The kind he'd never get in prison.

Why the hell did he have a gun though? And where did he even get it? At the hospital, a cop said Jack would be charged with a more serious felony because he'd used a gun while committing a crime, and another felony because the gun was fired during a robbery. It wasn't intentional, Sean knew it wasn't. Jack probably just got spooked. He couldn't have known who was coming through the front door and when the door flew open, it probably scared him. If he'd known it was Sean, he never would have pulled the trigger.

It was stupid to rush into the store like that in the first place. He should have done something to get Jack's attention first, done something to distract Michael Morelli so Jack could run out the back door. But things went to hell long before he even got to the store. If Sean would have just done a better job of talking Jack out of the whole thing—of finding a way to help him pay TJ back—none of it would have happened.

A tap at the living room window shattered Sean's reverie. Brooke was supposed to bring him some edibles once she got off work—something to help him sleep a little better.

He pulled back the curtain to find Jack standing on the front porch.

Sean slid off the sofa and hobbled toward the front door, carefully maneuvered onto the porch. "What the fuck are you doing here?"

"Bro, I'm so sorry." Jack stared at Sean's leg. "Shit, dude. I'm so fucking sorry. How bad is it?"

"I'll be okay."

"Can you walk?"

Sean leaned against a crutch, shrugged. "With crutches."

"Shit, bro." Jack paced back and forth. "I didn't mean for any of this to happen."

"Why the hell did you have a gun, dude?"

"I dunno, bro. I went to my mom's to get some tools, and I found it in the shed." He reached into the pocket of his jacket and produced it. A small, chrome pistol. "I thought it would be good protection."

"Jesus Christ." Sean looked back at the front door. "Put that away."

Jack shoved it back in his pocket, out of sight.

Sean limped, shifted some of his weight so he could lean against the wall of the house. "Why do you still have that thing?"

"For protection, bro." He paced some more. "TJ's lookin' for me."

"Are you really going to shoot him if he finds you?"

"I dunno, bro. I'll do what I have to do, you know?"

"You need to ditch the gun, man. It ties you to the robbery. They find that gun and they've got proof you did the Morelli's job."

"Shit, bro. I never meant to use it. I don't know what happened. I didn't shoot at you on purpose. You know that, right?"

Sean nodded. "I know."

"Everything's just outta control right now. The cops were already searchin' my mom's place and shit. They know it's me, bro. I don't know how they know, but they do. You didn't say nothin', did ya?"

"I didn't say shit."

"Cool. Yeah, I didn't think you would. Fuck, bro. I don't know how they know, but they do." Again he paced. "I'm so fucked. I'm getting outta here. Like, tonight. I just wanted to tell you in person, you know? Let you know I didn't mean to do that shit to you."

"Where you gonna go?"

"Back to Saint Louis, at least for now. Some friends there will let me crash with them."

"What about TJ? Are you even close to having what you owe him?"

Jack shook his head. "Not at all." He stopped pacing and faced Sean. "Look, bro. Do you know anyone who can get me a little something? Just a little bump."

"Meth?"

"A teener, or maybe an eight-ball. Anything, bro. Just enough to get me on the road and all."

"Dude, don't even fuck around with that shit right now. If you're leaving town, just leave. Too many people are looking for you. You shouldn't even be here."

"I know, I know, but like, I just need a little something. Just to hold me until I get back to Missouri. Till I get settled there."

"Dude, you've gotta go. Just get out of town."

"Shit." He paced. "I know. You're probably right. Okay, bro." Jack extended his hand.

Sean shook his hand, but Jack pulled him in for a hug, nearly pulling him off his crutches.

Jack slapped his back. “Okay, bro. I’ll, uh, see ya around, I guess.”

“Yeah, dude. Take care.”

reagan

She and David's bags were packed so they could head back to Chicago tonight after dinner. However, Ma wasn't ready to let go yet and insisted that they stay one more night so the entire family could watch a movie together. She'd already talked Donnie into it, and Sean was in no position to go anywhere else, so all the pressure rested on Reagan's shoulders now. Either she shattered her mother's heart, or they called their bosses, gave some lame excuse about not being able to work tomorrow, and stayed in Laytons Grove one more night.

Ma was obviously stalling—trying to extend the time her whole family was together under one roof, trying to hang onto the moment, to relive how things were before everyone moved out. Reagan couldn't fight that. Aside from the fact that leaving tonight would crush a wonderful woman who'd done so much for her family, Reagan wasn't in a particular hurry to leave anyway. Now, maybe more than ever, being near family seemed important.

Reagan plopped her bag down beside the bed and turned to her fiancé. "You really don't mind staying one more day?"

"Not at all." He wrapped his arms around her and kissed her. "But if you want to leave, you can use me as an excuse. Say that my boss is being a hard-ass and requiring me to be in tomorrow."

She shook her head. "No. I want to be here."

"Then I'm happy to stay."

She took his hand and walked toward the stairs. In the living room below, Dad and Donnie sat in front of the TV flipping through a long list of possible movie options available to them on several streaming services.

Dad stopped when he spotted her at the base of the staircase. "You two staying?"

"We are." She smiled. "Did you find us something to watch?"

Dad shook his head. "Nope. It's not as easy as it sounds." He chuckled. "I'm afraid we've had a number of stipulations placed on this selection."

"Like what?" Reagan sat down on the chair and curled her legs beneath her.

Dad handed the remote to Donnie as he turned to face her. "Well, the movie has to be something that everyone will like. So, that means not too much violence, but also not too much cutesy romance. Not too much swearing, but also not some sort of chick flick."

Ma shouted from the kitchen where she'd been popping popcorn and gathering snacks. "And it needs to have a happy ending."

Dad turned his palms upward as he shrugged. "You see? It's quite a difficult task."

Ma joined everyone in the living room to announce there weren't as many junk food options in the cupboards as she'd promised. Seeing it as a good opportunity to get away from all the family madness for a little bit, Reagan volunteered herself and David to go to Sullivans Market to gather more goodies.

She stood and pulled her phone out to make a shopping list. “Okay, for movie night, we’re obviously going to need Milk Duds. What else?”

Sean was the first to speak. “I need a Snickers.”

Dad smacked his palms together. “Yeah. Double that, please.”

“Got it. Donnie?”

“I want something fruity. Like gummy worms, or some Sour Patch Kids.”

“We can do that.”

David sidled up beside her. “M&Ms, please. Peanut.”

“Got it.” She typed his request into her phone. “Ma?”

“Oh, whatever, dear. I don’t really need anything.”

“Sure you do. Strawberry Twizzlers? That’s your favorite, right?”

She smiled. “It is.” She sat down on a chair and watched the TV as Donnie scrolled through pages of movie options. “So, have you guys decided what we should watch?”

Dad shook his head. “We can’t even agree on a genre.”

Ma nodded an understanding nod, then pointed toward the TV. “I’ve heard good things about that *La La Land*.”

Sean made an audible grunt. “A musical? No, thanks.”

Ma didn’t protest. “How about *Oppenheimer*? It won lots of awards.”

Donnie scoffed. “It’s like ten hours long though, and way too much like sitting through a history lecture. How about *Joker*? The first one. I still haven’t seen it and Sean said it’s awesome.”

Sean nodded emphatically. “It’s freakin’ incredible.”

Dad liked the idea, David said he’d watch it, but Ma wasn’t convinced it was something she’d enjoy in the least.

She shook her head in protest. "I don't think I care much for comic books and superhero stuff. Plus, it sounds very dark, and probably violent."

Sean jumped in to defend the movie. "There's honestly not a ton of violence, and it's not really heavy on the comic book aspect. It's mostly a commentary on the lack of mental health care in the country."

Ma looked at Reagan. "What do you think?"

"I haven't seen it, but I have heard that it's really good."

Dad nodded in agreement. "A guy at work loves all that Marvel stuff and said it's a good flick."

Sean rolled his eyes. "Joker is from the DC Universe, not Marvel."

Dad chuckled. "My apologies for mixing up the various categories of geek things."

Donnie interrupted. "So, we doing *Joker*?"

Ma nodded. "I guess I'm willing to give it a shot."

"Cool." Donnie grabbed the remote and began typing the title into the search bar. "Well, crap. It's not on any of the streaming services we have."

Reagan's shoulders slumped. It'd been a miracle that everyone agreed on a movie, and now they'd have to restart the search for something else. "Can we rent it from one of the services?"

Sean interrupted. "Screw that. I've got it on Blu-ray."

Reagan turned to face him. "Do you have it with you?"

"No. It's at my place."

Donnie laughed. "You're like the only person in the world that still buys movies on discs."

"Well, everyone else is stupid for not buying discs."

Donnie rolled his eyes. "Why would anyone clutter their homes with antiquated things like that?"

"Because owning a real copy is better than relying on streaming services, and because no one can censor it later, and because you can watch it whenever you want without hoping to find it online."

Sean reached for his crutches.

Ma's eyes narrowed as she watched him stand. "Just what do you think you're doing?"

"I'm going to go get the movie, if someone will drive me."

Ma shook her head. "You're not going anywhere, especially up any stairs."

Reagan had seen enough and decided to offer a solution. "How about David and I go to Sullivans to get the snacks, and while we're out, we'll stop by Sean's and grab the disc, how's that sound?"

Sean sighed as he repositioned on the couch. "Fine. Keys are in the front pocket of my coat."

Reagan consulted the notes on her phone. "Okay, Snickers, Sour Patch Kids, peanut M&Ms, Milk Duds, Twizzlers. Anything else?"

Donnie turned to look at her. "Peanut butter cups."

Sean added on too. "How about some potato chips? Barbecue."

"And peanut butter cups, and barbecue chips." Reagan added them to the list.

David retrieved the keys from Sean's coat. "Where in your apartment would I find the disc?"

"It might be in the player. I watched it recently. Otherwise, there's a stack of movies on the edge of the TV stand. Should be in there." Sean shifted his gaze to Reagan. "Don't mess with any of my shit."

"I won't." She chuckled. "I am, however, going to lick one thing, and you'll never know what it was."

David set out down Monroe toward Rockford Avenue as Reagan watched the city pass by through the window. For weeks, she'd been trying to find a good way to bring up the subject but hadn't yet.

Now seemed as good a time as ever, so she turned to him. "What do you think of this town?"

"I like it a lot. You know that."

She smiled. "Sorry my family is so nuts."

"I love your family." He chuckled. "More than my own, frankly."

"Can you see yourself living here, someday?"

"In Laytons Grove?"

"Yeah."

"Sure." He nodded in agreement with the idea. "I could see that. And I could see liking it. Why do you ask?"

"Well, we'll be parents soon, and I don't know... I guess I'd just like our kids to grow up here and have the things that I had growing up, like family, and a big yard, and streets safe enough to ride bikes on all summer long."

He reached across the center console and grabbed her hand. "Sounds perfect, babe."

"Yeah? Are you serious?"

He squeezed her hand. "It makes sense. There's nothing keeping us in Oak Park, not really. I mean, I like it there, but aside from our jobs, we have no real connection to the place. And raising children in a small town like this makes a lot of sense."

"Are you sure? I mean, obviously I agree with all of that, but would you be bored here?"

"I think I'd love it here."

"Can we make it work though?"

"I don't see why not. Sure, we'd have to find new jobs, and pack and move again, but it's nothing we can't handle. If this is what you want, it's what I want."

"Thank you." She smiled. "Plus, you know, having grandparents, who are willing to babysit anytime, just a few blocks away, can't be a bad deal."

He chuckled. "I guess there's a practical side to it too." David glanced at her briefly. "Mind if I ask what brought all this on?"

"It's been building for a while, and I guess this week really reminded me about the importance of family. Ma has always told us it's the most important thing. 'Family first,' she's always said. For a long time, those were just words, but this week... Well, this week has been a reminder of how small our family really is, and of how quickly things can change. I want our son or daughter to be around family. To know them. To have their love."

"I want that too." David pulled into the parking lot behind Sean's place, put the car in park, and leaned over to kiss her. "I love you. If you're serious about wanting to move here, then I'm all in."

"I am. *Someday*. When the timing is right."

"Why put it off? If this is what you want, for you and our child, why not just do it now?"

"What about work? And what about our apartment? We basically just signed the lease."

"Leases are easy to break, and we'll figure out the work situation. You should be home with the baby anyway, and worst-case scenario, I commute to Chicago for a while. Just until I find something around here."

"You'd do that?"

"Forever? No." He chuckled. "For a few months, maybe even a year? You bet I would."

"Not just the commuting. You'd change jobs just to live here? You love your job."

"I do, but life is about a lot more than having a job you like. I'd much rather my wife be happy, and our child be safe and around people who love him or her."

She kissed him. "I really didn't know if you'd be okay with the idea."

"I love it here. I love your family. And if I'm honest, I don't know that I want to raise children in a massive city. I know lots of people grow up in big cities, but this just seems... I don't know. Better? I guess. Safer? Whatever it is, it feels like the right thing for our family."

She kissed him again. Feeling overwhelmed with emotions, she shifted topics to avoid the waterworks developing behind her eyes. "Okay. Tell you what: I'll go up to Sean's apartment and get the movie while you head over to Sullivans and get the snacks. Deal?"

"You sure? I can just go grab the movie while you wait here."

"Have you ever seen Sean's apartment?"

He contemplated the question. "I guess I haven't, no."

"It's going to be a disaster up there. Trust me. And even though he says the movie is somewhere near the TV, I *promise* you it'll take me ten minutes of hunting—and cleaning—till I find it. I may even have to fight a rat over it."

He chuckled. "It's that bad, huh?"

She nodded aggressively. "I'll text you the list. Go get us some snacks, then come back for me before I'm eaten alive by movie-hoarding rats."

Reagan flipped the light switch on and one dim bulb in the dining area flickered on, shedding a small amount of light on what looked like the aftermath of a tornado. Clothes cluttered the floor and seating areas. With shirts and sweatshirts draped over almost every piece of furniture, it was impossible to discern which ones were dirty and which were clean, if any of them were actually clean.

Fighting the urge to tidy up, she headed toward his TV and opened the Blu-ray player. The disc was not in the tray, and given her brother's total lack of organizational skills, finding the movie was going to be a challenge.

She moved the first layer of debris from the top of the TV stand but that only uncovered more clutter. She bent down to look in the storage slots below the TV but found only video game controllers and a couple remote controls.

A noise from across the room startled her. She turned to see someone coming out of the bathroom. "Well, fuck. I knew you guys would find me."

She gasped. "Jesus, Jack! You scared me."

"Why? I should be the one afraid of *you*."

"Why is that?"

He shouted angrily. "Don't give me that shit! I know you're working with them."

"Working with who?"

"CIA. DEA. With the goddamned FBI." His voice rose at a sharp level. "Yeah. It's the FBI, isn't it? You guys have been on me for days."

"I—I don't know what you mean, Jack. It's me, Reagan. Sean's sister."

"Oh, I know who you are." He threw something against the wall. It shattered and the debris scattered across the cluttered apartment. "Don't play dumb with me."

"Jack, I—I'm not—"

"Shut up!" He rushed toward her, stopping inches from her face. "How'd you find me here? Who told you I was here?"

"No one. I—I'm just here to get a movie."

"You lying bitch!" His hand rose quickly.

Grasping her throat, he pinned her against the wall.

mary

She rang Michael's doorbell and waited on the porch, examining the landscaping between the lawn and the house's foundation. He'd removed some bushes since the last time she'd visited and added some rubber mulch and a stone border.

The door opened. Michael spoke through the screen door. "It's about time you came to visit me."

Mary faked a smile, pretending to be amused instead of angry. "Sorry. I know I'm here kind of late, especially when you're trying to rest up."

"It's not late at all."

"Can I come in?"

"Of course." He pushed the screen door open and held it for her as she stepped into his living room. "If I'd known you were coming by, I'd have made some coffee or something."

"I don't need anything." Mary glanced at the pill bottles on his coffee table. "How are you feeling?"

"Just fine." He chuckled. "Luckily it was just my head that I hit, huh?"

She faked a laugh and sat down on his sofa.

Michael walked toward the kitchen. "Sure I can't get you something? Pop, water? I've got some wine too."

Mary shook her head. "No, thank you. I won't stay long."

The numbers didn't lie. For months, Michael had been skimming profits and covering up his crimes by keeping two sets of books. The deeper she dug, the bigger the scope of the problem became. Last month, Morelli's missed a payment to one of its top vendors, and as she reconciled the actual receipts, it became clear they were going to have trouble meeting obligations this month as well.

He returned to the living room with a glass of water in his hand. "So? What's up?"

She released a deep breath. "I found the ledger book."

He broke eye contact with her but didn't say anything. His body language confirmed all of her suspicions though.

Mary scooted to the edge of the sofa cushion. "I've gone through the numbers, Mikie. You've been stealing from the store. From your own family."

He exhaled sharply. "Look..." He drew in another large breath and released it slowly. "It's not like that."

"So what then? I've got it all wrong? You haven't been keeping two sets of books, doctoring deposit slips, and taking money from each night's deposit bags?"

"I'm not stealing anything. I..." He sat down in a chair across from her and exhaled slowly again. "I'm just bridging some other investments. It's a loan, is what it is, basically." He wiped his eyes with the edge of his palm. "It's a bridge loan."

"A loan? One that you never asked Papa for. One that none of us knew about."

"I'm a part owner."

"So what? What does that have to do with anything?"

"I didn't think I needed permission to borrow money from a company I own."

"You *just* said it yourself, Mikie. You're a *part* owner of the store. I'm also a part owner, and Papa's is the majority owner, so yes, you needed permission. Besides, don't you think the other owners have a right to know what's going on with the store's finances?"

"I just— I dunno. I needed a temporary loan to get me through some stuff."

"Okay, fine. Then go to a bank. Ask your family. Hell, pawn your belongings. What you did... Jesus, Mikie. What you did goes way beyond taking out a loan. You took money that didn't belong to you. Money that belonged to your family, and even worse, you tried to conceal what you were doing."

"It was supposed to be quick." He stared at the floor. "Look, I'll be honest: Courante Systems—that company I invested in—well, it's had some setbacks. I was just trying to buy some time to get around those bumps in the road, so I borrowed some cash from the store to bridge that gap."

"Without permission. That's the problem here. None of us knew you were 'borrowing' from the store, and you did all this without any thought about what would happen to the store. We can't pay our bills now. You know that, right? Three vendors are going to stop making deliveries within the next couple weeks. We can barely afford to pay Amber or James for the hours they've already worked, let alone schedule them for any more shifts. We're effectively going to have to lay them off."

"I— I'm sorry. I thought things would turn around quicker. Courante was kicking ass. We were just about ready to launch the new app, but then we got hit with a cease and desist order from some California company. They're claiming we're infringing on their technology, but we're not. I know we're not. It's just a stall tactic by them because they know that our app will cut into their market share."

"Do you hear yourself, Mikie? You care more about some app than you do your own family. More than you care about the employees who've worked hard for us for years, at least in Amber's case. She depends on that income to help feed her kid."

"I don't care more about the app than I do any of that stuff, it's just... I know the app will be huge, at least once we're allowed to launch it. That delay is a big setback, so we just needed some quick funding to get us over that obstacle. I thought the loan from the store would cover it until we cleared things up. Once we launched, and once the revenue started coming in, I was going to pay every cent back. I promise you, that was my plan."

"Mikie, the way you went about things... Aside from having no regard for your family, or the future of the family business, or our employees... Aside from all of that, what you did is massively illegal. And that aside, even if things had gone as you planned, you were still stealing from your family. But things didn't go as planned, and now we're screwed. Do you know how much you've screwed us? If we'd gotten a tax audit, or if we'd tried to get a bank loan to expand the business like you wanted, we'd be totally fucked. And that's another thing. All your talk of expanding, how did you think any of that was going to work? How are we going to open a second location with no cash on hand and falsified books?"

He stood and paced the room. "I told you, I really thought things would turn around with Courante. Not only was I going to pay everything back, but I was going to personally fund the new Utica location."

"Why? So you could steal twice as much money?"

"Oh, come off it already. A few years ago, when Emma needed braces, you borrowed from the store to pay for them."

"Yeah, Mikie. I went to our parents for financial help, and Papa suggested loaning me money from one of the store's accounts. Papa—*the owner*—made the offer and he knew all about it. See the difference there? The owner knew he was loaning the money."

"And I *am* an owner of Morelli's. One who made a similar loan, but to myself."

"Jesus, do you really not see the difference? None of the other owners knew what you were doing, and you cooked the books to make sure we didn't. That's the difference, and it's a pretty fucking huge one, don't you think?"

"Whatever."

She stood. "That's your response? Are you six years old?"

"Look, it's not the big deal you're making it out to be. I can pay most of it back right now. Okay? I talked to my partners at Courante and they're willing to buy my shares."

"Aren't your shares worthless at this point?"

"No, they're not worthless. They're *worth less,* two words. But Courante still has plans for other software to launch, even if we're not able to launch the main app right now. Anyway, my point is that they've agreed to buy me out, and I'll put the money straight into Morelli's."

"I hope you do, Mikie, because if you don't, I think this is the end of Morelli's Convenience. Three generations and it all ends right here with us. That would crush Papa."

He sighed as he sat back down on the chair. "Do they know?"

"Papa and Mom?"

"Yeah."

"I haven't said anything. I wanted to talk to you first."

"Good. They don't need to know."

"Mikie... They have to know."

"Why? I said I'd fix it. This has nothing to do with them."

"I disagree. I think they should know, and I think they should hear it from you."

"What purpose does that serve? As long as I get the problem fixed, they don't need to know there ever was a problem."

"Jesus, Mikie, I'm not going to argue about this. Get your shares sold and repay the store. We'll go from there." She stepped toward the door. "Fix it, Mikie. Soon."

"I will. Next week. I should have the cash by the end of next week."

"I hope that's true."

"It is. I promise. I'm sorry. I really am. I hope you know how sorry I am."

She reached for the doorknob. "Just return the money."

Mary stepped onto the porch and glared at the new landscaping, wondering if the family had unwillingly funded that project too. The digressive thought was interrupted by her phone ringing. On the other end, Officer Duffy explained that LGPD had just been dispatched to a home on Monroe Street about an assault that occurred at a nearby apartment.

"Okay." Her tone was blunt, but she had too much family drama to deal with and didn't see why he'd called her. "This linked to one of my cases?"

Duffy cleared his throat. "Uh, maybe. Thing is, the apartment belongs to the guy who was shot at your family's store. I thought you'd be interested in that part."

"Who was the victim of the assault?"

Papers ruffled as Duffy looked for the info. "Reagan McKenna."

Though the assault occurred at Sean McKenna's downtown apartment, Reagan called LGPD dispatch from her family's home on Monroe Street several blocks northwest of the crime scene. Mary hadn't asked Officer Duffy for too many details. It was always best to hear them straight from a witness' mouth, and she knew Reagan well. They'd worked on a few community projects together over the years, so she hoped to use that connection to get Reagan to open up and be forthcoming with her. Mary didn't know Reagan's brother nearly as well, but it seemed beyond coincidental that Reagan had been assaulted in his apartment just days after he'd been shot during a robbery.

Mary pulled up to the curb in front of the McKenna's house and parked behind one of the LGPD cruisers already on scene.

Kathy McKenna, the family matriarch, answered the door and directed Mary to the living room where Reagan sat on a chair with other members of her family gathered around her. A young man about her age, presumably her partner, sat on the arm of the chair next to her.

"Hi, Reagan." Mary knelt in front of her. "Are you okay?"

She nodded. "I'm good. Just a little shaken up."

"Did he harm you?"

She shook her head. "I'm okay."

The young man spoke. "I still want to take her to the hospital. I want to know that the baby's okay too."

Mary returned her attention to Reagan. "You're pregnant?"

Reagan nodded as she placed her hands over her belly. "We're both fine. Mostly, he just scared me."

"Is this your husband?" Mary motioned toward the young man.

"I'm David. David Moran." He extended his hand to her. "We're engaged."

Mary shook his hand. "Congratulations, on the engagement, and on the baby." She returned her gaze to Reagan. "Did the man you encountered lay hands on you?"

She nodded.

David interjected. "More than that. She was on the floor when I walked in and the guy was standing over her, choking her."

"You witnessed the assault, Mr. Moran?"

Reagan interrupted. "He stopped it."

Mary turned to David. "It's a good thing you were there."

"I wish I'd gotten there sooner. Hell, I should never have let her go in there alone in the first place."

Mary shifted her focus back to Reagan. "I know it was probably a scary situation, and I hate to make you relive that trauma, but could you walk me through what happened tonight?"

"I already told him everything." She pointed at Officer Duffy.

"I know, and I'm sorry, but us cops, well, sometimes we're redundant. I just want to make sure I know exactly what happened tonight. The apartment you were at, it belongs to your brother?"

Sean spoke from a chair in the corner. "Yeah. It's my place."

Mary stood and walked to him. "Good to see you again, Sean. How's the leg?"

"Healing."

"I'm glad to hear that. My brother is healing too."

Sean didn't bite at the bait, but it didn't matter. Now wasn't the time to dig into Sean's role in what happened at the store, so Mary returned to Reagan's side. "Ms. McKenna, you went to your brother's apartment alone this evening, is that correct?"

"Yeah. We were all going to watch a movie, and David dropped me off at Sean's so I could go grab the DVD."

"What happened then?"

"I dunno, really. I was kind of cleaning the place up, and digging through stuff looking for the movie, and I guess he was hiding in the bathroom."

"Jack Hoffman? Is that the 'he' you're referring to?"

She nodded.

"And Mr. Hoffman attacked you?"

Again she nodded.

"Did you recognize him at the time?"

"Yeah. I knew it was him."

"Is Jack Hoffman the same man you told Detective Flanigan about the other day?"

"Yeah." She glanced over to her brother. "He's the same guy."

"Okay, so Mr. Hoffman was hiding in the bathroom. What happened next?"

"He just started shouting at me. He was pretty wound up. He kept saying I was an FBI agent or something like that. He kept saying nonsense about how he knew I'd find him and that he wasn't going to let me arrest him. I'm pretty sure he was high on something."

Officer Duffy spoke from behind her. "We found methamphetamine paraphernalia in the bathroom. It looks like he'd been camped out there for a while."

Mary returned her attention to Reagan. "That sounds like pretty typical behavior for meth users. They can get pretty paranoid, and oftentimes, they start imagining things." She crouched in front of Reagan. "What happened next?"

"He mostly just screamed at me, and he wouldn't let me leave. I didn't know what to say or do. He just kept yelling at me, then he charged at me. I don't really know what happened, but we ended up on the ground. Thankfully, David came in and stopped him."

David patted Reagan's shoulder. She reached up and squeezed his hand before wiping tears from her cheek.

Mary patted her knee. "Ms. McKenna, I wish I didn't have to make you relive what happened to you this evening, but if you don't mind, it would really help me if you could be more specific. What happened once you were on the ground with Mr. Hoffman?"

"He kind of tackled me, and he was on top of me, pinning me down. He had me by my throat. But not long after that, David came in and they fought."

"Were you in fear of your life?"

She nodded, then wiped another tear.

Mary turned toward David. "Mr. Moran, can you tell me what happened once you entered the apartment?"

"I don't know. It was all kind of a blur. I'd gone to Sullivans to get some snacks, and when I came back to pick Reagan up... Well, I actually sat in the parking lot for a minute or two kinda waiting for her to come out, but when she didn't respond to my texts, I went upstairs. I should have just gone up there as soon as I got there."

"Sounds like you still arrived at just the right time. Can you tell me what happened once you entered the apartment?"

"I knocked on the door, but then I heard him shouting inside and I thought I heard Reagan say something, so I just kinda burst in, you know? Then I saw her on the floor with that asshole on top of her, and I just kind of snapped."

"Snapped how?"

"I charged him and kinda tackled him to get him off her. Then... I don't really remember what all happened. We traded some punches and eventually he just stood up and ran away."

"I'm very sorry both of you had to experience this. We're going to do everything we can to ensure the man who did this is punished." Mary walked toward Sean. "Mr. McKenna, you've known Mr. Hoffman for several years, is that correct?"

Sean nodded. "Since high school."

"Did you allow Mr. Hoffman access to your apartment tonight?"

"No. I didn't even know he was still in town."

"At any point did you provide Mr. Hoffman with a key to your residence?"

"No." Sean let out a long sigh. "Look, I know where he is."

"You do?"

"There's a house on Seventh Street, in between Iowa and Missouri. I don't know the address, but it's a gray house with white trim. It's a rundown place that's been foreclosed on or whatever. He's been living there for months."

"So you've been in touch with Mr. Hoffman?"

"Not really."

"Then how do you know where he is?"

"He's got nowhere else to go. His mom's done with him, and I'm done with him. It's the only other place he has left to go."

Mary believed him. He seemed close to tears, like it physically hurt him to share the information. "Is this vacant home where Mr. Hoffman has been hiding since he robbed my family's store?"

Sean nodded. "Yeah, I think so. For what it's worth, I didn't have anything to do with that. I wanted to stop him. I tried to, actually."

"Sean!" David stood up quickly. "That's enough. Don't say anything else."

"Why? What's it matter? All of this is my fault. All of it."

The Seventh Street neighborhood was silent, made even quieter by the recent snowfall that blanketed the lawns of the homes. Mary shattered that silence by pounding on the plywood that covered the door to the abandoned house.

A dog at a nearby home reacted, its bark echoing throughout the neighborhood. "Police! We have a warrant!"

Her hand on her gun and her ear to the plywood, she listened for noise inside the home. It too was silent.

She stepped aside as two uniformed officers ripped the plywood free from the door frame. Officers clad in tactical gear rushed inside, guns drawn, flashlights lighting their way.

A sergeant gave the all-clear, and Mary stepped inside. The place sat empty. Empty of people at least. The floors were littered with trash: beer cans, pizza boxes, takeout bags. Several mattresses lay scattered across the living room floor, with more in the bedrooms. The walls had been tagged and spray-painted, and large holes had been kicked and punched in the plaster throughout the residence.

In one bedroom at the rear of the home, officers located a crowbar and several screwdrivers—items possibly used during recent break-ins at businesses in the area. Next to the crowbar sat a blue vinyl deposit bag from the First National Bank of Laytons Grove. Inside the bag was a deposit slip bearing the name and address of Morelli's Convenience Store.

One item not located was the Raven Arms MP-25 pistol that Vickie Hoffman had reported stolen from her shed. It was a small, cheap handgun known to cops as a "Saturday night special." While low quality, the firearm was harmful, nonetheless. It'd already injured two men—directly and indirectly. The idea it could still harm others left her feeling unsettled. Perhaps its next victim wouldn't be as fortunate to escape with their life.

Mary sat in her car, reflecting on the events of the evening. Even though they hadn't located Mr. Hoffman at the abandoned house, maybe Sean was right: maybe Mr. Hoffman hadn't left town, and if he were still in town, so was the gun.

Sean seemed to know a lot about Mr. Hoffman, and maybe there was more he hadn't shared yet. She put her car in drive and made a U-turn. It was getting late, but the McKennas would likely still be awake.

As she turned onto Monroe, she gazed ahead toward the McKenna home. Many of the lights remained lit, so she pulled toward the curb to park. Something caught her eye though. A shadowy figure dressed all in black walking down Monroe from the other side of the street. The sight of Mary's headlights caused the individual to dash between two houses though, disappearing into the darkness.

Throwing the vehicle in park, Mary hopped out and cut through a yard to the alleyway in back. She walked west, toward the last known direction of the individual in black, but the crunching snow below her feet made too much noise in the still night air, so she stopped and positioned herself between a fence and a utility pole. In the distance, the crunching sound of footsteps coming her way.

Pushing her jacket away from her body with the back of her hand, Mary rested her palm on the backstrap of her Glock. She inhaled a deep breath and steadied her nerves, but the sound stopped. Leaning forward, peering around the pole, she saw the shadowy figure climb a chain-link fence into a yard. The McKennas' yard.

She turned around and headed east through the alley, retracing her steps back to the sidewalk on Monroe. Approaching the McKennas' home, she drew her gun, keeping it low, but ready.

A light flipped on in the McKennas' detached garage. The frosted windows embedded in the garage door prevented her from seeing inside though.

Acutely aware of the sound each footstep caused, she slid past the truck in the driveway and made her way to the side of the structure toward an unlatched entry door. Pushing the door open with her leg, she entered.

"Police! Don't move!"

In the corner, a slender male in a black coat stood by a workbench, digging through a drawer.

She trained her gun on the man and commanded him to turn around slowly. "Jack Hoffman?"

The man nodded, his hand resting just below the right-hand pocket of his jacket. The pocket that likely contained the gun.

"Hands up! Let me see your hands!" Mary adjusted the grip on her gun, preparing for the possibility she may need to fire it. "Don't make any sudden movements or you'll be shot, do you understand?"

"It's over." Hoffman shook his head slowly. "I'm fucked either way."

"Hands up!"

Hoffman's hand slid closer to the pocket. Mary adjusted her arm, slid her finger from the trigger guard to the trigger, aimed the sight at Hoffman's chest.

He stared toward her. "I'm so fucked."

"On the ground, now! Get on your knees! Hands in the air!"

From the house behind her, Mary heard shouting. Multiple voices calling back and forth to one another. Then the door opened, revealing Kathy McKenna in the doorway.

Mary returned focus to Hoffman but shouted instructions to Kathy. "Go back inside your home, ma'am!"

The sound of crutches clinking on the pavement behind her distracted her. "Go back to your home!"

"Jack?" Sean advanced into the garage. "What the fuck are you doing here?"

Hoffman didn't respond. He continued to stare at her, his hand inches from his pocket, inches from the gun.

Mary watched Sean approach in her periphery. "Sean, go back inside."

He ignored the command and approached Hoffman. "Dude, give me the gun."

"Mr. McKenna, go back into your home. You're impeding a police investigation."

Hoffman shook his head. "I'm so fucking fucked." His hand slipped closer to his pocket.

Mary applied pressure to the trigger, taking in the slack, but Sean wandered into the line of fire, and she let up. "Everyone on the ground, now!"

Sean ignored her and moved closer to Hoffman. "Dude, give me the gun."

Hoffman pulled the small pistol from his jacket pocket. "Fuck, bro. I—I'm so fucked."

Mary stepped to the side, closer to the door. She had a direct line of sight on Hoffman's head, but there was a strong possibility she'd hit Sean if she fired.

"Jack, c'mon." Sean extended his hand. "Just give me the gun, man. We can fix the other stuff."

Mary backed into the doorway where the entire McKenna family had gathered outside the garage.

Sean lunged toward Hoffman, grabbing the gun in the process. Mary repositioned and retrained her gun on Sean.

Hoffman began to cry. Sean pulled him in for a hug, the gun at his side.

Mary approached cautiously, her gun still trained on Sean. She reached for his hand and took the gun from it.

Retraining her gun on Hoffman, she again ordered him to get on the ground.

Hoffman dropped to his knees.

"Hands on your head!" Mary moved in behind Mr. Hoffman, holstered her weapon, then removed the magazine from the small pistol and cleared the chamber. Once it was made safe, she grabbed her cuffs and clamped them around Hoffman's right wrist, then the other.

Mary turned her attention to Sean. "Mr. McKenna, you're under arrest as well."

reagan

Ma *pulled* the pot roast from the Crock-Pot and set it on the cutting board.

Reagan peered over her shoulder. "That looks delicious, Ma."

"I think it will be good. It's very tender." She pointed toward the Crock-Pot with the fork in her left hand. "Would you mind pulling the veggies out? There should be a large skimmer in the bottom drawer by the dishwasher."

"You got it." She turned toward the drawer. "Want me to pop the rolls in the oven when I'm done? Or should we wait until Dad and Sean are back?"

"Let's wait. You know he loves fresh bread, and they won't take very long."

Reagan nodded as she stared mindlessly at the veggies in the Crock-Pot. "Shouldn't they be home by now?"

"I don't think it will be much longer, dear."

Dad had taken Sean to meet with an attorney. They probably had lots to discuss since the DA had already indicated more charges could come after the detectives concluded their investigation, but it seemed like they'd been gone too long at this point and Reagan feared that maybe Sean had already been charged with more things. She didn't want to say it aloud and make Ma worry more than she already was, but if the charges were severe, they could have arrested Sean again and the entire process would restart.

Reagan's phone buzzed in her pocket. Another call from Mary Morelli. She slid the phone back in her pocket. She knew why Mary was calling. Mary wanted her to come in and answer more questions about the attack at Sean's apartment.

Reagan had nothing else to say. She'd already told Mary—and a bunch of other cops—what happened that night. They knew everything Reagan knew, and with each passing day, it felt like the cops were using that info against Sean, rather than Jack.

She'd once considered Mary somewhat of a friend. They'd worked together to save small businesses in town, to keep developers from demolishing the Alice Theatre, to keep Laytons Grove a great place for families, and now the woman was trying to rip the McKenna family apart.

Obviously Sean had done some bad things, and maybe he deserved to be punished for his actions, but he'd already gotten shot because of those things. He'd also given Mary what she needed to find and arrest Jack. Without Sean's help, Jack would probably still be out there, maybe he'd even commit more crimes. Maybe none of that fully erased the bad things, but it was more than most people in that situation would have done.

The front door creaked open. Reagan rushed to the living room, and Ma followed, apparently just as anxious over Dad and Sean's delayed return.

Donnie muted the TV. "Oh look, the felon is home."

Ma slapped his shoulder lightly. "Stop it."

Reagan hugged her brother. "We're glad you're back."

Sean chuckled. "You realize it's only been about two hours, right?"

"Can't I just be happy to see my brother?"

Ma stepped closer. "What did the lawyer say?"

Dad kicked his boots off by the door. "Lots of things. Some good, some less so, but it smells like dinner is ready, so we can discuss it as we eat."

"It will hold." Ma leaned against Dad's chair. "At least give me the bullet points."

Sean hobbled to the sofa and plopped down. "Looks like I'm gonna have to testify against Jack."

Reagan walked to the sofa and sat beside him. "When?"

He shrugged. "Could be months from now."

Dad sat down in his chair. "The lawyer said it's a possibility, but he also said that it might not happen at all. The cops are still gathering evidence against Jack, so more charges are almost certain to follow. Once that happens, the lawyer thinks the DA will offer Jack a plea deal, and if that's the case, there won't be a trial."

Ma stepped toward the TV to face Dad. "What about Sean? Will he have more charges?"

"We don't know yet." He turned his head toward Sean and Reagan on the sofa. "The lawyer said Sean could get a plea deal too though."

Ma gasped. "He'd have to plead guilty?"

Dad nodded. "Probably to something, but that could be a misdemeanor. We won't know for some time."

Reagan waited, but no one else asked the biggest question, so she spoke up. "Would he have to go to jail?"

Sean shook his head. "The guy said he didn't think that would happen."

"*Think*?" Reagan sighed. "Doesn't that imply there's a chance you'd have to go to jail?"

He nodded, stared at his shoes. "He said it was still a possibility, yeah."

Ma gasped again.

Dad stood to hug her. “I don’t want you worrying about that. The lawyer said that while it wasn’t *impossible*, it would be quite unlikely given Seanie’s lack of criminal activity and his cooperation in this case.”

Ma pulled away from the embrace. “Does he know about the shoplifting stuff? Won’t that play a role?”

Dad shook his head. “That happened when he was a juvenile, and it was a misdemeanor.”

Sean sighed. “Yeah, but the dude said a judge could still decide to use that as a factor in sentencing.”

Dad nodded again. “And he also said it was unlikely that he would.”

Ma sat down in the chair. “But the fact remains that Sean could have to go to jail?”

The room fell silent. It seemed both Dad and Sean had run out of ways to sugarcoat the situation.

Reagan stood. “I have some good news.”

It was a shameless attempt to lighten the somber mood, and with everyone staring at her, she reached into her pocket, retrieved the folded flyer, and opened it. “I was going to wait until David got back from the mortgage place, but we’ve made an offer on that little bungalow on Keith Drive.”

She held the flyer up for everyone to see.

A smile slid across Ma’s face. “Is that the one with the original hardwoods and the big yard?”

Reagan nodded. “That’s the one.” She pointed to one of the photos in the flyer. “The kitchen is slightly hideous, but a little paint will go a long way, and at least the appliances are newer.”

Ma’s smile grew wider. “That one’s close, right?”

Reagan chuckled. “Nine blocks away. We counted.”

Dad stood and hugged her. “That’s amazing news. And I’m happy to help with anything you two need. Painting, resurfacing those floors, whatever.”

Ma hugged her next. “When do you expect to hear something?”

She shrugged. “Could be as soon as later today, but I guess I don’t actually expect to hear anything until tomorrow at best. We offered a little below their asking price, but our agent said they need to move out of state soon, so we offered a fast closing. Hopefully that sways them.”

The room erupted in chatter as Ma and Dad planned everything from repainting the entire house to the logistics of loading a U-Haul to move their things from Chicago to Laytons Grove.

Sean stood, fumbled with his crutches, hobbled toward her, and hugged her. “Thank you.”

“For what?”

“This.” He pointed his chin toward the living room. “Distracting them, taking the heat off me.”

She smiled. “My motives were that obvious, huh?”

“To me at least.”

“You’ll be welcome at our placc any time, I hope you know that.”

He nodded. “Appreciate that.”

“Maybe you and Brooke could come for dinner some night? Once we get settled that is.”

“Yeah. That’d be cool.”

Reagan returned her gaze toward her family and smiled as Ma and Dad discussed the necessity of things like baby gates and cabinet locks to protect a child they hadn’t met but already loved, proving that she’d made the right choice to come home.

mary

The grand reopening of Morelli's was a lowkey affair, and that'd been by design. Mary didn't want to draw too much attention to the awful things that happened there. No matter what, people would talk about it—not just the shooting but how one of the owner's children nearly bankrupted the place—so Mary thought it was best to get back to normal as quickly as possible, and without fanfare.

With Amber taking care of the morning customers, Mary settled into the chair in the office to finish some paperwork. The same tattered chair had been there longer than she'd been alive—and probably about as long as Papa had been alive. In many old family photos, Grandpa Carlo sat in the same chair, sometimes with Papa on his lap.

Though she'd helped around the store all her life, Mary was thirteen when she worked her first real shift at Morelli's, stocking the aisles, helping customers locate items, and even ringing them up and giving them change. At the time, it was fun, and it felt like Papa had entrusted her with tons of responsibility. Even back then she could see how important the place was to him, and she felt lucky to have his trust. Michael had been given the same trust, but he'd treated it very differently. His actions threatened the very existence of Morelli's Convenience, but even worse, it'd caused a massive rift to form between Michael and Papa.

When Michael came clean about what he'd done, Papa said nothing. Mary expected him to be hurt, and sad, but she didn't expect it to harm the man as much, or as deeply, as it had. In the days since that conversation, Papa had barely left the house and hadn't worked in the store for more than an hour or two at a time. Mary didn't know what he felt because he wouldn't discuss it with anyone, but best she could tell being in the store made him too sad.

A knock at the door shattered her reverie. She looked up to see Michael standing in the doorway to the office.

"Hey, you. If you're looking for Papa, I think he's at home."

Michael leaned against the doorframe, his hands in his pockets. "Yeah. I just came from there." He shook his head. "He still won't talk to me. Not much at least. Mom let me in, and I tried—I apologized again—but he just sat in his chair paying more attention to the TV than me."

"Well, I don't know what to tell you, Mikie. It's going to take some time, and if I'm honest, things may never get back to where they were."

"Yeah." He nodded as he stared at the ground. "Anyway, I just wanted to let you know that I'm leaving town."

"Like, for the weekend? Or do you mean permanently?"

"Permanently. There's nothing here for me anymore."

"No? What about your family? Our mother, your nieces?"

He sighed. "I didn't mean it like that, and I'm not going far. Just to Chicago. Kim got a job up there and is moving, so I'm going with her."

Her eyes widened. "You're moving in with her?"

"I know, you don't like her, and you probably think it's a bad idea, but she makes me happy and I want to be with her."

"Okay." She raised both hands as a sign of surrender. The fight wasn't worth having. "When is this happening?"

"Next week. I'm meeting with a real estate agent later today to see what I need to do to list the house. We've rented a little place in the West Loop for now. Once I get this place sold, we'll probably buy something up there."

"Sounds like you've got it all worked out." She released a deep breath. "At the risk of sounding indelicate, don't you still owe this store a couple grand?"

He sighed and rolled his eyes. "I gave Papa a check before coming here. We're square, and I'm officially no longer part of the family business."

"I'm sorry to hear that."

He snorted. "No, you're not. It's what you've always wanted."

"Mikie, that's not true. The only thing I've ever wanted for you is for you to be happy. And all I want for this store—for Papa's legacy—is for it to thrive, feed our family, and serve this community for years to come."

"Well, I guess you're free to see that through now. Once Papa deposits my check, you should be able to pay the last of the overdue invoices."

"What about the other part? Are you happy? I mean, with Kim and the move to Chicago?"

"It doesn't matter how I answer that. You hate her and I'm sure you think it's a big mistake to move in with her."

"I don't hate her, Mikie, but whatever you do, just promise me that you'll still come back and visit your nieces. I want them to know their uncle. And our parents... No matter what you think, they love you and it would break their hearts if they didn't get to see you often."

"I know. We'll see how things go, but for now, I've gotta go meet with my agent."

She stood and hugged him. "I love you, Mikie."

sean

The ride from the courthouse was a quiet one. Dad drove him, and even sat through the proceedings, but since they'd walked out of the building, he'd said very few words, so Sean sat quietly and stared out the truck's window.

Today's hearing was mostly a legal formality, at least that's what his lawyer said. As part of the deal the guy got him, Sean promised to cooperate with the DA—to tell the truth about his knowledge of the robbery at Morelli's. In exchange, the DA agreed not to file charges against Sean related to the break-in at the sports memorabilia warehouse in Mendota, even though the cops claimed they had evidence to prove he and Jack were behind it.

Travis' lawyer made a similar agreement with prosecutors. He might also have to testify against Jack, but in exchange, he'd receive a suspended sentence for the shit with the watches, keeping him out of prison as long as he didn't get arrested for anything else.

Jack, meanwhile, was close to getting a deal of his own. The cops said they had evidence that linked him to the theft of the watches, and the DA seemed certain that Travis' testimony would secure a conviction in the case. But if Jack took the plea deal, Travis wouldn't be forced to testify against him, and Jack would serve much less time in prison than if he were convicted at trial. Still, he was facing several years behind bars.

The cops also said they had plenty of evidence to prove that Jack and Matt were behind at least two smash-and-grab burglaries in the Illinois Valley, and they were supposedly close to tying them to a third. The plea deal the DA offered also combined the sentencing for those cases, as well as the attack on Reagan, allowing Jack to avoid some of the most serious charges and preventing Reagan from having to testify as well. That was the best news because it meant she wouldn't be forced to relive that night in a courtroom with a bunch of strangers staring at her and listening to every word she spoke.

Dad pulled into the driveway of Reagan and Dave's new house. For weeks, everyone had gone on and on about how solidly built the house was and how safe their daughter would be in the neighborhood. McKenna Blake Moran wouldn't be born for at least a couple months, but once she did arrive, she'd grow up with her entire family nearby, and everyone in the family was super stoked about that part.

Dad turned in his seat to face Sean. "I've got a few things to finish up here. I wouldn't mind your help with them."

Sean nodded. "Sure."

"I want the place to be perfect when they move in next week."

Sean slid his crutches beneath him and maneuvered up the two steps of the porch. Once inside the house, Sean looked around at all the work Dad had done since he'd seen it last. It'd been painted, the wood floors had been resurfaced, and the nursery was about finished too.

Dad pointed at a pile of boards and metal brackets on the floor. "That's supposed to be a crib. Hopefully when we're finished it will resemble one." He chuckled.

Sean chuckled in return and sat down in front of the pile of lumber. Dad joined him, and they worked in near silence, screwing boards together, mounting supports in place, tightening screws.

Sean wasn't in a talkative mood by any means, but he wasn't sure why Dad was so quiet. He was probably still mad—or disappointed, whatever parents called it. Or maybe he was just sick of him by now, sick of him living in their house, taking over the living room.

Dad examined the pieces in his hands. "I need what the directions call a 'back rail,' but looking at the diagrams, I can't tell which of these is the back rail and which is the 'left front post.'"

Sean took the directions from his father and examined them. "The one in your left hand is the back rail."

"How the hell can you tell that?"

"See how it has the two notches. The front posts have holes drilled through them." He held the directions up for Dad to see.

"If you say so." He shrugged. "If all else fails, I've got a roll of duct tape in the truck. It'll hold. Babies are small."

Sean smiled and even laughed a little, the first genuine laugh of the day—probably the first in weeks. Over the past few weeks, he'd attended various court hearings—some his own, some Jack's. Those were the hardest. Every time he glanced over at Jack, his face looked sad, empty. It seemed like he didn't care what happened to him. Jack's mom was in the courtroom for most of the hearings as well. She looked detached most of the time though. She never cried. In fact, her face wore no expression at all. She sat quietly, barely reacted to things said about her son, no matter how negative they were.

Dad stood up and wiped his hands on his jeans, inspected their work. "Not bad."

The pile of parts had transformed into a crib.

Though the thing was brand new, it looked weathered, like it'd come from an old farmhouse. Apparently, that's what Reagan loved about it though, and it also had a feature that allowed it to be converted from a crib to a full-size bed when McKenna was a little older. Admittedly, that part was kind of cool.

Dad turned to him. "Not bad for a day's work, eh?"

"Yeah. Looks good."

"You hungry?"

Sean shrugged. "I guess."

"I've gotta stop for gas, then how about we go over to Johnny's? I'll buy ya a burger and a beer."

Sean nodded as he stared at the crib. "Yeah. Cool."

It too was a quiet drive, and Sean fell especially quiet when they stopped at the Morelli's pumps.

Was Dad fucking with him? It was the first time he'd been back since the shooting—since everything in his life changed. Dad pumped gas and Sean hobbled out of the truck to smoke a cigarette. Gazing through the windows of the store, things looked the same as when he'd found Jack inside that day, but today, he only saw the old man behind the counter.

Dad finished pumping and Sean hobbled back into the truck. They sat in silence again during the short drive to Johnny's.

Outside Johnny's, Dad parked on the street, close to the front door to make it easier for Sean to get inside. They claimed a table up by the small windows at the front of the joint, and Sean leaned his crutches against the wall.

Dad ordered a bacon cheeseburger. Sean got a club sandwich. Dad tacked on a basket of onion rings for them to share too.

The waitress smiled and said she'd get the order put in.

Dad finished a swig of his beer, wiped his mouth. "You thinking about your friend?"

"Yeah."

"It's a good deal the DA's offering. Probably too good."

"What do you mean?"

He drew in a long breath and exhaled it quickly. "I know he's your friend, and I know you care about him, but the things he did... What he did to Reagan, and what could have happened to my granddaughter..." He exhaled sharply as he stared into his beer. "I'm sorry, but he should pay for what he did, and the deal that's being offered is just too lenient in my opinion."

Sean shrugged. "Maybe."

Dad stared at the table. "I understand why you're concerned about him. If he were my friend, I'd be worried too, and I'm not saying it's wrong that you're worried about him, but you have to understand, when David found Reagan at your place, and when I saw you with all that blood everywhere..." He shook his head slowly from side to side. "Both of those things scared the living hell out of me, and both of those things made me very angry. Madder than I think I've ever been. You'll have to forgive me for wanting some justice."

"No. I get it."

That part was easy to understand. Sean felt many of the same things. When Reagan told them what happened, Sean wanted to hurt Jack, wanted to make him pay. But he'd played a role in the direction Jack's life took too. It was one thing to be in high school pulling stupid little heists, rip off the school, have some fun, feel some adrenaline flow. Most people leave shit like that behind them after graduation, but Sean never wanted to leave it behind, and he'd dragged Jack along for the ride. Or perhaps Jack had willingly come along for that ride, but the jobs they pulled only helped fund his drug use, and it wasn't like Sean had done anything to dissuade Jack from using either. He'd mostly ignored it, allowed it to grow out of control.

Dad patted him on the shoulder. "Hey, it'll all be okay. Like I said, the deal the DA gave him is a good one. And once he's sentenced, you can go visit him, you know?"

Sean nodded. "Yeah. I guess."

"I know you don't want to hear this, but this is probably the best thing for him. Sounds like the facility they're talking about sending him to offers a lot of rehab help. He definitely needs that."

"I don't know what to think. I know he messed up, but he's not a bad guy. Not like the guys he'll be in prison with. He didn't kill anyone or anything."

Dad sighed.

Sean exhaled a deep breath. "I mean, I know he could have, but that wasn't him there that day, not really. He'd just hit a bad string of luck, and he was high as hell. He didn't know what he was doing when he shot me."

"I know, son. Drugs are terrible, but who's to say that that bad string wouldn't have continued? And then maybe he would have killed someone for their wallet or something, ya know?"

"I just wish someone would have gotten him some help before all of this. He probably shoulda been in rehab a couple of years ago. I should have said something to him, you know? Maybe tried to get him to go or at least mentioned it to his mom or something. Instead, I just kinda let him spiral out of control."

"Sure, but on the other hand, if you'd tried to get him some help, you don't know that he would have accepted it. You can't spend all your time thinking about what could have happened. Those what-ifs will keep you awake for days, that much I know. And if Jack didn't want help, it probably wouldn't have mattered what you did."

He made some good points. Jack wouldn't have listened even if Sean had tried to get him to stop using. If their roles were reversed, Sean wouldn't have listened to Jack, and he probably just would have gotten pissed at Jack for trying to run his life. Still, Jack needed help, and Sean hadn't done anything for him. If he'd told the cops the truth after the shooting, Jack would have been arrested that night. He could already be on the way to getting help, and he would never have had the chance to attack Reagan.

Sean cupped his hands around his beer. "I get what you're saying, but none of it makes me feel any better, you know? Jack's had a rough life, and he made some bad choices, like carrying that goddamn gun."

"Why did he have a gun anyway? If you don't mind my asking."

"He was afraid of someone. A guy he owed money to. So when he found it at his mom's place, he decided to grab it. It was a total last-minute thing that's going to send him to prison for years."

"Well, Seanie, I don't know much, but I do know that you can't blame yourself for the decisions of others. You just have to worry about your own choices."

"How do you mean?"

"Well, your friend Jack saw things one way and acted accordingly. You, thankfully, saw them another way and chose to stay out of it. Ultimately, those moments are what define our lives. Most of the time, the thing that guides us through life is our perception of things, how we view any given situation at any given time. Those moments—those choices we make in those moments—those are what end up defining our lives."

"Sure, but how is it that one bad choice leads to *years* in prison? That just doesn't seem fair."

"Jack didn't make *one* bad choice though. He made a bad choice when he started using drugs. Another bad choice when he decided to rob Morelli's, and another bad choice when he decided to take a gun with him to do it."

"Yeah. I get that."

"None of that means he's a bad person in his heart. He just had a bad record of decision making, both now and in the past. It's unfortunate, but sometimes our pasts haunt us for years, or even our entire lives. Hopefully, this will give your friend some distance from his past, and when he gets out, he can start fresh, not to mention completely sober."

Sean nodded as he stared at the plastic checkered tablecloth. "If I'd just called the cops early on, none of this would have happened. Not to Jack, not to Reagan."

Their food arrived just as the evening regulars began pouring in, taking their spots on the stools encircling the bar.

"Look, son. Yeah, you messed up, but you also owned up to it and did what was right when the time came. That says a lot to me." He patted Sean's arm. "I'm proud of you. I know it's been tough. I know it's been eating at you. I'm watching it eat at you right now, but you did the right thing. Everyone's okay, and your friend is going to get the help he needs now."

"I guess so."

"I mean it. I'm proud of you. We haven't always gotten along perfectly, and no family does, but we've come through all of this—you, me, the entire family. We've made each other stronger, you know?"

"Family first."

He smiled. "You do listen to your mom, don't ya?"

Sean nodded.

The motto made sense now. Family did matter. Through everything that happened, his family had stuck by him, because that's what families did, no matter how difficult things got.

ACKNOWLEDGMENTS

Writing a novel is a long process. I've written that sentence before, in the acknowledgments of my first published novel, *The Gentle Slope*. That book took around seven years to go from a budding idea to a printed book. That's a long time, but *Laytons Grove* took even longer. This book began as a short story—the first I'd written in my adult life—in 2002. It saw many iterations as a short story, then as a novella, and then as a novel. As a novel, it changed several more times over the years until the version presented within these pages.

Given the two-decades this story—and its characters—resided in my head, I have lots of people to thank, people who provided support, guidance, feedback, amusement, and comic relief.

First, my longtime friend Gaetana Jessen who was my first reader for one of the earliest versions of this story as a novel. In fact, she read it nearly in real time as I wrote it. When I'd finish writing a chapter, I'd email it to her from my home in Colorado to her home in Victoria, Australia. Most days, by the time I woke up, an email from her awaited me with thoughts, proposed changes, and words of encouragement that kept me wanting to write each day. Without that instant feedback, I'm not sure I would have finished the draft as quickly as I did and I am forever grateful to her for her time and help.

Also, I must thank Gaetana's husband, a lifelong friend of mine, Jeremy Jessen for allowing me to take up so much of his wife's time with my nascent storytelling. For the record, this makes up for that time in middle school when he body slammed me onto his neighbor's driveway (although, admittedly, I completely deserved it).

This novel is set in a fictional town that is located in a very real part of Illinois called the Illinois Valley. It is a place dear to me; a place I have long consider my home. This is perhaps odd because I've never lived there for more than a few weeks at a time, but I've never felt as at peace as I do during my visits there. So, thank you to all my family there who always made it so comfortable and welcoming for me. This includes my Grandfather Keith Lowery, my Great-Aunt Galena Lowery, my Aunt Bernie and Uncle Terry who always opened their home to me and allowed me to stay as long as I wanted. All of them have left this world, but they will remain with me throughout my lifetime, stored among my happiest memories.

Immense thanks to my parents Greg and Sandi Lowery for years of support and for handling my angsty teen years with patience and love, but most importantly, for allowing me to find my path free from the pressures of predefined expectations.

Thanks to Clare Moran Heilman for years of friendship and for lending me the Moran surname for this story. Marilyn Tarpey for being an early reader of a long (and somewhat terrible) early draft of this novel, but especially for not holding the less-than-polished writing against me. To Juna Dykes, Doug Gilchrist, Katie Gilchrist, and Jana Traynelis for all the late-night taco and/or Guinness runs that gave me a needed break from hours spent writing this book.

Last but most: endless thanks to my wife Aimee Lowery, my partner in every sense of the word. She makes me laugh, allows me to disappear for hours at a time to write, reads my work, and helps me polish it. She's the best first reader anyone could ask for, and she not only puts up with me but she also seems to enjoy my weirdness. Most importantly, she allows me to be myself, and there's no better gift.

ABOUT THE AUTHOR

R.M. Lowery is the award-winning author of the Jakob Larsen Mysteries: *The Gentle Slope*, *We Kill Our Own*, and *Time Fades Away*, as well as *Tough Messes: Eleven Stories of Crime and Desperation*. His short fiction has also appeared in Black Cat Mystery Magazine, Workers Write, The First Line, and others. Lowery lives in Colorado with his beautiful wife and their clowder (of cats).

www.ingramcontent.com/pod-product-compliance
Lightning Source LLC
LaVergne TN
LVHW010645110826
845149LV00014B/2957

* 9 7 9 8 9 9 3 3 9 6 2 1 7 *